WILD GIRL
RUNNING

WILD GIRL RUNNING

REGINA WATTS

PAINTED BLIND
PUBLISHING
LITERARY ALCHEMY

PAINTED BLIND
PUBLISHING
LITERARY ALCHEMY

For the McHardys:
To Simon, for the suggestion;
And to Clare, for reading.

ESTELLE

THE WILD GIRL had no name before Ulysses Cochran found her—but then again, before she was seen by that first and most important of men, she didn't need a name. A name distinguished one thing from another, and the wild girl was part of it all. The babble of the brook was the sound of her voice; the singing of birds, the rhythm of her heart; the rising sun and moon, the story of her soul. None of these things had names to her, either. All were simply part of the kaleidoscope of experience through which she wandered in a dream-state.

Dr. Cochran woke her from that dream, for better or for worse.

It was not just that the wild girl had never seen a man before. She had never seen any other human before. In fact, so integrated with the wilderness as she was, it had never occurred to her that there were other humans, or that she was a human herself. It was true that she often saw animals in pairs, and those pairs soon yielded smaller animals whose big, watery eyes and docile softness moved her heart in almost painful ways—but, somehow, the wild girl had never put things together enough to consider that she, also, might have a partner somewhere in the forest.

She did, however, understand that she was different from the other creatures there. For instance, she knew she was cold all the time and had to cover herself or else become wickedly ill. Mother wolf kept her warm for years, as did her sibling wolves, but the wild girl couldn't spend all winter huddled in the den with her yipping, nipping litter-mates.

When she had been walking on her hind legs for four or five winters, she finished dinner with her siblings one night and at last made the connection. Fur! Fur was the problem. The wild girl needed fur. So, using her teeth and tiny hands, she stripped the tatters of hide from the gutted deer and wrapped herself in these unclean blankets.

They made her warm until they rotted. Every time her family hunted she therefore made herself new coverings. Slowly, as more seasons passed, she became better at it. She learned to scrape away meat and fat with the rib-bones of the animals who had donated the skins; and, one summer, she discovered that skins which had aged too much and been tossed out in the heat changed their texture if they had been properly cleaned.

She experimented with this over time and gradually found that scraping the skins of fur and washing them in the river many times made a new kind of covering: one that was better for the hot summer seasons when the sun beat down but biting bugs precluded her natural state during anything but a dip in the stream. When she was very little she had worried that she wouldn't be as good at hunting or playing or simply existing as the other animals, but these days she had taken to wondering if she wasn't maybe a little bit better. After all…what other animal stole skins this way?

The wild girl discovered soon that she was good at hunting, too. At least, she was very good at scaring animals into the waiting maws of her family. All she had to do was step out of a bush. Most deer who knew what was what would bound away, disappearing into the trees from which they would scream. Delight always surged through her: she would dash through the trees to find her family already at the feast. Mother wolf would wag her tail and kiss her adopted daughter's face and nuzzle her with a bloody snout that left venison remnants across the girl's joyfully flushed cheek, and the girl herself would take her turn at the meal with a glad heart.

Alas, not even the wild girl's childhood was full of endless joy.

One day, mother wolf began spending more time in the den and let others do hunting for her. She produced no new litters of pups. After a few seasons of this, she got up very early and went outside.

For some reason, the wild girl followed her. Mother wolf breathed haggardly, heavily, her body extended along the earth and her tail flat with it. The wild girl kissed her ears and petted her mane and held her body, by then all bones beneath thick, coarse fur. She lay her head upon mother wolf's back and dozed off to the sound of her unsteady breaths.

When the wild girl woke up, mother wolf wasn't breathing anymore.

The wild girl had seen other animals die, but somehow it had not occurred to her that mother wolf could die, herself—that mother wolf, specifically, could die without being hunted by something the way she once hunted hoofed spirits of nature. Yet, such a horrible thing had happened.

There had been no stopping it: no way to protect her, nothing to fend off.

Grief and pain like none the wild girl had ever experienced shot through her whole body. The wild girl looked around in search of that thing that had stolen mother wolf.

Though no great creature had come in the night to claim mother wolf's meat, the displaced human felt certain that something had taken her protector. Something unseen and invisible had come into their territory and annihilated mother wolf's essence, leaving behind little more than bones and meat and fur.

The wild girl wept: not just in sorrow, but fear. Fear that the invisible thing that came for mother wolf still hung around, and would come for the wild girl next.

But surely, whatever this evil thing was, it only preyed on living meat. Her family did the same: when they found a deer lying dead in the woods they ignored it unless hunting had been very, very poor that season. Therefore, the wild girl had a strange idea that comforted her as much as it protected her—best of all, it was a way for mother wolf to always be with her.

The wild girl waited for her adopted family to find their dead mother. The wolves snuffled her still form, howled and mourned as the wild girl did, tails low and ears drooping.

It pained the wild girl to see them all so sad, and pained her all the more to wonder if that invisible thing might come for them, too. This hateful predator!

Perhaps the scheme might lead it away from her pack. If the predator only hunted living things, then the living wild girl, wrapped in her mother's furs and crowned with the cleaned, sun-baked bone of her skull, might confuse the unseen spirit that had taken mother wolf away. After all, it had already killed mother wolf, but her fur would go on moving, and her skull would continue resting upon a living being—a living being that disguised itself with the tatters of death. Perhaps the invisible spirit would feel so confused it might follow the wild girl hidden within the wolf: follow her and watch her, rather than take her or her family in the darkness of the very early morning.

Therefore, though it pained her to think all this meant mother wolf was truly dead, the wild girl skinned her dead relative and carefully cleaned the bones. Because it saddened the girl so much to think of her mother dead, even while wearing these pieces of her, the wild girl took what was left outside of the fur and skull. She arranged it all very carefully in the cradle of some twisting tree roots near her favorite spot of the forest, a place by the stream. Thereafter, she had a place to be with mother wolf; to close her eyes and feel as though the fur wrapped around her had come to life again. She cleaned mother wolf's fur so carefully, so thoroughly, that it lasted season on season—even once, sometime around her twentieth summer, the wild girl was discovered by Dr. Cochran.

In an effort to keep the invisible predator confused and away from the rest of her old pack, the wild girl lived apart from them after her mother's death. She no longer had hunting partners, and this meant things could be very hard. She learned strategies that helped. The wild girl learned about the berries growing in the bushes and saw which ones birds favored. She watched mushrooms spring up in humid seasons and saw which ones killed the deer who ate them—and which other ones simply made the deer who ate them wander around in frightened circles for hours on end before collapsing in an exhausted heap.

Sometimes, after eating these other mushrooms, the deer looked very happy and rolled about in the grass, stubby little tails wagging with pleasure. Sometimes, when the deer ate the mushrooms together, they did a strange kind of embracing that the girl had once or twice noticed mother wolf permit the strong male wolf of the pack—each time, a season before the arrival of a new litter. The wolves had never eaten mushrooms, which made the wild girl nervous about trying these strange ones; but then again, they had never eaten berries, and the wild girl loved to devour those by the handful.

When at last her curiosity got the better of her and she tried that funny kind of mushroom, all manner of strange things began to happen. The trees began to move—not as though blown by the breeze, but as though they breathed like her brethren animals. The heartbeat of the sunlight streaming upon her became apparent, and somehow the wild girl realized for the first time that, without that sunlight, she could never live.

She thanked it, blessed it: blessed it for all it did for her by way of warming her flesh and drying her skins and helping her to see. Indeed, it seemed to her that the sun itself was what kept that hateful, invisible spirit at bay. Mother wolf had died before the sunlight came that day, after all.

Had she made it to dawn, would she have lasted even a day longer?

The wild girl's mind whirred with the advisements of the mushrooms, which she came to believe were teaching her about the value of the sun and the living nature of the plants in the forest. All things were nature and all things were a part of her because she was part of nature—yet the mushroom also taught her something else. The mushroom showed her how mighty she was compared to other animals.

When the strange fungus made her flush with heat and sent sweat dripping out of every pore, she removed mother wolf's furs and realized that she had somehow forgotten the furs were separate from herself. She had re-purposed the furs, but they were not hers—not something that sprang from her body. They were only something she had learned to use.

What else could she learn to use?

In the end, it was the mushroom who taught her to make spears from the bones of dead animals. Mother wolf's femur, once snapped and fastidiously shaped, was but the first. The wild girl made many carefully designed weapons and soon was a better hunter than her family had ever been. She became rich in furs and meats and lived a happy, peaceful life, especially once she had the idea of making her own den out of cured skins and fallen tree branches.

Seasons passed. Blood sometimes came out of the wild girl, and it frightened her terribly because of the pain this caused, but the storm always passed to leave her feeling better than ever. Gradually she accepted that this was the way things were with her, and she began using these incidents to keep a basic kind of time.

Each cycle of the sun up and down became a specific indicator to her, and after a few seasons of watching she copped to the fact that the blood came about once every twenty-eight passages of that fiery orb. She learned about the world, about death, about her body and its keeping.

But, still—still, somehow, the wild girl felt like something was missing.

She longed for her family and sometimes went to see them, but by this time many more litters of pups had come and gone. Now, not all of them knew her. The younger ones were kind to her because the old ones were kind to her, but they were far more cautious and less friendly than her old siblings. Then, when once she came to the pack and discovered her favorite sibling was missing, she knew the invisible spirit had taken it away.

She wept with that same old sorrow felt for mother wolf. Perhaps she had been visiting too often. The spirit that haunted her had followed her back to the den. Taken another wolf.

She resolved to separate, and not to visit them again for their own protection.

For many more seasons, life was just the wild girl and the bones of mother wolf. Every season, the tools with which she hunted became more expert and interesting. She enjoyed the problem-solving that came with figuring out how to attach one thing to another thing in order to kill a third thing.

Her cured skins became better quality and, through trial and error and a happy accident or two, she discovered that the application of animal brains made these cured skins into a hardened armor that reminded her of bark, or the thick shells of regal beetles making their slow and confident way through the forest.

The wild girl learned where all the other animals made their homes, where the sweetest berries grew, where her friendly teacher mushrooms preferred to hide in the shade. She even learned how to banish the darkness with fire, for she had come to believe that anything nature could do she could also accomplish in her turn. And, having once seen a thunderstorm strike a fire in some brush, then later seen a spark when a bit of flint she'd been crafting into a spearhead was struck at just the right angle, she became inspired and learned the sacred art of bringing the sun to earth.

She learned all of this: and then, when at last she thought she had nothing new left to experience, she learned what men were.

It happened one day that she had hunted well. Her prey roasted over the fire, which she found made it delicious and also made her stronger. Sometimes the raw meat her family ate made her feel queer, but when it was heated and cooked until the juices ran clear she was almost never sickened by her food again.

The scent of cooking meat filled all the forest and occasionally drew in a bear, but the black bears who lived nearby did not seem to her unkind creatures and she had come into the custom of leaving fat, organs and scraps of less-used meat in a pile for them some distance from her camp in order to buy their peace. They never bothered her, perhaps understanding that if she wished she could have hunted them much like the deer she donated to their appetites.

The wild girl felt very safe with a side of venison roasting over flame, a new skin drying on the nearby rack, and the sun still high in the lovely sky. She let the meat roast while she bathed nearby, which was something she only did when happy and safe. As she did when she was warm, she removed her skins and placed them upon the earth, then arranged mother wolf's fur atop these.

In recent years she had acquired fresher, thicker furs to wear about because she did not want to risk snagging mother wolf's sacred fur upon thorns or tree branches; mother wolf's fur thereafter became a blanket, a bedroll, a comforting pad that kept off of the dirt of the cold ground. She did not mind the dirt, the wild girl, but she had found it was invigorating when she could wash the dirt off her body in the sun-warmed water of the stream, then lay upon mother wolf's fur to dry in the sunshine like one of her own deer skins.

It was a soothing, peaceful feeling, this sun's kiss upon flesh beaded with water droplets. Inevitably it lulled her into a sleepy mood that made her think of how hard she had run that day; how sore her muscles were after committing to the hard task of stripping down the deer. Her hand resting upon her heart as she lay beside the riverbank, the wild girl dozed off to the scent of the cooking meat emanating from the nearby clearing where she lived.

She awoke at the snap of a twig.

The wild girl jolted upright. Another deer? She might spear it now and cook it, too, and avoid having to hunt for some time. Her body pounded with immediate, hopeful adrenaline as she looked toward the sound.

Thrill turned to fear.

For a few seconds, she thought she looked upon some kind of bear. The wild girl struggled to make sense of the wide-eyed, open-mouthed creature standing on its hind legs, its body wrapped in a strange collection of furs and skins she had never seen before, one pale paw lifted in the midst of its surprise.

Its open mouth stuttered out some kind of sound.

How much it sounded like the noises she could produce! Noises she had never heard from other animals in quite the same way. She was amazed, but—

The strange creature took a slow step toward her.

Frightened, the wild girl sprang back from mother wolf's fur and hurriedly gathered it up in her arms, shielding her sensitive body with it if this strange creature got the idea to attack her. Instead, it stepped back. Its paw lifted to its heart.

Somehow—perhaps because she had herself just been dozing in the same posture—this gesture made the wild girl recognize what this creature was.

She was looking at a being like herself.

A chill washed through her. Something changed inside her, though she couldn't understand what it was. It were as though some earth within her shifted and she felt the invasion of her territory along with the offering of a new one: in an instant, she became aware of the existence of things she had never imagined. Never even had the context to imagine, had she wished to imagine them.

Fright filled her anew. Was this the spirit that had taken mother wolf? It stepped toward her again and the wild girl cried out, lifting a hand toward it before dipping down to sweep up her spear. No! This spirit, this thief— now that it had made itself visible in a form so close to her own, it surely meant to lure her away.

It would not take her. She loved her home, her forest, and did not wish to know where mother wolf had gone when the predator took her out of her body. She did not wish to be dissolved, dismembered, have her skin used as some other creature's protection.

Shaking her head in feral fright, she turned on her heel and ran to her camp. There, seeing the creature had not followed her, she hurried to dress in a second set of skins she had already cured. With a glance to mother wolf's skull sitting protectively atop her den, the wild girl hurried with her ancestor's furs into the dark parts of the forest and left her cooking meat behind.

Perhaps, like the bears, it had come to bargain with her: to request a meal in exchange for her security. It could have the roasting meat, have whatever it wanted of her camp—if only it would leave her alone and let her continue living beneath the eye of the sun! If only, if only.

Hidden in the undergrowth, the wild girl trembled and held herself. The image of the spirit made visible rolled through her mind again and again. What kind of animal furs had those been? Where had this being come from? Why was it here now?

Worst of all—why had it been so pleasing for her to look upon?

Only when the panic passed did she try to sort through her impressions. It had indeed been very beautiful to her, perhaps because there was something in its face that reminded her of her wolf family—the spirit's keen eyes, high cheekbone, long face.

Yet not so long. In fact, well—in fact, the spirit's face was very much like hers, albeit harder and subtly lined like the tanned hides she had donned in her panic. It seemed to have its own fur, too, a great gray cluster of it puffing out around its mouth. She found herself wondering if it was soft fur; found herself wondering all kinds of strange things about the spirit.

Strangest of all…she hoped to see it, this death-spirit, again.

It had permitted her to live the first time, after all. Permitted her to see it and live. Perhaps, if she was lucky, she might be permitted to survive a second time.

For some bizarre reason, she thought it was almost worth the risk.

ULYSSES

DOCTOR ULYSSES COCHRAN was sure he was dead. At least, he had to be deeply dreaming. Yes: he had been wandering in the West Virginian forest, separated from his guide so long that some bear had gotten to him. Now, in his death-fugue, his soul presented him with an angel whose mere existence lessened the blow of his passage into eternity.

All that raced through the anthropologist's head the first time he saw the wild girl.

If he hadn't been so dehydrated from spending the afternoon without his guide, maybe he would have had a more rational explanation. The doctor was a man of science, after all; he was not the type given to superstitious leanings.

Yet, in later days, he would look back and wonder what man could have looked upon Estelle and not thought himself in the presence of a truly sacred being.

But maybe that was just what all men felt when they first saw the woman they were destined to love.

"I'm sorry," he said to the shocked creature, quite stunned himself. She stared continually on, her great, dark eyes as wide as surely were his own. "Please, excuse me—I didn't mean—I'm afraid I'm lost."

The researcher struggled to keep his eyes on her face. The rest of her supple young body called to his in a way he had never felt. Never had he seen a woman so spry, so charming. In an age when women strove to be pale as possible and applied all number of sickening remedies to achieve the pallor of bone, this golden goddess gleamed in the sunshine that had the good fortune of kissing every centimeter of her radiant flesh. He struggled to keep his focus and, stupidly, took a step toward her while trying to ask, "Do you know—"

More skittish than any deer, the girl leapt up and clutched the fur upon which she'd lain to her breast. He marveled, falling back a step again. A native woman, perhaps? He was not aware there were any left who were permitted to live in harmony with nature—not once Andrew Jackson had finished with them, anyway. The doctor looked a little closer at the areas he could stand to look without feeling terribly indecent.

Just before she stooped to whisk up some carefully hand-crafted weapon of hers, he got the sense from her features that her origins were perhaps closer to his own. By genetic lineage, at any rate—as she stood upright with the spear gripped in her hand, he couldn't help but think they were the clashing citizens of two completely different forms of reality.

"You don't have to be afraid of me," he told her softly, hand resting upon his heart. "Oh, please—don't be afraid of me. I would never hurt you."

At once, the lovely creature turned tail and dashed into the thick netherworld of the trees.

Ulysses's heart sank. It was like watching an undiscovered species of bird fly off before one could so much as sketch a feather. Oh, God! How cruel You were to show him this, this perfect woman—then take her from him. The keen flint daggers of her eyes had made a terrible wound in his heart. All the love that now came oozing out would surely be what killed him. Perhaps his original theory was right: perhaps he really was dying.

For a few moments, Ulysses waited, ears straining. The snapping of twigs and the rustling of bushes were her footsteps from him; soon thereafter a new path was beaten to the greater distance and finally made it far enough away to seem silent. He ached with disappointment, love, starvation.

Not metaphorical starvation, either. He really was extremely hungry, having not eaten since breakfast. Jason Blackthorn, Ulysses's guide, was an erudite Cherokee clearly as interested in seeing the abandoned sites, skills, and customs of his heritage cataloged for posterity as Ulysses was in cataloging them. He was also interested in keeping his employer alive. When the bear had come, Jason had instructed Ulysses to run back to the river and await his arrival.

Well…Ulysses *had* waited.

Almost two hours, by estimate of his pocket watch.

He had waited and waited; then, feeling terribly exposed, alone, and lost in these treacherous American woods, the European researcher had decided the best— perhaps only—option was to walk along the riverbank until it brought him to people. There were always people along a river somewhere. Surely, one way or another, he would come upon someone: hunters, trappers, an obscure miller living in fairy tale solitude. Even an encampment of intrepid researchers like himself.

And he did, of course, come upon someone. He just hadn't expected that someone would ever be as splendid, as sacred on first sight, as was Estelle. The scent of her cooking food lured him in, but during the time he spent looking upon her, Ulysses forgot all about his hunger. He forgot everything—everything. His own name, why he was in the forest, why he had come to America at all. Even the very land whence he had arrived.

All those things disappeared until she also disappeared; and then, as though he had been stirred from a dream, cruel reality again set in.

Perhaps it was her cooking that he smelled. Perhaps if he approached her more carefully he could bargain a bite to eat out of her. Even find a little out about her. Removing his hat, Ulysses moved slowly in the direction of her footsteps, tracking her through broken branches and disrupted leaves until he came to an empty clearing.

Well—empty of people. From an anthropological perspective, however, Dr. Cochran had stumbled upon an extraordinary find.

A lean-to, draped in animal skins and obscured by the shelter of a broad-trunked tree, exhibited signs of longterm habitation. At the very least, it must have been this woman's home during the summer months. A sort of bedroll from rabbit fur formed a comfortable carpet, and nearby a hunk of venison roasted over a stone-enclosed campfire.

He marveled not just at that but at the array of weapons leaning upright against the same tree as the lean-to, most of them crafted of bone but a few contrived of flint. Spears and daggers; he was not sure she had mastered the concept of the bow and arrow, though the hard intelligence of her eyes left no doubt in him that she would have taken well to the introduction of the concept.

There were other small items of interest interspersed around the campsite, as well...but by far and away, the anthropologist was most fascinated by the altar.

The aged bones of some mighty animal—a wolf, he thought, though wolves had allegedly been eradicated from West Virginia a few years prior—were arranged in a structure that was clearly religious in intent. The entire skeleton, save for the skull, was stacked upright against a mossy willow. Interestingly, it was poised upon its hind legs as though to indicate the animal possessed some degree of humanity in death.

A bit of flesh sat between its skeletal paws and Ulysses had the immediate sense that this was a deliberate offering, perhaps out of gratitude for the good hunt or thanks that it and its kind left the wild girl's camp undisturbed. He could not decide on first glance whether it was a gift or a ward of some kind, but it seemed fresh from that very day; no doubt, part of the same deer whose leg roasted over the lashing tongues of the fire.

The doctor's stomach rumbled. He glanced all around, peering through the trees in an effort to see the girl again. After frightening her off, the last thing he wanted to do was take food out of her mouth...but he was famished. It was now almost three in the afternoon and he hadn't eaten after having porridge at four that morning. Since then he had been wandering through the forest, mostly alone and certainly high-strung with the terror of mortal peril. Now, in a location that seemed at the very least peaceful, Ulysses could think only of sating his hunger.

With a reluctant look toward the skeleton, he bowed and said to it, "You really must understand…I haven't any choice."

While the headless wolf made no protest, the doctor turned his attention to the cooking meat. He sat his hat and jacket, (long-since shrugged off and reduced to a burden over his shoulder), down beside the edge of the lean-to. Then he turned to examine the spit that this strange woman had crafted. It truly was admirable—one could even turn it, albeit not for very long at a stretch without beginning to feel the crackling heat in earnest. He did dare to turn the cooking meal, hoping perhaps that the girl watched. When she did not emerge with some shout of protest at his interference with her food, he settled down to watch the fire.

Well…it had been an interesting encounter, anyway. Permitting the fire to entrance him with its bright, crackling peaks, Ulysses studied the meat and only occasionally turned it. Mostly, he wondered how he was going to get back to Blackthorn.

This discovery aside, night would fall eventually. The anthropologist would be left in the cold darkness without so much as a blanket. Then there would be the matter of future meals, of clean water, of escaping hypothermia. He shuddered in fear to think that this might be one of his last days on earth—might have been *the* last, if he hadn't stumbled upon that woman.

Ah, he had to stop ruminating on her! It made his soul hurt to think that he might never clap eyes on her again. To distract himself, the anthropologist sang a few hymns he had learned during his study of American Evangelism—and soon he considered that such singing might catch the acute ears of his traveling companion, so he sang a little louder.

Protestant hymns had distressed the researcher because they made him think of death's cruel inevitability, as did all forms of prayer, but in that moment the songs proved the opposite. His ability to remember and recite the songs was evidence that he was alive; still in-touch with his reason and healthy enough to think.

He had just turned the spit over again and taken up his meager interpretation of a folk ballad taught to him by his Irish valet when a rustle caught his attention. His heart leapt up with his head.

She had returned.

At once, his singing stopped. Once more enchanted as he'd been the first time, Ulysses assessed the leather armor with which the girl had dressed herself and could not help but immensely admire its quality. And how beautiful she was! Her dark hair fell wild, uncombed around her face and tumbling back over her shoulders, wisps grazing her cheeks like the seaweed locks of some dream undine. The soft petals of her damp, pink lips parted with awe to watch him, and he had the strange sense that she remained as shocked to see him as he was to see her.

Gingerly, the doctor lifted his hand away from the spit.

"I don't mean to intrude," he told her, keeping his empty hands raised to show her he had no weapon. "I'm lost, you see."

The girl stared on, one nervous hand lifting, the edge a thumb pressing against a lower lip his mouth suddenly ached to kiss. Oh, God! What cruel creator would put a woman like this in the world? She was too fair to look upon! Ulysses couldn't long admire her without feeling as though his entire body was about to burst into flame. He looked away again, into that better-contained cooking fire and the venison whose rendered fat provoked the crackling flames to leave the meat a bit charred. That was fine. He didn't care. He couldn't help but think it was going to be the best meal of his life—certainly with the finest escort, if she would condescend to join him.

"Do you know English?" He watched her face, waiting for some brand of recognition. "*Parlez-vous français?*"

Nothing. He tried a few more times: stilted Italian, halting Cherokee, helpless German. Nothing reached her.

"You don't speak at all," he observed, quite astonished. "Not a word. You must have lived in this forest for a very long time…oh, my God. What a shock this is!"

The anthropologist laughed a little, gently, shaking his head. Though at first the girl's body jolted with the sudden sound, soon her tawny limbs relaxed. The rhythm of her breathing seemed to slow beneath the leather panels of her armor.

Slowly, cautiously, she edged back into her own campsite. With the girl clothed he felt less abhorrent for admiring her—more able to rationalize his interest in this feral goddess of the woods. Her eyes were plastered to him in turn…though, he assumed, largely out of fear. He made not the least move, therefore, as she slowly walked the perimeter of the camp, watching him the whole time. Then, behind his back, she unfurled the wolfskin she'd taken with her upon the bed of rabbit carpeting her lean-to.

"This is a very impressive arrangement you have," he told her. Even if the language did not get through, the tone of his encouraging words might set her at ease. "You must have made all this yourself—is that right? Your lean-to doesn't look large enough to fit another person. You must be alone."

The girl, uncomprehending, said nothing. She stared on, wincing slightly as he turned to see her. "I'm friendly," he told her softly. "I promise. What can I—here, I know, here. Let me give you a gift, let me see."

Slowly, steadily, he rose, having to lift one hand to keep her still when the motion of his standing frightened her. Though she now appeared tense, ready to spring off again at any moment, she did in fact remain where she was. While her lovely hand braced against the tree for support, Ulysses slowly, carefully patted his pockets. His handkerchief? No, that would not be interesting to a girl like this. Something from his billfold? She might be interested in the illustrations of his money, but so overwhelmed by the object itself that she couldn't even detect the faces upon them.

The pocket watch ticked in his waist coat.

Yes—yes, that could be something to catch her eye.

Still moving slow as ever, Ulysses gingerly drew the watch from his pocket and unclipped it from its place upon his vest. "Here," he said, carefully extending the timepiece toward her, letting it dangle from its chain like a mesmerist's prop. "Here—take this, have it. I want you to know that I'm friendly...go on, it's fine."

It took her a long few seconds before she understood what he was doing. After a look into his face, the girl rose somewhat unsteadily to her feet. His heart raced as she edged away from the tree and toward the center of the clearing. Toward him and the fire.

Her eyes flashed rapidly between his face and the device he held for her, but when she was within range she extended her arm and carefully ran her fingers over the watch's cool case. A sweet gasp rose from her lips to boil his miserable blood; she looked at him all the more sharply. It occurred to him only as she took the device out of his hand that she might have thought he had made it himself somehow.

"Have you ever even seen another human before?"

Now that she stood so close, her eyes plastered upon the silver case she turned over and over in her hands, he could examine her every feature and thrill at the thought that he was the only man who had lain eyes on them. Chapped, shocked lips; freckle-kissed cheeks; pretty round nose; sweet doe eyes that lifted toward his again in new appreciation.

"No," he decided at last, the intense scrutiny she applied to his face somehow exciting to him. "No, I don't think you ever *have seen another human...at least, not a man. May I—*"

She cringed away from him as he lifted his hands toward hers. He drew back, remembering himself, redoubling his efforts at slow motion. "May I show you something?"

Hearing his ultra-soft tone, the woman looked into his face, then down at his still-waiting hands. Now he reached forward and she did not step away...though, as his palm fit against her knuckles, he could feel her very fingers tense with readiness to flee.

Holding his breath, Ulysses took another slow step closer to her, the shockingly soft knuckles of her delicate hand cradled in his fingers. One would have thought a lifetime in the sun would leave her flesh as tanned as the hides she wore, but far from it. Even feral as any animal found in the forests where she lived, the woman was nonetheless touchable. Gorgeous. All-consuming.

They had been staring into each other's faces for a few seconds: he broke her gaze with a shy sort of chuckle, glancing down to the watch she still held.

With the hand enveloping hers, he worked his thumb

over the latch of the pocket watch and said, "See? This is how you open it."

The lid sprang open and she jumped in surprise, fumbling the device and knocking his hand away for a panicked few seconds. Then, realizing that no ill fate had befallen her, the wild girl studied the device in her hand and frowned in adorable curiosity. Careful, gentle, she turned it over in her hand and lifted it high to her face. Her eyes widened somewhat when she saw the second hand ticking forward; soon she lifted the watch to her ear to listen to the sound. She laughed.

Her laugh! Oh, it stole his soul from out of his mouth. A giddy laugh, almost childish for how pure it was. Uninformed by the laughter of other humans or their discouragements, it was a bright, loud sort of laugh that the European seldom heard women produce. It soon faded into a crooked smile and she lowered the device again, turning it around in her hands, shutting its lid, making it open again as he had.

"Ah," said the girl, a pleased noise that absolutely slayed him. She smiled up at him, showing him her accomplishment by waving the open pocket watch for his approval. "Ah, ah!"

"Oh, God"—he tried not to groan in lovesickness, but could not help at least the smallest gasp—"you are so beautiful, so beautiful. I'm almost glad you don't speak English, so I can say such a thing out loud to you...who are you?"

"Aha..."

The girl laughed again, softly, fondly, lifting the watch to her ear to listen to it as though it were a shell from the seaside. She gave the watch a little shake and Ulysses laughed, gently catching her arm, saying, "Careful," as she jumped once more in surprise.

Soon, though—faster every time—her body relaxed.

Rather than pulling away, she studied his hand on her forearm. This connection between their bodies.

The girl looked into the face of the anthropologist, who took a sharp breath and released her. "I'm so embarrassed by myself, my goodness—ah, I'm sorry, so sorry. I certainly ought not to take advantage of you when you don't even speak my language, any language. Oh! I don't know what's come over me—"

Shaking his head in humiliated displeasure for his unprofessionalism, Ulysses decided the hunger must have been getting to him.

He glanced over at the meat upon the spit, which he studied before saying, "Really, I *do* wish you spoke English, or anything…I wish you could understand how hungry I am!"

She might not have understood that, but she did seem to understand the concept of fairness—of reasonable exchange, one thing for another. He could have taken his evidence for that from her altar; but, after seeing his gaze drift to the meat, the young woman glanced at the watch in her hand, then back up to his face.

"Ahum," said the girl, more an abstract sound of comprehension than a deliberate linguistic device. Upon gently resting the watch on the wolf fur in her lean-to, she stepped with new confidence into the center of her campsite and stooped over the warm-smelling meat.

After poking it a few times with a bold finger and evidently deeming it finished, the feral woman reached out with her other hand to grab him by the wrist.

"Ah?"

The angel gestured toward the roasting meat. He nodded, swallowing dryly to form the word, "Yes, please— I'm famished, if you wouldn't mind—"

To his relief, with a flint knife drawn from the leather of her deer hide loincloth, the lovely creature tore off a hunk of the venison's flesh. She pressed it into his hands, her black eyes darting in a reflexive glance—not to the timepiece still ticking open upon the wolf fur but the skeleton with the selection of organ meats arranged before its headless memorial.

Perhaps she thought he was some sort of god. The notion struck him as her eyes darted away from his along with her step back. It was hard to avoid the thrill, the burst of power—he willed it to go away and leave him in peace, morals in-tact. To further humble himself, he sat on the ground and ate with his hands beside this simple, simply beautiful specimen of untouched human.

Where had she come from? What had happened to her to leave her adrift in this way? Good God, how he wanted to know!

Yet he would never know.

Not really.

He would be able to make guesses, maybe. Approximations. But he could tell already, tell just by looking at her, that she didn't know the answer herself.

Then again—did anyone really know where they came from, really, before the Earth was born?

"You're very kind," he said after eating his fill and wiping his hands with his handkerchief. "Thank you, goodness, ah—I wish you had a name."

This beautiful creature, this shining star of Bethlehem that had led him to rejuvenation, smiled softly at his tone. He had a terrible headache from wandering all day and his entire body was exhausted on the verge of collapse, but every time he looked at this marvelous woman his soul was so full of energy that he felt he might have taken down a bear.

Ah! He was mad. He was going mad. He had found a feral woman in the woods and fallen in love with her—why? Because he was too crippled inside to deal with a woman who could speak? Because he fetishized primitivism? Because he was just so lonely anymore that even an anthropological specimen of the rarest sort might serve as a vessel of his feelings?

He sighed heftily and studied her radiant face.

"Now if only you could show me the way back to town. What a hike it's been—even if he finds me tonight, Blackthorn's going to take two, three days to get us back. Good thing I've gotten sort of fond of camping."

She listened with interest, perhaps trying to parse his sounds into meaning. The close scrutiny of her eyes, her slightly parted lips—oh, he wanted to kiss her.

Clearly, he was just excited by his discovery. Yes! That was it. He was confusing his feelings for this living example of primitive cultures, this woman from a completely different time, with thoughts of love or romance.

It was natural, he was sure. After all: Dr. Cochran loved his job. He loved learning; loved exploring the early traditions, both spiritual and cultural, of all mankind. When it came to this kind-hearted young wild woman who had just fed him, it was only natural that he should feel a fondness.

And perhaps it was only natural that she listed toward him the way she did, having stared into his face so long. He stared back into those dark eyes burning with intelligence, alertness. One might have expected her breath to be rancid or her flesh to reek of never having had a proper bath, but instead he found her so immensely alluring that his heart throbbed in his chest.

She smelled like earth and seawater. Like pure female flesh.

Her delicate hand lifted; now it was his turn to flinch in surprise. Ulysses laughed lightly at himself, then stilled again to see her fingertips' renewed course to his beard. Those golden fingers trailed lightly over the hair of his cheek, inspiring a tiny gasp from her mouth. His heart throbbed in his chest.

What was the harm, really? She looked like a perfectly mature and independent young woman. And the way she *looked* at him! The way her curious eyes flickered back up to his while her fingers stroked the hair of his beard.

"Well, here I was thinking of going for a shave when we got back to town…maybe I'll just trim it."

He laughed a little at himself. The wild woman laughed, too. She laughed, and looked into his face, and—

"Ulysses? Ulysses—"

The moment withered and died like a premature flower caught in early morning frost. Startled, the girl looked in the direction of Blackthorn's cry, eyes wide as she sprang to her feet.

"Oh," said Ulysses to her, reaching up for her hand again, "no, please stay—"

But she slipped away from him at once and was gone. Hidden again by the trees.

Ulysses sighed wretchedly. He stared up at the blue sky visible amid the trees around circumference of the clearing. "Here, Jason…I'm over here."

A few rapid cracks and crunches announcing his arrival, the researcher's guide burst into the campsite. Jason's look of relief quickly transfigured into shock, then interest. "I didn't think I'd left you alone for *this* long, Dr. Cochran."

Despite himself, Ulysses laughed. "Well, by now you know how I am…the sort of man who tries to make the best of a bad situation."

"What is all this? Did you meet somebody?"

"I did, thank God—oh, I did."

Stumbling to his feet and glancing over his shoulder at the lean-to, Ulysses dusted off his hands, turned away from the pocket watch still sitting there, and said, "Let me tell you about it…do you know of any peoples still living out in these parts, by the way?"

Blackthorn shook his head with another intrigued look and then a long, close study of the same wolf altar that had first captured Cochran's imagination. "Can't say that I do. Trappers, sometimes—woodsman. Forest spirits."

"But no indigenous peoples?"

"Not here, no."

With a thoughtful stroke of his beard and a pleasant shudder for memory of her tender caresses along it, Cochran said, "Well…maybe I'd better just tell you about her and see if you can help me sort it out."

Ulysses told Jason as much as he could, but there wasn't much to sort out. The native man suggested they could ask around the town where the researcher had paid for a hotel suite, but both already knew there would be next to nothing to learn.

Ulysses, especially. Having seen her and talked at her—having seen the ingenious engineering of her tools and the extremely primitive treatments of her furs and tattered leather—he suspected that she had been alone a very long time. The fact that she had survived at all was astounding as it was an indication of that same tenacious intelligence that burned from her eyes.

How long had she lived this way? The question drove him absolutely mad. She must have found herself in the woods at a very early age to be sublingual like this. *How had she survived so long? Had someone taken care of her? When had that stopped, and why? Had they died? Had they taught her some things, or was she self-educated in all the survivalist ways in which she was evidently quite adept?*

The doctor's mind twisted and turned. Exhausted as he was when they at last stopped to camp during their way back to town, he barely managed to sleep at all. He lay there staring at the stars, listening to Blackthorn's snores, replaying the intensity of her stares.

"This is a very interesting opportunity," the doctor posited when he and Blackthorn were a bit closer to town the next day. "From an anthropological perspective, I mean—it's like a glimpse back in time. A way to see in an almost enclosed setting the development of man's very early technology."

"Sure, but it's not like she can tell you anything. If she can't speak, well—then you'd might as well have just come across an abandoned site."

"That's true…but I was thinking about that, too. This is also an interesting opportunity to study the development of language, both in the brain and in a culture. Does she have *any* language? If she's never been with another human, then maybe not. She certainly looked at me like she'd never seen a man before, at least. Like she was terrified of me."

"Lots of women look at men like they're terrified."

With a humorless chuckle, Ulysses said, "Yes, well, that's true…but I mean, this was different. An existential terror, confusion—like she was looking at some kind of monster."

"I'm sure my ancestors felt that way, too," said Black-thorn absently, scratching his cheek before, with a glance at the sky, slightly correcting their path a bit more east-ward. "Sounds to me like she's probably right to be afraid of you."

The doctor couldn't help his scoff. "What on earth do you mean?"

"Well—you just stumbled across her, and already you're talking about her like she's an abstract discovery. Something to be experimented on."

"No, I—well." Ulysses's lips pressed thin in conster-nation. "I can't help but be interested in an interesting young woman," he said at last, earning a sidelong glance from his guide.

"What man can?"

Yes, well. Ulysses understood what it looked like from the outside at first glance—what it looked like to twenty times bitten, forty times shy native peoples such as Blackthorn—but the fact was that, by the time they finally emerged from the forest and found the path back to town, the researcher had convinced himself. He was enamored not with the girl but with the opportunity. Studying her was a service to mankind; a service to its understanding of itself.

Moreover, it was a service to the girl. The lovely wom-an who had saved him. As strong and wise as she obvi-ously was, there was still no doubt that her life was going to be very limited if she remained living in the forest alone.

Sooner or later, something would get her. Cold, heat, predators, starvation, malaria. She had managed to sur-vive quite a long time already, but anybody could look at her situation and see that her life expectancy was not what it should have been in the year 1905 AD.

And wasn't it unethical to meet a girl like that, then just leave her in the forest? Wasn't it wrong to find a human being who had never experienced civilization and *not* attempt to share with her the luxuries that developed humans had made for themselves? Houses, beds, telephones? Basic medical discoveries like vaccines, antibiotics?

It was unethical to have met this splendid, albeit primitive young lady and leave her quite literally out in the cold.

When Blackthorn and he parted ways for the meantime after making it back to the hotel, Ulysses collapsed in his bed but once again could not sleep for as much as he wrestled with the issue. Was it better to leave her alone, untouched?

Or was it the decent thing—even the Christian thing—to bring her into society?

A little voice in his head pointed out, as Jason had implied, that Ulysses would not be bringing her into society out of the goodness of his own heart. It was true. There was so much research that could be done—so much knowledge that could be yielded from attempts to educate her in the ways of modern man.

Of course…all that assumed she was willing to leave the forest. Leave the forest with him, no less. Ulysses's heart fluttered foolishly at the thought. If he was going to approach this ethically, it wasn't as though he could very well kidnap her…so he was going to have to convince her to come along. That might take a little while; at the very least, some sort of grand bargain.

And how did one bargain with a wild woman who did not speak anything, let alone English? How did one approach such a splendid creature and convince her to join a world of which she had absolutely no conception?

He had seen *A Trip to the Moon* just a couple of years before. Sweeping that girl off into modern society would be the equivalent of putting a human being in a rocket and sending them to meet a lunar race with absolutely no context at all.

But there were meeting points. Places where her desires and interests surely intersected with those of modern humans—modern women. There were ways to communicate that stood beyond issues of language and culture.

Ulysses Cochran was not a man who believed in the concept of destiny—not before he met the girl. But that moment, that first moment of stumbling upon the unashamed perfection of her naked body, the awe and fright and mortal bafflement of her eyes—

Some things in life really were meant to be, he told himself. Some things were presented to human beings for their betterment as well as society's: and if they did not take the opportunity, then somebody else would. Maybe they would take the opportunity in a less acceptable, ethical way. If the girl continued to stay in the woods she was not just in peril from nature, but from mankind.

And the thought of someone else finding her as he had?

No.

He had to do something. If he was ever going to return to England with his sanity in-tact, Ulysses could not leave the girl behind.

Somewhere in the forest, his timepiece ticked away in her camp.

Heart aching, Ulysses got up and at once began to make a great many arrangements.

3

ESTELLE

NOTHING WOULD EVER be the same again. Not after that spirit came to her.

The wild girl returned to her empty camp when she was sure the spirit and whatever other entity it had summoned were well away. Mother wolf was undisturbed. The remainder of the roasting deer still dripped upon the fire. For some reason, the girl looked around the clearing and felt immensely saddened by the stillness.

More than that, she was saddened by a kind of change.

What was it, this change? It was too early for the turning of the season—much too early for that. It was not time for the blood to come, either. Before it came, it sometimes made her feel queerly…but not in this way.

No—somehow, the feeling of this change made her remember how she felt when mother wolf was taken by the invisible spirit.

This just firmed the wild girl's resolve that what she had encountered was the same spirit, at last made visible. If only she could have learned why it had taken mother wolf, yet left the wild girl behind!

And left this strange treasure behind, too.

After ensuring she was truly alone, the wild girl knelt beside mother wolf's fur and gently took the spirit's offering into her hands. She lifted it to her ear once more and focused on the steady clicking that emanated from within. What was this object for? What did it mean? It smelled like the spirit—like dark, rich warmth. Like mystery and fascination.

She pressed the cold device to her mouth and frowned at the taste, pulling it away to look at it again. Little marks decorated the inside. Some sort of whisker steadily twisted from mark to mark.

Was this part of the spirit, somehow? It seemed to be living, though in a way that did not make sense to her. After all—it did not breathe or make noises other than its ticking. Yet all the same it moved.

How strange! How mighty. The wild girl wondered if she, too, could make things move on their own this way.

Perhaps the spirit was a teacher in the way the mushroom was. The mushroom helped her understand that, just as she could re-purpose furs and hides, so too could she use bones, sticks—whatever else was around her in the world.

Perhaps this spirit was attempting to indicate to her that she could create more intricate, fascinating things. Things that moved on their own. Things that once had no life but now took on motion or made sounds.

The wild girl looked hopefully up at the bones of mother wolf, the cold little device pressed to her heart beneath her hand. Maybe. Maybe.

Long into the darkness of night, the wild girl lay awake contemplating what the device meant—what the spirit meant. The relief she felt at still being alive in the world after such a visit was second to the question of this change.

It were as though she had discovered something she was missing—something she had missed all her life and never knew existed. The horrible feeling reminded her of how she felt when she saw stags who had shed one antler but not the other. She always wondered if they were bothered by the imbalance. It was the same imbalance she felt now, or so she thought. Like she had always been missing one antler; like she had forgotten to give mother wolf her food.

The wild girl did fall asleep eventually, but the next time the sun rose to gently awaken her, the feeling of lack had somehow only grown.

At least the offering from the spirit remained to console her. After toying with its cool, slender chain, she discovered a little mouth on the end—a mouth that led nowhere, but that could pinch the end of her finger or grip another part of the same chain to which it was attached. With this tiny mouth she affixed the chain around her neck and let the cool object (some kind of stone, maybe?) rest upon her heart.

There it ticked away, a quiet and steady companion all throughout the day and night. The noise was so soft that she had to pause her steps to properly hear it, but whenever she made it out amid the babble of the forest, the wild girl found it strangely soothing.

Would the spirit come again? She wished and feared it would. The next time she saw it, she sensed that the change that had already started upon her would be all the more tangible.

Would she be forced to leave her body the way mother wolf had left hers? What would happen to her bones, her skin? Where would she go when she left it?

The questions became so frightening that, overwhelmed by them, she let a deer get away and had to settle for rabbit. After stripping the little thing of its skin and roasting up its meat, she cried like she had when mother wolf died. Now, though, the wild girl was crying for herself, and for all the things of nature she would miss when she was forced to finally depart from it.

The sun rose and fell again. Each cycle of its passage seemed longer than the next, although by this point in the season they should have been just a little shorter every time. It didn't matter. Whatever had altered her had altered the very reality around her. Strange urges came upon her. She wanted to touch the fur on the spirit's face again.

She wanted to hear the spirit sing again, like the birds or the wind through the leaves.

Yes—perhaps meeting the spirit again would bring about her passage from her body. But the mere thought of its face filled her with such longing that surely, wherever it might bring her, that place would be a better one than this. She could not imagine a better place than this, so the thought that there could be something better excited her immensely. The ticking gift seemed to indicate this better place and all the strange, fanciful things it held in store for her.

The ticking gift indicated that—and so did the box she found.

The sun had made fourteen passages up and down following the appearance and disappearance of the spirit. Having put him out of her mind as much as she could, the wild girl went about her day-to-day and celebrated this extra period of life in her forest. She became so focused on living in careful awareness that she almost forgot her hope of the spirit's return until the day she found her camp disturbed.

Gingerly, the wild girl removed mother wolf's skull from her head. Something small and red and still sat in the center of the clearing. Frowning, not frightened so much as confused, she set the skull in its customary place atop the roof of her den so as to stoop over the little thing.

Six-sided and smooth on each side—smoother than anything the wild girl had ever touched. She marveled, her fingers running all across it until they encountered a seam of some kind. When she shook it, it softly rattled.

Thinking of the pocket watch around her neck, the wild girl set the item down and, realizing it could open at the seam, lifted the lid.

Strange! Very strange. The small box was filled with an assortment of what looked like big brown berries. What kind, she wasn't sure. They were not all brown, either. Some were red like the container that held them; some were golden like the fur of foxes prancing through the forest; some were dusted with soft green that reminded her of the trees overlooking these curious proceedings.

The wild girl picked one up and sniffed it. What a strange smell! Very strange. But not in the way of harmful plants or rancid meat. It was a good smell, rich and wonderful; it tickled her nose in a way that it had never been tickled before. Her mouth watered as it did when she found things that were good to eat.

With a befuddled glance around, the wild girl put the berry into her mouth and, after a second of delay, gasped at the overwhelming rush of flavor. Oh! Oh, what flavor—the watering of her mouth increased and she chewed in astonishment, a happy hum rising from her lips as the berry burst to release its syrupy contents over her palate.

Just what was this? Where had it come from? The wild girl had no idea—only that it was by far and away the most exceptional thing she had ever tasted. The blackberries growing in little bunches amid coiling brambles, they were nothing beside these rich, delicious things.

With another glance around, the wild girl swept the box up and brought it with her into the cover of her den. There she ate them all with sheer delight: she only considered that she ought to have saved a few when the box was empty and mere crumbs remained.

No reason for regret, though. They had brought her joy while they were there. She licked the berries' syrup from her fingers and soon enough dozed off, indescribably happy.

The next morning, on waking, the girl thought that perhaps this was a gift from mother wolf. After all! Offering meat to mother wolf brought good hunting, kept lightning from striking near her camp—even gave her pleasant dreams at night.

Perhaps mother wolf had finally been offered so much that she had regained the ability to bring her daughter delicious things to eat. The mere thought made the wild girl yelp with joy; she placed the box before mother wolf's bones and kissed her paws many happy times before, the skull once more affixed upon her head, she dashed off with her best spear to hunt in her protector's name.

Once more, the hunt was successful—once more, she returned in the evening to find something waiting in her clearing. This time, she recognized it on sight.

Oh! The wild girl gasped in astonishment and let fall the hefty doe around her shoulders. She hurried forward and knelt before the new fur, reverently running her fingers over its ultra-soft surface. And how soft! Soft and thick.

She hefted it upright, expecting the usual tatters of meat and fat that needed to be scraped away. Instead she discovered a strange substance lining the fur's other side—one that was almost softer than the fur itself. Amazed, humming, the girl petted that substance, then wrapped this new fur around her body.

How heavy! Yet comforting, too. It made her feel as mother wolf and her den mates must have felt to be wrapped in their thick coats. Cooing with pleasure, the wild girl thought to herself that the fur would be fantastic for the winter; she slept in it that night, when the sun had been gone for awhile and the air began to cool. Ah, the soundness of that sleep was second to none!

Excitement filled her the next morning at the thought of what she would find next. Perhaps, when she returned to her clearing, mother wolf herself would be waiting for the wild girl! How happy it would be to see her again, bones once again wrapped in fur, snout lolling in a pleased smile for her daughter. Just in case she would need it, the wild girl left mother wolf's skull behind that day—the first time she had hunted without wearing it in years.

As it was the day before, hunting was good. She did not normally hunt quite so often, but the goal of her hunting had changed.

Now she was not hunting to feed herself, but to feed the hungry spirit of mother wolf. The wild girl took down another deer, a buck much too large for her to carry back. She spent a great deal of time that day gutting and preparing the carcass in the spot where it had dropped.

Soon, tired from running the animal down to the state of sheer exhaustion that had finally permitted her to kill it, she strung the remainder of the meat in a tree and took with her a leg and a head.

The leg was hers to eat, her prize—the head and its antlers were for mother wolf, who would surely be there waiting for the wild girl's return. And, in fact, as she neared her camp, she grew certain that something moved within its perimeter. Her heart pattered with eagerness at the thought of her offerings having worked. Joy warmed her every molecule and she hastened forward, the leg over her shoulder and the head gripped under her arm.

And the wild girl dropped them both when she discovered the spirit had returned.

Her heart sank, twisted, thrilled all at once. How could she know what to feel? The spirit had come again—it had come to take her away for good. She knew it at once, especially in seeing that it had come with another spirit. This second entity looked at her with the same surprise the first spirit had; the two spirits glanced at once another and made a series of soft noises before the one that was familiar to her, with another study of her person, carefully approached.

The wild girl stepped back toward the treeline, spear clutched tightly in her hand. She glanced toward her den and the skull resting there. Never again would she leave mother wolf behind, never! What a mistake. Her eyes whipped back toward the spirits standing in her camp. The one that knew her lifted a steady hand, rising slow and flat between them. Then, that same hand lowered again into the furs it wore.

It removed another red box.

Once again, the wild girl was overwhelmed by an intermingling of joy and sorrow. So it was not mother wolf leaving these treasures for the girl! So all along it was this spirit—this taker of life.

But, as the box rattled in his hand, the wild girl could not help but remember what she had thought to herself before: that, wherever it was this spirit planned to take her, it was perhaps a better place than this. Did the forest have berries so sweet as the ones it extended to her now? Furs so thick and soft as the one sitting in her den, too heavy to wear on the hunt but perfect for keeping her warm while she slept?

Biting her lip, glancing down at the device upon her bosom, the wild girl edged into the clearing. She watched both spirits carefully—most especially, the one who offered her the box. The spirit smiled at her in a way that seemed even gentler than the smiles mother wolf had worn; the box shook gently and the spirit made soft, pleasing noises. They reminded her of the kinds of noise she made while playing with her litter-mates or attempting to call them from the den in the morning.

Made measurably more bold by the comparison, the wild girl edged closer and took the box from the spirit's extended hand. No move was made to grab her or to shift in place as though to ready for a run; instead, the spirits watched as, with an uneasy look between them, the wild girl slid open the box and discovered it was once more full of berries.

"Ah," she said, cautiously pleased, examining the plainly brown ones that had proven to be her favorite before glancing over her shoulder at the meat she'd dropped near the clearing's edge. Perhaps the spirits might take something other than her—might exchange meat for the sweet berries without also demanding her life. She gestured at the leg and deer head. "Ha?"

The spirits made the same sort of noise that the wild girl made when watching squirrels fall out of trees or seeing her litter-mates fight over scraps. The two strangers exchanged a look and then, after studying the girl together, the one with no fur on its face bent over the empty fire pit.

With a noise of surprise, the wild girl clapped her hands and waved at it like a bird until it went away—she didn't want it to burn itself if any of the coals were still hot from the morning, though by now it was usually cool. When the two entities were safely apart from the pit, she set about making her fire. Again, they made the noise of levity.

Soon, the blaze rising high and ready for a meal, the girl presented mother wolf with the deer head. The spirits watched but made no move to take her away: she thought it was very kind of them to let her say good-bye to mother wolf. In her heart, the wild girl tried to explain to mother wolf that she would not be able to give offerings here anymore. It occurred to her that, if nothing else, perhaps wherever the spirits took her she would also find her mother waiting.

That encouraged her, as did the sight of the spirits sitting placidly by the fire. It was hard to say what their intentions were or how they made their decisions about what things they took and what things they didn't, but she had the feeling somehow that if she really put up a great struggle—if she demonstrated and demanded and maybe even fought—they wouldn't take her away with them.

Then she would be there, in the forest, alone with her strange feeling of missing an antler.

The fur-faced spirit smiled slightly up at her while she set the leg above the fire. Soon all three—wild girl and these two spirits—surrounded the cooking meat, watching the flames and breathing deep the aroma of dinner.

Distracted, the wild girl almost forgot entirely about

the box of berries that had been their peace offering. Instead she sat with her knees to her chest, listening carefully to the noises the spirits exchanged. Although it was hard to tell because she had never seen such entities before, it seemed they had something more in common with the big father wolves of the pack than they did with svelte, wily mother wolf.

Finally, the spirit she recognized turned to study her again. He made a noise and touched his chest. The wild girl stared.

He made the noise again.

He pointed at his companion and made another noise.

He touched his chest and made the first noise again.

She squinted in search of the pattern. Slowly, bit by bit, amid his patient repetitions, she began to hear a distinct set of noises within the singular sound. It reminded her of how, when she was very young, the calls of birds had been meaningless blurs to her—then, gradually, she pieced together which call belonged to which bird and why they were making it. Now she knew when the birds told each other 'good-morning' and 'good-night' and 'there are berries' and 'the wild girl is walking through.'

So, thinking of such lessons, she listened carefully with that same ear to the sounds the spirit made. His companion spirit made a noise that elicited a kind of click of the lips and a strange hiss along with another word. Then, looking somehow determined, the fur-faced spirit looked back at the wild girl.

"Ulysses," he said clearly, precisely, touching his heart. "Ulysses. Ulysses."

For a second she thought he was talking about the thing that beat in her chest; that beat in the chests of all animals she had killed. The red organ keeping its time in her—was it called 'Ulysses?'

"Jason," said the first spirit then, gesturing to its companion. "Jason."

Aha! Aha. At last! Yes, she got it now. They were talking about themselves. The spirits had noises that indicated the spirits themselves! It was amazing. Clarity expanded the features of her face at this idea and, with a little gasp, she reached out and touched him. She laughed a little when he winced, then smiled softer as he relaxed beneath her touch. Were these spirits afraid of her? How funny!

"U-lissus." She touched him, her hand shifting to lay flat upon his chest.

How warm! Warm and somehow hard beneath the soft texture of the furs he wore.

While she commenced to gently pet him, he inhaled and pressed her hand to his chest with a sound of delight. He made a few more noises that sounded eager; happy.

"Ulysses," he said again, then gesturing to his friend. "Jason."

"Jason?" The girl looked over at the less-familiar spirit and smiled when it lifted its hand in greeting. "Jason," she said again, now with even greater pleasure. "Jason—Ulysses."

The girl tapped Ulysses in the chest and grinned all the wider. He sighed like she sometimes did after a long day of hunting, when at last she was able to lie down in the warm embrace of mother wolf's fur.

Together the spirits exchanged more sounds while the girl reveled in her new understanding. Did the spirits have noises for other things? She marveled around her, amazed at how distinguishing these two spirits into the two separate categories of 'Ulysses' and 'Jason' opened up the rest of the world and its potential for other, even clearer categories.

Did they have a sound for her, for instance? What about for the trees enclosing her clearing? For mother wolf? For mother wolf's bones? Perhaps, if a spirit such as these watched the wild girl's mind, it would have interpreted her thoughts into such noises for benefit of its own understanding—but to her, the world was a hazy miasma of interlocking experiences, nameless and indistinct until that moment Ulysses introduced himself to her. Now she looked all around, feeling again that missing antler sense that, all this time, she had been lacking something very obvious. Somehow, she had not been looking at the world around her correctly.

The spirits continued on with their noises, exchanging between them one set at a time and waiting for a response noise. For as many varied noises as the girl heard in that span of time, she could not help but think the spirits had developed many words for many things. Maybe even things she had never seen before—things from their world, rather than hers. These noises in themselves seemed to be from their world, separate from her own existence. They staggered her with their implications.

How did a spirit learn so many sounds and the meanings behind them? Was it possible for her to learn these sounds in the same way? Vague, empty desire gnawed at her. She felt strangely hollow, as though her head was a rotting stump: open at the top and ready for the receipt of steady rainwater.

Yet that hollow feeling didn't stop at her head. It hovered, too, around her heart and sometimes down her stomach. Especially when she looked at the spirit, the first spirit, who had found her in this place. Especially when he looked back at her in return.

Now that she was less afraid of him—at least, convinced that she was not in imminent peril when she was near him—the wild girl could look at him with abandon. As he spoke with his companion she stared intensely into the features of his face. It occurred to her that he resembled her reflection as presented in puddles and easy-going streams.

At the very least, he had two lovely blue-laced orbs that flashed between his conversational partner and the wild girl. He had a mouth that made sounds and ate food, and two ears that, she imagined, permitted him to hear as well as she did.

But then there were so many differences. There was something hard about his face, something pleasing. These hard features and the low timbre of his voice were what made the wild girl relate him somehow to the father and brother wolves of her old pack, fur on his jaw aside. She loved to look at these features of his—these high cheeks, this strong brow, this softly graying dark blond hair that was brighter atop his head than it was upon his face.

Was it as coarse? She cautiously touched his mane and smiled a little when this made him laugh. To her pleasure, the spirit leaned toward her to permit her exploration. Beaming ear-to-ear, the wild girl petted his fur much as she did that of her brothers and sisters, all the while making a noise of delight to find that the pelt atop his head was much softer than the one upon his chin.

The spirit called Jason made a few noises in a funny sort of tone. Ulysses scoffed. Upon uttering a few sounds of his own, he leaned back from the hand he gently removed from his head with a tender pat. The touch seemed to linger. The wild girl studied her hand before busying herself by carving meat off of the leg.

It turned out that both spirits ate just as she did. They slept, too. She had just been wondering when they would try to take her away when Jason yawned, stretched, made a few noises to Ulysses, and gestured out of the campsite. Ulysses nodded his head and said something in an agreeable tone while the baffled wild girl watched.

To her further confusion, Jason waved a hand at her again, said something while gesturing to the leftover meat still warmed by the fire. Then he got up and left the clearing.

For whatever reason, relief swept over the wild girl. It seemed much easier to deal with one spirit than with two, and she liked the furred spirit very much. Not just because he was the first who had come to her, either—she liked him very much because of the way he looked at her, and the way he looked to her, and the way he moved so gently when he was around her.

And, of course, he had given her those funny berries.

Ulysses made some noises that she didn't understand, but she did know his tone was even gentler now that his friend was gone. She tried to find some meaning in them but, after deciding the pattern of sounds didn't repeat in any way she could discern, the girl simply let them wash over her like water over the edge of a muddy bank. After seeing that the wild girl more or less stared into space at him amid his constant sounds, the spirit fell silent and looked around himself.

Aha! An idea brightened his face. He patted her knee before he clambered to his feet, stretching a bit and muttering some noise under his breath while striding over to the den. There, he stooped and delicately picked up the red box he had most recently given her. After returning to her side, he sat down again and opened the box.

What had happened before was now repeated; only now, instead of touching his chest while repeating a sound, he touched the box. This sound was longer than 'Jason' and either as or more complex than the sound 'Ulysses.' She couldn't help but wonder at the invention of such sounds—was she capable of making such sounds as that, inventing them from out of her head?

She was distracting herself. She tried to focus. The girl had the sense that he wanted to teach her something.

Seeing she wasn't fully understanding, Ulysses opened the box and pointed to one of the berries inside. He once again made the complex sound and she frowned, trying to repeat it.

"Chocolal," she mumbled out, looking up at him uncertainly.

To her relief, he chuckled even more warmly than he had when she petted his head. After producing a few amiable sounds, he plucked up the chocolal and offered it to her.

"Chocolate," he repeated, adding emphasis on the 't'.

"Ah," said the girl, "chocolate."

With pleasure, the spirit praised her again. The wild girl smiled in pride. Only at his slight gesture with the 'chocolate' did she understand he wanted her to take it. She carefully extended her palm and cooed as he dropped it in her hand.

Chocolate! Was that what these berries were called? Well, whatever they were called, she loved them more than anything else she had eaten. This second encounter with them sealed that opinion. What tree in the forest produced these delicious little fruits? What bush sprang with berries the spirits called chocolate?

Her mind whirred desperately. If she had sounds with meanings she might find a way to ask. How frustrating! How did spirits learn these sounds? How did they learn to make them to each other?

"Ah." The girl pointed at a bush, hoping to get the message across.

Ulysses followed her gaze and uncertainly asked, "Jason?"

Though she was momentarily confused—did Jason mean something she didn't actually understand?—soon she realized she had pointed in the same direction the other spirit had gone. Ulysses thought she wanted to know about it, apparently. No, not really. All she wanted to know now was how to get more of that delicious chocolate stuff.

"Ah," she repeated, now gesturing to another bush.

Ulysses hummed in consideration, trying to get her meaning. Eventually she had to scramble up and slap a few leaves of the bush with her open palm. "Oh!" Laughing, he told her, "Bush. Bush."

"Bush," repeated the girl, the word bursting out of her somewhat violently. "Bush…chocolate?"

Again, it took a few seconds for her meaning to come through clearly. When it did, he laughed in a merry way and shook his head. More words flowed through him; she didn't understand them. Finally, when they had finished, he picked up another chocolate berry and extended it for her to eat. "No chocolate bush," he said, repeating a word she'd heard him use a few times, 'no.' She had little experience with it, yet still managed to piece together the disappointing reality easily enough. Frowning, the girl leaned forward and, using her mouth, took the berry from his hand without thinking of it.

Ulysses gasped softly as her lips brushed his fingers. "Oh," he said, drawing his hand away as though in shock while looking into her uncomprehending face. A few meaningless noises flowed from him—meaningless to her, anyway. She worked on chewing the berry and, just as she was going to indicate her desire another, he put the whole box in her hand with a few more noises.

He got up.

He put on the object that had been set aside, that he wore the way she wore mother wolf's old head.

He made another noise and turned to leave.

Panic fluttered in the wild girl's heart. No! He couldn't leave. If he left, she'd be alone again. Alone with one antler. Looking at him, sitting beside him, it were as though she had two perfectly-matched, towering antlers: tree branches rising from her head and her heart. Hurriedly setting the box aside, the girl sprang up and caught his hand.

"Ah," she protested before remembering, "U-lysses—Ulysses—"

A noise fell from his lips. The spirit turned to look at her, somewhat surprised, then all the moreso when she threw her arms around his waist and held him as close as she could.

For reasons she didn't understand, her eyes filled with tears. Maybe it had something to do with the thought that she was more willing by the second to leave her life behind—or maybe it was more. For some reason she was not just saddened at the thought of the spirit leaving, but also afraid. Afraid that something might happen to him. Then she would never see him again.

And oh, how she wanted to see him again! He was so kind. Kinder than she would have expected for something that had taken mother-wolf in the night like that. With a gentle coo, the spirit wrapped his arms around her. The wild girl inhaled sharply the curious, complicated scent of his warm body. She had never been held by anything that resembled herself before.

She had petted wolves and snuggled up with her litter-mates; she had roped deer that she then wrestled to the ground; she had even had a close brush with the black bears before she got into the custom of leaving them scraps far from camp. But never had she been held, touched, petted by a being in return. Certainly never with so much kindness.

Tears welled rapidly in the wild girl's eyes and spilled over twice as fast as they did when the teacher mushroom showed her so many brilliant things. The girl made a noise of longing—a noise of hope that he might stay with her in the safety of the camp and continue holding her like this. Why, after all, did the spirit need to go back whence it came? Why did it need to take her? Couldn't it stay there in the camp?

If the spirit had really come for her, couldn't they be together there instead of elsewhere?

The tone of his voice still as gentle as anything she had ever heard, Ulysses made a series of melodious noises—the same singing that had lured her back to the clearing when she'd abandoned it in her fright. Her breath hitched sharply, then froze. She shut her eyes and listened, not just to the spirit's voice but to the sound of his beating heart.

"Ah," cooed the girl softly, looking up into his face. It almost hurt her to look at him so close for so long! A hard hurt to explain. There was no wound in her, but there was still a terrible ache—a flame in her chest burning brighter every second she spent admiring him.

The longer he looked at her, the more his singing faded. He looked on her silently, somehow troubled.

Did he feel the same ache?

The girl rested a hand upon his chest, that same spot that so ached in her. The spirit once more gasped as though she were the frightening one.

He gently patted her hand, then unwound his other arm from her body.

How she loved to be held! She wanted the experience again; longer. As much as her chest burned, her flesh tingled with the tangible memories of that tender touch. In search of it again, she caught him by an elusive hand and attempted to draw him back into the camp with her. Maybe they could sit under her roof? She wasn't sure the spirit would fit, but if it meant he would stay then she would have happily slept outside in the cold—she would even have given him the fantastic fur that she was now certain he had left.

Finally, with a look around, the spirit extricated his hand from hers and made a gentle noise. He lifted one finger and the girl's heart dropped, not understanding the gesture. Somehow she thought it was a kind of negation and, though he then eased both open hands toward her as though urging her to stay in place, she couldn't help but worry and take one step after him. "Ulysses," she said again.

But the spirit only repeated its gentle noise and vanished into the trees.

A sad cry lifted from the girl's lips—the cry of her aching heart. She watched him go, hand on that pained organ, and wilted upon the ground like a flower in the dry season.

Oh, come back! His gentle hands upon her had given her such a sweet feeling of symmetry—a bright inner glow of fulfillment that normally only came with hard things, like crafting sharp weapons or taking down a great animal. His touch reminded her of the safety of the den: being snuggled with her family while waiting for the hunters to return.

The wild girl glanced at mother wolf, then realized with a start of shame that she had not offered any of the sweet chocolate berries to her.

Mother wolf! Bring the spirit back, bring Ulysses back! Hurrying over to the box still resting on the forest floor, the girl selected one of her favorite colors of berry and rushed back to offer it. She had just knelt to kiss the wolf's s bony paws when, to the joyful surge of her heart, a few leaves cracked in the night.

Ulysses reappeared from the trees.

ULYSSES

ULYSSES WAS PROFESSIONAL. He was a trained anthropologist who had spent years in school. He had come to America with grant money awarded to him by Cambridge. He had written many books and was well-respected within his field.

Yet he had to ask himself, as he returned to the wild girl's camp, what exactly he thought he was doing. Jason asked it aloud when Ulysses found him and informed him that he would be spending the night in the clearing with their subject.

"You'd better leave this part out of your book," was what the guide suggested wryly while Ulysses left him for the night.

Maybe so. But he had noble intentions, Ulysses. He had a scientific interest in the girl, and he had to gain her trust. If they were really going to convince her to leave with them the next morning, the doctor had to assure her that she could rely on him—that she wouldn't be abandoned in the middle of the woods.

And, anyway…she had been so terribly, heart-wrenchingly sweet. His name slurring from her lips, the tight embrace of those arms packed with lean muscle but smooth to the touch.

The pain in her face at her obvious understanding of his intention to leave.

No. He hadn't been able to leave such a sweet girl alone for the night. Not when she wanted him to stay.

But now they were alone together. The terrible male fear of being left alone with a beautiful woman gradually crept over him: an abstract pressure weighted upon him, the urgings of nature combating with the wisdom of human consciousness. He was grateful that the girl in all likelihood did not fully understand the origins of animal life, let alone the recreational aspects of the process. If she had shown such interest in him, the anthropologist might not have been able to resist her.

Thank God, the girl was wholly innocent, and her intentions toward him quite wholesome. He had returned with his bed roll and, seeing him arrange it along the fireside, she produced a pleasurable chirp and hurried to her lean-to. First she removed the mink coat he had left for her—he tried not to cringe while she lay it temporarily upon the ground, but the situation was soon rectified. From within the lean-to she removed a wolf's fur and, after kissing it with all the sweetness of a child for her favorite doll, the wild girl arranged this more clumsily-produced but still admirable fur upon the ground beside his bedroll. Over this, she pulled the mink like a blanket. Then, with a thoughtful and happy sound, she demonstrated that the mink could fit over both the wolf fur and the bed roll. Ulysses strove to see only her innocence, her generosity of spirit.

"Yes," he said at her gesture toward the bedding, "yes, that's very nice…thank you, my dear. How thoughtful."

She had no comprehension of his words, but she could understand his tone very well. She smiled at his praise and then, happy as could be, flopped down amid her furs with the box from the chocolatier.

"Ulysses," she said, patting the bedroll to encourage him to sit. With a chuckle, he slipped off his shoes and did. While she once again opened the box, she surprised him. Rather than nibbling on the chocolate she selected, she instead held it out to him.

"Oh," he said, laughing in surprise. "for me? That's very kind—"

He had not been expecting her to press it straight to his lips, but…well. He supposed one had to expect boundaries to be rather different for an innocent creature who had no social contact. Obediently opening his mouth, Ulysses let her push the chocolate in upon his tongue and—rather amazingly—didn't even think about her grubby fingers. They were lovely fingers, lovely hands. Lovely wrists, lovely eyes. Eyes that gazed into him, oh! How she stared—like an owl, like a cat. His heart gave a queer flutter even as he chewed the chocolate.

"Delicious," he told her once he swallowed, yielding a giddy smile from her happy lips. The girl picked up another chocolate and attempted to feed him a second time, but he laughed and gently pushed back against her hand. "No, no, that's enough for me. They're for you. The chocolates are for you."

"Chocolalate," the girl mumbled thoughtfully, glancing into the box and eating her selection herself. It was funny—she was wild, of course, or at the very least uncivilized. But she was so *careful* with things.

Perhaps because she had to be. She turned the little chocolate all around, pinched between her fingers, examining it in the firelight before taking it into her mouth. A squeal of pleasure rose from her lips as the chocolate burst to release its fudgy center. She grinned, more eagerly masticating the candy while giving the box a happy shake.

Interestingly, the girl had some sense of conservation. She shut the box back up and held it to her heart, then set it upon the earth beside their bedding.

Then—again, to his surprise—she turned back to lean against him, sliding beneath his arm with a sweetly animal coo. "Ah," she said with a pat of the bedding. "Ah, ah!"

"Yes," he agreed, not knowing what else to say, "yes, it's a very nice bed."

She bit her lip. He wasn't quite sure what she was getting at. "Ah," she said again, folding his arm around her body and inspiring a surge of absolute adoration.

Oh, she was so sweet to touch! So good to hold. The girl fit in his arm as though made for it; the weight of her head upon his shoulder seemed like something out of a dream he had once had and then forgotten at the moment of waking. Even that earthy scent of her hair, a far cry from the florally perfumed locks of European and even American women, filled him up with simple pleasure.

He breathed of her deeply, paying no mind to thoughts of fleas or lice or ticks or dirt or grit. She was perfect, perfect to him, and it saddened him very much whenever he had to remind himself that she was the subject of research and not a potential lover.

There was no reason he couldn't be kind to her, however—couldn't be fond of her. At her encouragement, he took up gently petting her arm, smiling at her sigh. "Isn't that nice? You must have been alone for a very long time."

Without so much as a grunt for response, the girl gazed up at him and then lifted a hand to caress his beard. Ulysses chuckled—how easily his smiles seemed to inspire hers!

"I wish you could understand me completely," he told her, his tone as soft as her touch. "I would like very much for you to come back with me. I just don't want you to be afraid, or confused…but I suppose at some point that's going to be unavoidable."

How she gazed! Those great dark eyes glittered with the firelight. What worked within the mind of this displaced engineer, this re-inventor of mankind's first technologies? How was the mind formatted when it did not have language with which to format itself? Did she even have a sense of self, really, as distinct from the forest around her?

"We need to think of a name for you," he said, more to himself than to her.

He had considered this subject quite a few times over the past two weeks of preparation, though he had still come up with nothing.

It wasn't really his place to name her, after all. Ideally she would name herself, or better still would come with a name already attached; but, with no moniker to distinguish her by, he supposed that he was as responsible for helping her establish an identity in the human world as he was for protecting her in that human world.

Because he would need to protect her—sadly, yes.

In the forest, she had been more than capable of protecting herself. But among the other human beings, it occurred to the researcher now that she would be unsafe in many new and different ways. He frowned at the thought. Watching his face as carefully as she did, she frowned along with him.

"Ulysses," she said, still petting his beard.

"Ah, it's nothing—just thinking. Well, what should we call you? Eva? Mary?" She stared blankly at him. Her non-response made him chuckle. "Yes, you're right…a little predictably Biblical."

Lost in thought now, going through the list of every woman's name he knew, (she certainly was not a Bernadette or a Rosa, but maybe a Dahlia or a Poppy would suit her), the researcher happened to glance toward the stars peeking into the clearing where the two sat in their makeshift bed. Even with the fire burning, the fast-fallen night sky swirled with a thicker network of glittering lights than one could see from any city or even any town.

When he glanced back down he found she had begun looking up along with him. The stars glowed in her eyes like the firelight had.

"Estelle," he said spontaneously, sliding the name over her to find that it fit like a glove. At his utterance, her gaze shifted over to him. He smiled. "Yes—Estelle."

The girl looked at him blankly until he touched his chest and said, "Ulysses."

While she looked on, the hand around her patted her touchable arm. "Estelle." Again, he patted her—"Estelle"—then himself—"Ulysses."

Her eyes widened in interest. "'stell," she asked, a request for confirmation. Ulysses smiled and nodded.

"Yes! That's right…Estelle, and Ulysses."

"Estelle," she repeated, clearer now, stumbling through the syllables in a mimicry of his enunciation.

"Perfect." The word drifted faintly from his lips, all the air stolen from his lungs by her great grin of pride. "That's perfect, Estelle."

"Estelle," said the girl happily, glancing down at herself with a smaller, more mystical smile before she abruptly sprang up. "Estelle, Estelle. Estelle…Ulysses."

Her foot knocked the box of chocolates and she frowned down at them. After hurrying to put them away in her lean-to, she then returned with a spear she rested beside the bedding. "Ulysses," she said with a pat of the spear and a look up at him.

He laughed a little. "You mean to say you'll protect me if something goes awry? That's for the best…I don't think I could fend off an animal attack, sad to say."

After clearly thinking about his words for a few long moments before giving up and deciding whatever he had said was meant to be pleasant, the girl straightened up again—

And began to undress.

"Oh," said Ulysses, coughing slightly, glancing away before he could once more see the fine golden body hidden beneath the layers of primitive leather. "Oh, aha, ah—"

"Ah," responded the girl agreeably, perhaps happy to hear him making sensible noises rather than overcomplicated words. While the doctor cleared his throat and continued watching the fire, armor fell at her feet piece by piece. Soon he could sense that she was naked. Dear, dear. This was going to become a problem when he got her back into civilization.

'Problem'—listen to him! He caught himself and repressed a scoff. What was the problem with a young woman sleeping naked during the summer nights? It wasn't *her* problem, really…it was society's problem. She was a perfectly natural girl, the natural human animal in its true environment.

If Estelle wanted to sleep in the nude and he thought strangely of it, wasn't that more a statement on his own immoral thought patterns than a condemnation of what Estelle should change in herself?

Oblivious to his internal dilemma, to the ways civilization had corrupted his views of nature and the perfectly natural human body, Estelle slid into their temporary bed and drew the mink fur over herself.

In the same set of seconds, she snuggled back into his embrace heedless of whetherhe was ready for her. Ulysses's heart seized in his chest at the sensation of her warm body pressing through his clothes, every inch as soft and sweet as was the girl herself.

"Ulysses," she said with a sigh of relief to be held. "Oh!"

The little moan that rose up from her as his hand once more stroked over her arm! It made his eyes squeeze shut. She didn't mean anything by the sound, of course, nor of the situation.

He understood: the anthropologist understood that, after a lifetime of loneliness—of thinking she was the only one of her kind in the world—surely to just be touched was an absolute relief to the senses. What was it like to spend every second of existence anxious for one's life? Ulysses couldn't imagine.

"You're a very sweet girl," he said to her softly. "I'm very glad I found you."

She cooed in response; her eyes were already closed. Not long after, she had fallen asleep in his arm.

Ulysses awoke very early the next morning, the softening blue of pre-dawn lightousing him more naturally than any wake-up call from a hired maid or the valet he'd brought to America with him. And the sight that waited for him upon awakening, ah, it was naturally far lovelier. Estelle dreamed with her back to him, her face hidden by locks of disheveled hair, her breathing steady with the peace of her dreams. Her free hand rested beside the spear. Ulysses thought of Siegfried, claiming to lay his sword between himself and Brunhilde to protect her purity in the night. Whether or not he truly did was up to the interpretation of the director.

Dr. Cochran, on the other hand, was faithful to his good intentions. How fond he was of the girl! And, yes— as a man, how admiring he was of her body. She was beautiful, lithe as a doe. He ached to touch her and, when he awoke, it was hard to deny that his mind whirred with a few profane fantasies he worked to banish.

All the more reason to protect her. Not all men would show such restraint. He almost hoped he had not already taught her to trust people too much by virtue of his kindness.

Gingerly, he touched her shoulder—now it was his turn to flinch. The girl sprang awake at once, snatching up her spear in an orchestration of muscle memory that would have been astonishing if it hadn't ended with a flint spearhead pointed at his nose. "Estelle," he cried, throwing up his hands as the veil of sleep at last fell from her face.

"Ah! Ulysses—"

Gasping to realize what she'd almost done, the girl dropped the spear right away and sat up. The mink fur fell from her body and he inhaled at the flash of flesh dimpled in the cold of the night. He hadn't had a chance to recover from the glimpse before soft hands caressed his face.

She knelt before him, cooing, petting him in contrition.

"It's all right," said Ulysses, encouraging her gently while the brush nearby crashed. Only then did the girl lower her hands to snatch up her spear again, but the doctor stayed her hand while his guide appeared in the encampment.

"Doctor Cochran! Is everything all—"

Jason glanced between the two of them and instantly wheeled away, slapping a hand across his eyes. "Excuse me! I thought I heard—uh—"

"There's no problem, Jason. I just woke her up too quickly, that's all. Don't worry."

While Estelle, with a lingering look of caution for the interloper, once more lowered her spear with no second thoughts for her nudity, the researcher added in a tone that he couldn't help but admit was a little defensive, "As you can see, she thinks nothing of basic cultural taboos such as nudity. Insisted on taking off her clothes for bed!"

"I'm sure you're just fascinated," answered Jason dryly, his back politely to the clearing. "Well, if she's coming with us, you'd ought to get her dressed again as soon as you can. I want to get started soon—if we hurry it up we might be able to make it back to town by dark."

The doctor's heart fluttered with joy, with hope. Oh! The thought of learning from Estelle—the thought of teaching Estelle, and showing her the joys of society. Smiling, Ulysses took the girl's hand into his.

"Estelle," he said, gesturing. "Estelle and Jason and Ulysses."

With the same hand that had gestured between the three of them, he now waved toward the edge of the clearing. The girl followed the motion, then studied his face more carefully. He said it again, then said, "Jason—why don't you go ahead and take her chocolates from over there. See if it helps her understand."

As the guide did what he'd been bidden, Estelle's sweet lips drooped into a frown. "Estelle and Jason and Ulysses and chocolate," the anthropologist said, once more waving between all three humans before gesturing toward the edge of the trees.

"Come with us, Estelle."

Somehow, on this second repetition, she got it. At least, she seemed to—but he wasn't quite sure just what she understood. Her lower lip sliding between her teeth to nibble there adorably, Estelle's big, dark eyes trailed between the two men before drifting to the altar of wolf bones.

"Estelle," she whispered to the orchestration.

Yes—somehow Ulysses got the impression that she *did* understand they would all be leaving.

Leaving, and probably never back again.

"It'll be such a nice—oh—"

Before he could so much as finish his thought, a sorrowful wail rose up from the girl's bosom. To his surprise, tears made an immediate and rapid trek down her cheeks. All thoughts of her alluring innocence were forgotten beside the immediate instinct to comfort and protect her.

While her shoulders shook with her hiccuping sobs, her grief for the thought of leaving this place, Ulysses drew her into his arms and tucked her head beneath his chin. He rocked her, patting her back with one hand and using the other to stroke her wild mane as she soaked his shirt with salt.

"Sh, Estelle…sh…there, there. I know how hard it is to change."

"I'm going to go break down our camp," said Jason with a lingering look toward Estelle. A frown twisted his somewhat stern mouth. No doubt he saw in her sorrow the very least of his ancestors' plights—yes, the very least. He turned away and made himself scarce to do as he'd said. All the while Ulysses gently petted the beautiful wild girl.

"I know it's hard," he said again, softer now. "But I can keep you safe—I can keep you safe and healthy, Estelle, and give you things you can't have here. I'm not a doctor of medicine, but I'm a doctor all the same, Estelle. Let me treat you kindly, as a doctor does his patient. Let me teach you to speak as much as I can. Let me teach you what it is to sleep in comfort and security in a room and the embrace of a soft bed."

Though she understood these words no better than any of the others he had spoken, Estelle's frantic tears slowly eased to a stop. Soon the torrent had reduced to the occasional pathetic sniffle of a pretty little orphan. And she was that, wasn't she? From his pocket, Ulysses withdrew his handkerchief to wipe her tears from her cheek. She gazed up at him through red-ringed eyes that glistened like the face he cleaned, her lips still drawn in emotional consternation.

"There…it's all right, Estelle. There's nothing to be afraid of. I know you think this world of yours is all there is. And it's a beautiful world. A simple world. But there's so much more out there, my girl…things you could hardly begin to comprehend in your current condition."

"Ulysses," whispered the wild girl, staring tearfully into his face.

"I'll take care of you, Estelle. I'll take care of you…and

in exchange, you can teach me all about yourself without even having to say a word."

Her pinkened nose sniffed sadly. "Ulysses," she said again, the sound as heart-breaking as any stream of tears.

Seeing her like that, so helpless and tender and emotional, the researcher couldn't help a small breach of professionalism in the name of easing his subject's mind. Slowly, carefully, Ulysses lowered his head. The lingering remains of her tears halted as she waited to see what he would do.

Very gently, the anthropologist kissed her cheek.

Her breath hitched in a soft gasp; Ulysses's entire body yearned for another kiss, another, and all the things that came with enough kisses lovingly applied to a woman's face—but, denying his urges, he pulled away. Instead he glanced at her nearby pile of armor and reached behind her, patting it to draw her attention.

"Come, now," he encouraged her. "Why don't you get dressed? Then, we'll go."

Her sensually sheepish gaze flickered over him for a handful of seconds, then back in the direction of her altar. She bit her lip and lowered her head. He half-expected her to put up some kind of fight, or to try to bargain somehow. In either such case, he would have let her stay where she was—no matter how it pained him to do so.

Yet, to his joy, Estelle got up to dress.

ESTELLE

IT HURT ESTELLE to think of leaving mother wolf. At the very least, she could bring part of mother wolf with her—the most important parts. After seeing the way Ulysses rolled his strangely-textured fur into a bundle, the wild girl had a clever idea.

Using mother wolf's fur in a similar fashion, Estelle took one of the bony paws with profuse apologies and many presses of her lips to the partially dismembered skeleton. Into this makeshift pack of fur she folded the paw, the cool and strange device the spirit had left in exchange for her first offering of food, and a dagger she had recently made. It was very kind of the spirits to permit her to bring anything at all with her—after all, mother wolf had been forced to leave everything behind. Her cubs, her body, her Estelle.

Estelle! Thinking of that word emboldened the wild girl somewhat. It was very strange to have a word applied to one's person this way. It made her feel different to think of herself as something specific—as an Estelle—rather than simply as part of the system of the world. Somehow it made her feel sturdy; firmer than she ever had, as if all this time she had been shifting forms and now Ulysses had caught her, put her into one single way of being. He watched her while she packed up those portions of her life that she wished to take, making no noise at all as she said good-bye to the many things she loved.

She petted her den's roof, which had so kindly protected her from the elements all season long; she dawdled many times to kiss and pet and say good-bye to mother wolf's body; she put a hand on the stones of her fire pit to extend her gratitude for all the nights it had kept her warm and dispelled predators.

Then, sad but satisfied, she set mother wolf's skull atop her head and turned to see Ulysses still watching.

"Ulysses," she said.

"Estelle," he said.

The spirit extended his hand and, with one last nervous glance at mother wolf's remains, Estelle stepped forward to take it.

Good-bye, camp! Good-bye, life. Were the spirits so kind and gentle to mother wolf when they took her away from her body? It was very generous of them for her to leave Estelle's with her. She admired the good spirit that had permitted this transition to be as painless and simple as possible—he was very kind. Very kind, and very gentle.

The girl remembered the soft caress of his warm hand along the bare flesh of her arm. For some reason her face heated, and in the heat was the craving to feel that touch again. Ah! She wanted those hands on every part of her, in fact. Surely if it felt so good to be touched along her arm, being touched along other parts of her body would feel even better. The girl studied their hands, their fingers interwoven, and the heat flooded down to her heart.

Together they beat a short path to the riverbank were first they laid eyes on one another. There, the spirit named Jason had made his own camp for the night. The remains of a fire were almost indistinguishable in the earth, and his back was burdened perhaps even more than was Ulysses's. The spirits exchanged some words until Jason, with a hefty sigh, marched into the trees toward the rising sun. Ulysses led Estelle along even though by rights she ought to have been the one leading them.

To a certain point, anyway. She did not travel far through these parts of the forest because this was where the bears lived—and although the bears were generous when it came to accepting their tithes and leaving her be, Estelle knew that they would not be quite so kindly-disposed if they came upon the travelers together in the forests. However, she could not help but think perhaps the spirits had some kind of magic to them: no bears found them as they made their way through the forest that day.

No wolves, either. It had been many seasons since she had visited her old pack, but the thought of not visiting ever again made her very sad. Perhaps someday they would also be taken by the spirits, and then the entire family would reunite. Mother wolf, too.

There were many other things she would miss about the forest, as well. Teacher mushrooms, for instance. Estelle noticed a cluster growing in the rotten wood of a fallen log. She gave a cry of recognition at the valuable, sentient substance that grew quietly and minded its business until an animal came to ask a question of it. "Ah," she said with an eager point, pausing to tug on Ulysses's hand.

"Hm?"

The spirit paused in following its companion, glancing off in the direction of her point. He made a few interested noises and she repeated her own more adamantly. With a thin smile that indicated a clear lack of comprehension, Ulysses turned to try to continue their path forward.

Estelle slipped her hand from his and hurried over to the mushroom patch. Knowing she would not be back, she picked the entire cluster and pushed them into her fur before Ulysses could stop her. When he made it to her side, he must have thought it had been the nearby flowers she was after: he smiled and picked a few of the violet-petaled plants, which he then handed to her with a look of pleasure and a tip of his headgear.

Well…it was a nice gesture, anyway.

The day was long and when the sun reached its peak the spirits stopped to rest, making spaces together on the mossy earth to share a meal. What it was, Estelle didn't understand. Some kind of meat, yes, but dry and shriveled; it reminded her almost of the different texture of a hide after she processed it to be worn. There was also something else, too…though, again, it was hard to say just what it was.

A cake of some kind of fat? A big chunk of something she had expected to taste like mud but found instead to be curious and pleasant, some dense kind of thing she would later learn was called 'hardtack.' Just then it was only another new thing that, while inferior to chocolate, was nonetheless superior to everything she'd ever known if only for reasons of novelty.

All the while, whether they rested or moved through the forest, the spirits talked: mostly to each other, but also to her. Ulysses in particular talked to her quite frequently, never deterred by a lack of definite understanding. He made all manner of noises through his smiles, all these mysterious word-sounds meaning nothing but a degree and style of vibration through the air. He was so warm to her! Warm even without touching her. She wanted to learn how to speak like he did, just as she once longed to sing like the birds.

The three of them had been walking for the whole sun cycle when the trees began to thin a little and the moss was replaced by thicker, more ample grass. On seeing this, Ulysses emitted an "Ah!" of relief: Estelle felt as though she were hearing herself clap eyes on mother wolf's old den the last time she visited.

Ulysses nudged his companion and said something excited, then turned to Estelle with a gentler, more thoughtful smile. He took her hand.

"Estelle," he said, saying something else.

Estelle was very good at pattern recognition. She did not think that she could ever learn all of these noises, but she was excellent and fast when it came to taking note of the pattern of a new bird call after but a few repetitions. She would make them to herself, softly, but they never sounded quite right to her.

The same was true of words. The noises the spirits produced were so fluid, so elegant, that she doubted she could ever quite achieve the same level of articulation. Surely, like birds, these spirits had been making such noises since birth.

Since her birth, Estelle had bared her teeth and nuzzled up to her family members and tried to howl with the pack. Her feeling was that it took all that time and more to produce fluid, meaningful sounds as did the beings who abducted her, but she could nevertheless understand general meanings if the context was obviously clear to her.

The problem was that the context was not clear to her at all. Never having been out of the woods, she did not understand the woods had an end. When Ulysses was telling her how excited he was to show her the world and how he hoped she wouldn't be afraid, she didn't understand a single word. She smiled patiently on, glad it pleased him to talk to her but not even partly comprehending—until what she had thought from a distance to be some vast clearing turned out to be the end of the forest.

She didn't understand.

"Ah," said Estelle softly when Ulysses had guided her from the woods by the hand. "Ah!"

The sight was so staggering that her brain literally could not take it in—not for a long period of many seconds. Expecting as it had to see more woods on the other side of a clearing, it faltered. The sea of meaningless purple stretching far out in front of her seemed somehow so deliriously sudden that it meant nothing, and her eyes instinctively lifted in search of the trees.

There were no trees. Not here. Not on the other side of the dirt road upon which they'd emerged. All the trees had been cut down to permit the growth of lavender, and as far as the eye could see there expanded a swath of purple and green glory. The scent caught upon the wind was the sweetest, cleanest thing she'd ever known: she cried out in astonishment.

Her hand tightening around Ulysses's and her mind captivated by the rolling purple field bathed in the setting sun's melancholy orange, Estelle did not even see the bizarre deer and the great box waiting along the side of the road.

Only when Jason called out to it did she tear her eyes away. Much to her surprise, a third spirit startled awake from where he napped in the front seat. He made a noise like a grumbling bear, scratched the patch of fur over his lip, then sat up.

This new spirit stared at Estelle in astonishment, rubbing his eyes as she often did upon her own awakenings. Ulysses smiled and said something—lots of somethings—that ended in, "…Estelle."

The man before the antlerless deer looked at her again before exclaiming something that was, even to the girl, the hallmark of amazement.

Jason, meanwhile, opened the box and tossed his pack inside. He extended his hands and Estelle permitted him to take mother wolf's fur. As Ulysses also divested himself, Estelle edged up to the pawing, fidgeting creature that had been attached to the box by some fascinating contraption.

When it came to the creature itself, it was the most beautiful deer Estelle had ever seen. Its mane and all its fur was sleek; these black, short, shimmering hairs showed their gloss as its hooves pattered uncomfortably back and forth along the dirt. It eyed her cautiously.

The man behind the creature made some noises. She wasn't sure what he was trying to get across until Ulysses appeared at her elbow, his hand sliding into the small of her back while his other gestured toward the creature before her.

The third time he said the word 'horse,' Estelle understood that this was the noise that distinguished this creature from the world in the same way that 'Estelle' was the noise that distinguished her. She smiled at it.

"Horse," she named it, beaming, less pleased with herself than she was with the animal for existing.

"Very good!"

This was also a noise she was starting to recognize when Ulysses produced it. Whatever it meant, it seemed to denote something nice—something like the pride her family would shower her with when she helped them take down a deer. Similarly, Ulysses patted her back or her arm when he made such a noise, as he did now before this other spirit.

"Mark," he explained with a few repetitions, labeling the third spirit who had been waiting with the horse and the box.

So many noises! It was amazing to her that all of these spirits each had their own noise. Surely, if that was so, there couldn't be too many spirits—how could they all have their own unique noises? Were there that many noises one could even produce? She rolled it about in her head while Mark got down from his seat at the front of the box to open it for her.

With one last look around—first at the horse, then at the lovely purple fields, then at her beloved forest—Estelle climbed into the box with help from Ulysses. She perched uncomfortably upon the edge of the same seat where her helper-spirit settled himself with a sigh. He removed his headpiece and waved himself with it before setting it in his lap. Estelle removed mother wolf's skull and held it to her heart for comfort.

This box…what was it for? Why were they here? She looked all around it, baffled, then all the more baffled by the strange hole that had been cut into its side. This hole permitted her to look out over the lavender fields, yet when she lifted a hand to reach out to them she encountered some kind of cool material.

When she looked over, she found another square on the other side, next to the seats where the spirits had settled in. Jason already leaned back, arms folded, eyes shut in an attempt to summon sleep. She pressed her finger to the transparent covering of the hole and looked over her shoulder at Ulysses.

Then, all at once, an earthquake struck. Estelle cried out while she lurched against her helper-spirit, clutching him and looking wildly about for an escape to safety. Jason groaned and made some noise under his breath but Ulysses made one that was far more pleasant, far more consoling. As the box began to lurch and shake he draped his arm around her trembling shoulders, his other hand catching up hers to hold and squeeze. Many sounds fell from his mouth, especially one in particular. "There, there," he told her again and again, often between other words.

Her heart hammering with fear, especially to find that the earthquake did not stop after a short period but continued on and on, Estelle dared to glance with fright to that strangely sealed hole. A gasp tore from her mouth: all around them, the world had begun to move.

On one side, the fields whizzed by, flying off and out of sight. On the other side, the trees of the forest dashed away, an entire army of trunks careening off into the distance. She gazed up at Ulysses in terrible fear, clutching the front of his clothing while he hummed and petted her. Gradually, seeing how the terror didn't leave her, he drew her head down to his chest and pressed it to his heart.

The rhythm of the beat within began, slowly, to soothe her. His heartbeat reminded her very much of mother wolf's, save for the fact that it was steadier—mightier somehow. Inhaling sharply, the wild girl clutched him tight and shut her eyes. Surely, if the spirits were not afraid, then Estelle had no cause to be afraid either. Whatever was happening was meant to happen—part of whatever process had happened to mother wolf, perhaps.

In the arms of the spirit, Estelle looked down into the open eyes of her mother's skull. Mother wolf never wanted the girl to be afraid. When thunder would crack and Estelle would weep with fright, the good-natured animal would wag her tail and kiss her daughter wildly. There, there, Estelle now imagined her mother wolf saying.

All this business—the rocking box and the whipping landscape—went on for quite a long time. Neither spirit showed any trace of fear and in fact Jason slept soundly, his snores filling the box the way the noisy sleep of wolves once filled the den. Anxious all the same, the girl peered up at the friend-spirit whose embrace was so comforting and whose presence had, just the night before, brought on her a richer sleep than any she'd ever experienced.

She found him fully awake and watching her. When their eyes met, he smiled and gently eased her back from his chest. Ulysses pointed at the transparent hole and the girl turned to see its presented vision with great dis-ease.

Yet, something marvelous had happened. The land around the box had changed. Now, instead of fields of purple flowers, a vast green sea expanded out in all direc-tions. Strange little trees no higher than one's waist stood between the box and this sea, and on the other side of these squat trees meandered the oddest deer the girl had ever seen. Astonished, she pressed her face closer to the transparent surface of the hole.

Remarkable! And here she had thought the horse was a strange deer…these fat, black and white deer with broad noses and big, placid eyes wandered around the field, always moving out of sight to be replaced by others.

She made a sound of surprise to Ulysses, who leaned over her shoulder to point with one hand and caress her arm with the other.

"Cows," he said a few times.

"Cows," repeated the girl, smiling, then sighing at the gentle petting of his warm hand. Warm though it was, it sent a chill running through her—a pleasant, exciting chill that seemed somehow to increase the longer he touched her, yet somehow stoked the flame in her heart. She sighed again, more contentedly now, and looked into the spirit's face. He looked back, and oh! She smiled just to be looked at by him.

Ulysses smiled back—then, abruptly, frowned. She looked at him in confusion but he only leaned away with one more pat of her arm, evidently feeling that he had instilled enough of a sense of confidence to leave her alone. Estelle was almost tempted to become afraid again just for the sake of being held, but she was so intrigued by the movement of the landscape and the funny shapes of these foreign deer that it would have been difficult to pretend at such a thing. There were even among them smaller fawns: funny little deer not quite as portly as their mothers.

Ah—'cows.' She had to remember they were cows. Cows and horses and Ulysses and Jason.

And Estelle, who, still watching the landscape fly by, leaned back against her helper-spirit's arm with a smile. Perhaps, much as she sensed, change was not all that bad. Not all the time, anyway.

ULYSSES

ESTELLE'S SPATE OF fear upon the rolling of the coach struck Dr. Cochran with terrible guilt. It was amazing to him she had survived in the wild and was, inside her heart, obviously so tenacious—her innocent features were so gentle, so expressive in their sensitivity, that even the movement of a carriage through the countryside had profound impact upon her.

Not that Ulysses couldn't understand why. It must have been incredibly overwhelming. He had recently read an article about strange encounters enjoyed by rural Americans with individuals purportedly flying some kind of airship.

Although he could not help but find the stories a playful bit of speculative fiction, they had their parallels in the wild girl's surreal experience. The nearer they came to the city, the more he realized he had to teach her. Her linguistic skills were like a small child's. An intelligent, precocious child's, but a child's nonetheless.

Would she be able to learn English—or any other language, for that matter—with any true degree of fluency? She was able to reproduce sounds and connect them back to the objects they represented well enough…but there were harder matters. Abstract notions like verbs, time. Love. Were these things she would be able to understand and speak on with any degree of success? Just last year he had read another, far more believable news story: an interesting piece about a deaf-blind woman who had comprehended language somewhat later than other children but had still, at the age of twenty-four, managed to graduate from Radcliffe. No doubt Ms. Keller would continue to impress and inspire…but she had also grasped these principles of language, of the world outside her sense-deadened prison, prior to her twenties.

It was difficult to tell how old Estelle was, but she was certainly an adult. If he had to guess, Ulysses would have put her somewhere between eighteen and twenty-two. The shape of her body and the general arrangement of features across her face gave reasonable indication to this effect—then, of course, there were the many accomplishments of her engineering talents, which were not the achievements of a mere girl but of a woman who had already spent a lifetime hard at work in the perfection of her crafts.

So had to be a bit concerned about her ability to speak. Reading and writing? Well…those would have to wait. Her education would be a long process.

He reminded himself that even a child as old as ten years could only read to a certain degree of efficacy. Ten years from now, with much work, she might reach that level—but he was far more concerned with her speech facilities than with her literacy.

It was funny. He should have been detached from the issue. He reminded himself that he needed a neutral stance toward the girl, wherein he neither wanted her to succeed nor fail but instead simply maintained a scientific interest in whether or not she could learn such things. But—he couldn't help it. He looked at her, at this softly smiling girl overlooking a field of lambs they passed by, and he wished to talk to her. He found not some base scientific interest but a far more acute, personal one. The desire to learn about another human being and discover the contents of their mind.

What had she been through? What had she done? What did she like and what did she hate? He wanted to know everything about her, everything! Clearly she had experienced some positive interactions with something in her life. Did she have any memories of a mother or a father? Failing that, perhaps she had encountered some beneficent animal. If every creature in her world had been unfriendly, she surely would not have been so gently disposed to Ulysses and his traveling companion.

Ah…the anthropologist had so many questions. So many. And the thought that they might never be answered filled him with such dread that, by the time the gaslights of the city glowed softly in the distance of the fallen night, he had committed fully to the issue of the girl's education.

One way or another, he would see to it that they could at least speak to one another. At least exchange basic thoughts, if not complex ones.

While the road beneath their carriage took on the stability of pavement and the ride, after one last clatter, became notably smoother, Jason stirred with a snort and a jolt that alerted Estelle more than even the transition of the road's paving. He looked up and, finding their carriage dark, glanced out the window.

"Hope Bonnie's still waiting around for us," said Jason. "We're lucky Mark is paid to wait around and run errands for you all the time anyway. My sister's much more impatient."

"I should have brought Mrs. Halbrook," said Ulysses with a sigh, then a frowning glance over at the oblivious girl. "She's going to be in for quite a surprise when we get back to England…I'll have to send her a letter soon."

"Are you really going to take this girl back to Europe with you? Bringing her on a ship sounds like a terrible idea. She already seems frightened enough of the coach."

"Now, I think she's adjusted just fine. Estelle is adaptable." At the sound of her name, the girl glanced over and Ulysses showed a smile of pleasure for her ability to learn so quickly. "After all, she already knows her name. Estelle," he repeated. She smiled slightly at him.

"Ulysses," she responded, glancing back out the window.

"You see? Even my name."

"I once saw a man with a parrot that would repeat whatever you said to it. In fact, it wouldn't stop talking until it got a nut or a fruit or something else to eat. That bird didn't know up from down, but it could have recited all the cardinal directions and your home address if you said them to it first."

"Estelle isn't a parrot," said the doctor, unable to help his terse tone. "She's a human being. Unsocialized, yes, of course, and very inexperienced when it comes to existing in the human world—but that doesn't make her any less human than you and I, nor any less capable of change."

"I suppose we'll see," said Jason with a grim glance at the girl. "I just think you're setting yourself up for disappointment, Ulysses…and for trouble."

Short-tempered for as hungry and tired he was after a long day of journeying, Ulysses wasn't in the mood to let his friend get away with these sorts of comments. "And what trouble is that, exactly? With Cambridge, you mean?"

"With Cambridge—with society." Thoughtfully looking between the two of them, Jason suggested after a few seconds, "If I see so clearly the way you look at her now, barely knowing her at all, how are you going to start looking at her a week from now? A month from now? How quickly are the people in Europe, who have known you for years, going to see the way you think of her written in your face?"

"Would you rather I treated her coldly, Jason? Do you think I ought to have trapped her in a cage like some kind of animal? Hauled her back to town in a net?"

"You bought her chocolates and a fur coat before she'd even left the forest," said Jason, remembering now to remove those chocolates from his jacket. As he passed them over to Ulysses, he said, "I think I'll leave it at that."

With a sniff of displeasure for these crude speculations of his intentions, Ulysses opened the box and glanced inside. He nudged the girl with his elbow. "Chocolates, Estelle?"

"Chocolate," the girl said. The word was a mumble indicating that, even as taken by the chocolates as she was, she was far more taken by the sight of the earthbound stars growing nearer all the time. Good God! What did she think was happening to her? Ulysses couldn't fathom the contents of her mind; the overwhelming confusion she surely experienced to look upon the encroaching city.

Gently, he rested the box of chocolates in her hands. Now snapped out of some spell, she smiled faintly at their contents. "Chocolate," she repeated softly, looking up at him and selecting one she tried to lift to his lips. "Ulysses?"

At Jason's noise—something between a scoff and a clearing of his throat—Ulysses felt obligated to gently refuse what was intended by the girl as nothing more than an innocent offering of gratitude. "For you," said Ulysses, indicating her. "Chocolates for you, Estelle. You."

"You," said Estelle, murmuring to herself, a parrot's little echo as she pressed the chocolate to her own lips instead of his.

"You," emphasized Ulysses again, touching her arm. "Me," he said, touching his chest. "Him," he said, gesturing toward Jason. After repeating this a few times and watching her understand the pattern, he began to elaborate somewhat: "Me, I am Ulysses. You, you are Estelle. Him, he is Jason."

"Is-Jason," repeated the girl, looking hard for the pattern that was being presented to her.

"Yes," said Jason, open to enlightening the girl with language even if he did not believe it was fully possible. "I am Jason, you are Estelle, he is Ulysses."

After a few more repetitions from both Jason and Ulysses, his little deaf-blind darling (No! Subject, subject, she was his subject, blast it—) at last glowed with the comprehension of water. "Ah! Ah—you, Ulysses!" She pushed him in the shoulder as if copping to some secret code. "Me—I am Estelle?"

"Yes!" The eagerness with which the word burst up from the anthropologist's chest and the clap of joy that accompanied this obviously caused the girl a little start of surprise. Only when she realized that he laughed did she relax and laugh a little herself. "You see," said Ulysses, tapping Jason's knee. "She's extremely intelligent. All language is just patterning. I'm telling you…if we are patient and very gentle with her, we can prove that no one in the world is beyond the reach of education."

"She is educated," said Jason, apparently as argumentative and short-tempered as was Ulysses after another multi-day hike to and from the girl's encampment. "Until you found her and got it in your head that she needed to be saved from her own life, she was perfectly educated to exist in the world. Her world. I still think we should have left her there. I feel awful about this, making her deal with this. She could have lived in peace. Instead—"

The Cherokee descendant, whose mother had avoided the Trail of Tears by working as the maid of a white woman and had filled her son up with story on story of the horrors inflicted upon their people, studied Estelle with sadness. Seeing her brow furrow with concern for his tone, Jason sighed and spoke more gently to Ulysses.

"It's not too late. If you told Mark to turn around, I could take her back for you."

But it was too late. It was absolutely too late.

Jason was very focused on how Ulysses was allegedly looking at and treating Estelle; but in that focus, he failed to see that the gazes were obviously mutual.

Estelle was fascinated by Ulysses—fascinated by everything she saw.

There had been trepidation on leaving the forest and fear at the start of he carriage ride: but now she exhibited only astonishment, nibbling on her chocolates and watching the country transform into houses, businesses, theaters, parks.

She pressed closer to the window again, her breath fogging the glass and her eyes whipping back and forth in a wild attempt to perceive everything they passed.

"Ah," she cried, pointing with a chocolaty finger through the window. "Horse! Horse, Ulysses—"

"That's right," he told her, delighted, allowing himself only one glance sidelong at Jason before removing her sticky hand from the glass to be wiped clean with his handkerchief. "Yes, Estelle, that's right, that was another horse."

"Horse," she repeated while the beast of burden passed out of their view, a wistful tone that carried on as she turned back to her new friends. "Estelle, horse."

"You like horses, Estelle? Well, I'm sure Mark would like your help brushing Herodotus up there...what's that?"

The girl had lifted the skull that she had insisted on bringing with them, the wolf whose other remains had formed her shrine to whatever spirits she held sacred. "Horse," she asked, looking hopefully up at Ulysses.

"Horse? Oh—no, no, ah—'wolf,' Estelle. That was a wolf. Wolf."

"Woof," she said, pronouncing it with a childishly charming drop of the 'l.' For some reason the girl smiled almost sublimely at that, cradling the skull to her bosom as though it were an infant. "Woof, woof..."

"Wolf," corrected Ulysses gently. The carriage came to a stop. "Wolf, my dear...all right! Here we are. Home— home for now, anyway."

"Not a moment too soon," said Jason with a sigh and a glance out the window. While the carriage rocked beneath Mark's dismount, Jason, disinterested in waiting for the valet, popped open the door and whistled to a woman walking far off down the street.

"Bonnie," he called, getting her to stop and causing the look of disgusted irritation for a cat-caller to fade into the recognition of her brother—and new anger to find him so late. He climbed out while saying, "Hey, sorry we're late—"

Marching back, her blue gown whisking around the ankles of her harshly clipping black boots, Bonnie said, "I've wasted time waiting around for two days now! If that doctor wasn't paying me, I'd be a lot angrier than I am. Tell me you got her, at least."

Ulysses, having also dismounted the carriage, now turned to offer Estelle his hand. With a nervous look at him and then up at his hat, she replaced the skull atop her head and gingerly rose from her seat. Hand sliding into his, she permitted him to help her out of the coach. Outside, she looked around wide-eyed, her head whipping from building to streetlight to cobblestones to Ulysses so rapidly that she didn't even see the woman who had joined them.

For Bonnie's part, setting eyes on the wild girl seemed to take some of the wind out of her temperamental sails. "She looks so frightened," said Bonnie, whose voice at last attracted Estelle's attention. "Poor thing."

"Ulysses," the girl said, seeking shelter beneath his arm. She looked Bonnie up and down, obviously somewhat befuddled by the flaring hemline of her gown and the bouffant hairdo tucked up beneath her stylishly wide-brimmed hat...along with everything else in between.

"Her, she is Bonnie," explained Ulysses, maintaining the same pattern he had before. "Me, I am Ulysses. He, he is Jason."

"Me, I am tired," said Jason with a wave of his hand. "Your problem now, Bonnie...good night. I'll check in with you all after I've had a couple of days to sleep."

When Jason made to leave, Estelle took a step toward him—then, noting her protector did not follow suit, she looked uncertainly into his face. "Jason, Ulysses?"

Knowing it was fruitless to try to communicate that Jason was going home to sleep off the long journey and whatever moral qualms he might have felt about this whole project, Ulysses simply patted her shoulder and assured her, "Yes, that was Jason. This is Bonnie, she is Bonnie."

"Bonnie," repeated Estelle softly, staring into Bonnie's soft face. The civilized woman glanced over at Ulysses before focusing on the girl for whom she had been hired, at least for the next month or so, to serve as a sort of lady's maid.

"Bonnie is like you," said Ulysses, trying to explain the difference between 'she' and 'he.' "She is a woman"—next he gestured toward Mark, who had gotten Ulysses's bed-roll out and held the wolfskin like he didn't know what to do with it—"he is a man. She is a woman, you are a woman—I am a man."

"Woman?" The girl looked down at herself, then peered at Bonnie. No doubt her style of dress was so absolutely foreign to the girl that she hardly perceived Bonnie as one of her own species, let alone one of her own sex. She was trying to figure it all out, however, and that was really as much as he could possibly ask for a girl who had just set foot upon paved earth for the first time in her entire life.

"That's right, Estelle, that's right, you are a woman… come along."

Gently, slowly so as not to startle her, Ulysses took Estelle's delicate hand. She smiled, then followed the motions of his other hand as he gestured toward the façade of the hotel towering before them.

"Let's get you settled in…looking at her now, Bonnie, do you think the clothes you helped us get will fit her?"

"They might even be a little big," said Bonnie, assessing the girl with her hands on her hips. "But I'll get a better look at her during her bath."

"That's just fine, just fine…"

Soon, Mark carrying the bags and Estelle looking all around, the quartet made their way into the resplendently furnished lobby of the hotel.

The desk manager looked up from his work, then did a double-take to see the dirty, wild-haired girl crowned with the skull of a wolf. Ulysses smiled politely at him, nodded, and continued making his way to the stairs and their penthouse suite.

"Ah!"

The girl stopped in place, her hand still clutching his. Her grip on his fingers tightened while her free hand lifted to point vigorously at the subject of her attention: an enormous twelve-point buck whose head overlooked lobby's sitting area.

"Ah," she exclaimed again, looking up to make sure he saw where she focused before asking, "Horse? Cow?"

"Oh—deer. That's a deer, he is a deer."

"Deer." The 'd' burst from her mouth almost violently and then, in the bright way of pixies, she laughed. "Deer! Deer."

"Yes, that's a deer…"

"She seems very smart," observed Bonnie. "Are you sure she doesn't know any language?"

"So far as I can tell, her first word was my name."

Trying not to let the thought stroke his ego too much, Ulysses went on while they mounted the stairs that gave the wild girl pause, "You're right, though…she is very smart. Used to solving problems and living independently even out in the woods. Who knows for how long… come now, Estelle, it's all right."

Gripping the rail to steady herself, Estelle took the first stair, then the next, then the next. She observed uneasily the way Mark climbed them two at a time—and, even when Bonnie lifted the hem of her gown to let the girl get a sense for the process of the average stair-climber, Estelle seemed unconvinced. Still clutching that hand rail and Ulysses together, she made her slow way up. The researcher smiled patiently at their companions.

"That's not to say, of course, that there aren't some experiential gaps for us to deal with."

Soon enough, however, they were back in the eighth floor suite that Mark unlocked with a snap of the hefty old key. Ulysses sighed in relief to see it after such a long journey, and instant yawn rising from his chest. Mark set the bags down to start the fire and in an instant Estelle had released her protector to whisk up her things again.

"Wolf," she whispered softly to it, hiding her mouth against the fur and shutting her eyes. "Wolf…Estelle…"

"I really wonder how this is going to go," pondered Bonnie, watching the girl for a long few seconds before removing her hat and all its pins with a mighty sigh of her own. "I guess, as long as she's happy and healthy… it doesn't really matter if she's able to learn anything or not."

"She's already learned quite a lot just in one day…think of how many words she'll have learned in the passage of twenty days. Of two hundred! I believe in her." He said all this with a tender smile for the girl who peered shyly at him from above the wolfskin. A hand on the back of her shoulder, he guided her toward the bathroom. "Why don't you let Bonnie wash you up, and in the meantime we'll have gotten dinner."

After smiling with Bonnie at the girl's amazed gasp and soft babbling to see the immaculately gleaming bathroom, Ulysses shut the door after them. He almost immediately dropped into the nearest chair with a sigh. "Would you pop back down to the front desk and order dinner for us, Mark? After what I had yesterday and all that jerky today, I think I'm in the mood for a real roast…" He named a few side dishes and then, seeing the valet hovered nearby, he asked, "What is it?"

"Do you really think this is a good idea, sir?"

Mark only called his employer 'sir' when he was trying to be diplomatic. That employer sighed in aggravation, saying, "Those two, now you—is everyone going to second-guess me on this? I'm a research scientist, you know. An anthropologist. It's my duty to research a subject like this when I can find it…and, frankly, this is an opportunity that no one before me has had to the best of my knowledge. It could be my chance to go down in history. If I don't seize this opportunity, someone else will at some other time. I'll be remembered for, at best, writing a textbook about ancient religions."

"I understand why you feel all that," advised Mark, glancing toward the shut bathroom door. "I understand why you're interested in her from a scientific perspective…but you won't be the only one interested in her, you know."

"I've already thought about that. I'm going to have to keep a very close eye on her—teach her that she can't just trust every man who comes along."

"I don't mean just men, Ulysses…I mean people. That P.T. Barnum fellow might be dead, but there's scores of others happy enough to follow in his footsteps. And that's just the shysters in entertainment and carnivals. There's also the rest of Cambridge."

"Meaning?"

"Meaning, when a man finds something of value, he's best off keeping it quiet to ensure nobody takes it from him. That goes for gold, for women, and for scientific discoveries in equal measure."

Point taken—but, as he was in America on Cambridge's dime, Ulysses was going to have to write back to them to explain his discovery one way or another. Sighing, the doctor spread his hands and suggested, "All the more important that I take her under my wing and teach her as much as I can before we're able to secure passage to England. When they see how she's blossomed under my care, I'm sure they'll—"

A shriek and a clatter pierced their conversation from the depths of the shut bathroom. With a clear of his throat and a glance over his shoulder, Ulysses forced himself back up from the chair and waved Mark away.

"Go on, if you please, I'm starved. Get yourself whatever you like if you don't feel like beef; I just want to get myself and my new ward fed, then get us both to bed. Sounds to me like she's as tired as I am…no doubt more."

When Mark was out of sight, Ulysses knocked on the door. "Are you all right in there, Bonnie?"

"No, damn it—"

Tutting, Ulysses turned the knob and tried his best to avoid staring at the water pooling all across the floor. Already, the front of Bonnie's dress was outrageously soaked; he might have laughed were it not for the sight of Estelle, naked and fresh and wild-eyed with fear, defending her high ground upon the cold marble counter. Seeing Ulysses, she leapt past the aggrieved maid and threw herself into his arms.

"Ulysses," cried the girl. "Ulysses!"

"Oh, dear, whatever's happened?"

"I don't think she's used to warm water for her baths… or baths in general."

Thinking of that first glimpse of the exquisite form he cradled to his breast now, Ulysses said, "Now, I think she bathes…but you're right, I'm sure the hot water is worrying to her. Poor Estelle! Oh—"

He had bent somewhat to take her lovely face in his hands: the tearful, frightened sight of it made his heart swell with love. How he wanted to console her! To protect her from all things, even her own irrational fears of the unknown. How he wanted to hold her with abandon and not cringe away from her fearful beauty in the presence of these other people…ah, it was unjust that the girl had no conceptions of love, of lovemaking. It saddened him deeply, but at the very least it would help him stay on the task of her education.

Forcing himself to look at the wild girl as a scientific subject rather than as a lovely nude woman, he wiped a few tears from her cheeks and said in a soothing tone, "Estelle, you're okay. It's nice. Nice to bathe. Nice Estelle," he said, petting her cheek, demonstrating to her that she should take a deep breath like him. She breathed in with him and he continued petting, saying, "Nice Estelle," before gesturing to Bonnie.

"Nice Bonnie," he said.

"Bonnie," mumbled the wild girl while the already challenged lady's maid rolled her eyes.

"Yes, nice Bonnie…bath." Now he gestured to the tub and, after guiding the anxious girl back toward it, he leaned against it and mimed petting its porcelain as he had her cheek. "Nice bath…nice."

"Nice." Uncertainly looking up at Ulysses, Estelle yielded her hand and permitted her doctor to manipulate it within his. He showed her how to fondly pet the tub in the same way he just had, repeating the assurance that the bath was a nice thing all the while. Gradually he realized she was looking at him, rather than the water. "Nice Ulysses?"

Laughing slightly, the doctor agreed, "Yes, I suppose so—aha—"

His laughter grew—and inspired some of Bonnie's—when the winsome creature slipped her hand out of his and petted his cheek, his beard. "Nice Ulysses," said the girl with greater confidence.

How she moved his heart! It was undeniable. Oh, he loved to see her, loved to see her smile at him. Loved to be touched by her. She was so good, so pure. Empty of pretensions and desires to do anything but learn, explore, exist. Did she even understand death, he wondered? Of course...did he? It obsessed him—he always thought that this grim cloud over his life was what had driven him to anthropology. The study of dead men, dead cultures, dead worlds.

Now, well...if he believed in destiny, he would have said that he went into the field so he would someday find her.

"Here, sweetheart," he said very kindly, lowering her hand from his beard and easing his touch along her back to encourage her into the water. "Be careful, now..."

With a nervous look—but, also, the admiring reassurance that he found so dear in her—Estelle stepped gingerly into the water. She almost slipped and he shifted his grip to her waist, saying, "Careful, careful," as he eased her into the bath.

"Look at how good you are with her," said Bonnie, waving one hand. "What do you need me for, anyway?"

"To protect her modesty...and, failing that, to promote a sense of propriety."

As the bath sloshed around her, Estelle produced a charming coo. She smiled down as the grit and mud of her body darkened the warm water. Bonnie looked over the two while Ulysses extricated his hand from the girl's: the maid's sharp eye took in the scene until she said, "I suppose I understand…but I personally think you could be trusted to take care of her, just going by what my brother has said and seeing you look after her now. You speak very gently to her."

"Everything is about tone," said the doctor, strolling to the tap to wash his hands and trying to make it to the door before—

"Ulysses," cried the wild girl, a pitiful noise that pained his very heart.

"Oh, dear!" He shook his head as she tried to fling herself up out of bath to follow him. Gently, he took her by the shoulders and settled her back down. "I'll stay," he said, taking a few steps away to lean against the wall. "Don't worry, Estelle. I am here. Ulysses is here."

And then, studying the door, Ulysses folded his arms and listened as Bonnie went to work.

"I wouldn't worry too much about 'propriety' if I were you, doctor," said the nursemaid while scrubbing the wild girl behind her ears amid many protests and whines. "I don't think it's possible for her to have a lick of modesty."

"Well, that's part of the question, isn't it? At what point does the cultural notion of modesty become important to her? I don't want to muddy the waters by making her think it's fine for me, or anybody else for that matter, to look with impunity."

"But that's not what you would be doing, is it?"

"Of course not. If you weren't here I'd be treating her just the same as you are. But, well—I've been advised more than once to watch out for her in this world of ours, and the thought has occurred to me independently as well. She needs looking after; tutelage, not just in human civilization but in making herself safe in it. I'm not sure she will ever feel totally safe, but we'll see. One of the ways I can help her feel safe is by promoting a sense of modesty—by showing her that a decent man won't look at her without invitation, and that her body is worth protecting."

"So you want her to start feeling the shame the rest of us do."

Unable to help his scoff—though he himself had been thinking something not dissimilar the night before—Ulysses cast a sidelong glance toward Bonnie and endeavored not to see the fine young woman she patiently bathed. "How's that?"

"You want her to learn that her body is something to be feared—something to shield from the world as though it's some kind of secret."

"That's certainly not what I mean."

"It'll be the effect, though. Especially if you're really going to be hands-off and promoting this…'propriety.' After all…the way to teach her healthy respect for her body is to teach her that it's something beautiful to be respected, not something shameful to be avoided."

"Shame has an important place in cultures all across the world. It moderates behavior; keeps us on the straight and narrow."

"And makes it easy to brainwash people. Me and my brother—we both had to go to boarding school for a long time. Too long."

He had heard some horrors stories about those hell-holes. Those conversion camps, designed to smash the cultural heritage out of every Native American on which the government could lay its hands—dens of abuse and injustice. It amazed him to think that something like that could be going on in America, where the former colonists had always put so much value on freedom.

"I wondered about that," was all he said to Bonnie.

She nodded without looking at him and went on while washing Estelle's back, "Neither one of us really talk about it. Our experiences must have been almost identical, though—they would beat me for anything, for sneezing in a way that sounded too much like our language. I was young enough that it worked...I barely remember any of it these days.

"But the point I'm trying to make...they loved to humiliate us, belittle us. Better still was when we learned to humiliate and belittle one another. There's those in every group who love to run off to authorities, hoping for some special treatment or some evasion of their own required justice. That's how shame works. Sure, sometimes it has its purpose...but really it's a sickness, humans against humans. We've been pitted against one another in the pettiest ways—and they'll only get worse as time goes on."

"What a harrowing story. But what does it have to do with Estelle, exactly?"

"Just be careful what you teach her," said Bonnie, picking up the girl's hand and examining her fingertips. "So...what are we going to do about these nails?"

ESTELLE

ESTELLE WAS NOT sure how much she liked Bonnie. After all the gentle kindness with which Ulysses had treated her, she wanted to see no other spirit but him. Certainly she did not want to be alone with any other spirit but him, yet soon upon arriving beneath the sign of the deer head, she found herself in a curious room with Bonnie and a gurgling font of hot water.

Though she had been leery of it at first, she did quickly learn to appreciate the warm bathwater. Its sudden eruption from the gleaming hook—made, she noticed, from the same substance as that initial gift from her friend—frightened her at first, but soon she grew fascinated to realize that either spirit could summon it up with a touch of their hand upon one of its companion hooks.

She even tried it and found she could do it herself, a discovery so incredible she laughed and did it a few more times until Bonnie made an aggrieved noise. Then, chuckling, Ulysses came over to move her hand away from the twistable hook with an affectionate pat.

How deeply Estelle liked Ulysses! It was slowly becoming apparent to her that there were a great many spirits in this world, and that they all seemed to have noises distinguishing them. Although the sounds they made were very complex, she paid close attention and Ulysses often repeated himself—she had the sense that he wanted very much to teach her, just as had the mushroom. Therefore, just as she paid attention to the mushroom, she paid attention to him.

Sometimes she didn't have a choice. Strange things were done in this new world to which she had been brought: for instance, Bonnie fetched an odd, gleaming implement from a pack of some kind resting upon a nearby surface. While this occurred, Ulysses took Estelle's face in his hands. They were so warm, his hands! Warm, as gentle as the bathwater.

The noises he made were so comforting to her and it pleased her so immensely to have his face near hers that she didn't realize, when Bonnie took her hand, that the woman was also manipulating that same sharp little instrument. A snip filled the air and Estelle cried out in discomfort and surprise, trying to look at what was being done to her hand, but Ulysses kept her face caught tenderly between his hands.

"Nice Estelle," he told her, petting her cheek while her eyes strained to see the source of this odd, uncomfortable feeling. "Nice Estelle…there, there, Estelle…"

When at last her hand was released, it felt strangely altered. She couldn't tell what it was that had happened to it until Bonnie took up her other one—then she glimpsed the pressure of the implement against her nail, and glanced down at her released and with surprise. Ah! They had shortened her fingertips and she cried aloud to have this basic tool taken from her, though she had noticed over the seasons that they grew back when broken.

Still, Estelle frowned up at Ulysses. He made a funny sort of click of his tongue and smoothed the hair back from her brow.

"I know," he said, a noise he had repeated several times through the course of the bath. "I know, I know…"

Had Estelle understood what he meant by this and been able to answer him back, she would have very firmly told him that he most certainly did *not* know. These spirits could never imagine how strange it was! She felt like one of her chocolates, a small round thing being put into a bigger box.

Sitting in the bathtub, her attention diverted by Ulysses while Bonnie clipped and cleaned her nails on hands and feet, Estelle had never before been so enclosed—so contained. It felt terribly unnatural; simply being in this big, square, gleaming white room seemed to somehow alter her mind, and she was aware of the alteration in a vague way.

There was no conscious sense of change, but there was a feeling; a feeling as though the expansive sides of her mind, which once stretched out across her entire reality to encapsulate all those other things of which she was a part, had been shorn and folded in on top of one another.

Now she was a separate thing: separate from her home, from nature, from the spirits. While they prattled on together she realized how terribly alien they were, no matter how they resembled her.

Yet, Ulysses did not seem as far removed as the rest. When he stayed near Estelle, she was less afraid—less separate from all the rest of the world somehow. This Bonnie spirit had spoken to her in tones that were clipped and annoyed, and she had heard Jason speak to Ulysses in ways that were similar; Ulysses had even spoken that way back.

But when Ulysses spoke to Estelle, every word was soft and gentle. To listen to him speak was like being wrapped in a warm fur—and, in fact, as she was led out of the water and given a soft fur with which Bonnie dried her, Estelle shivered amid the new cold of the room but stayed so focused on the gentle tone of Ulysses's voice that she hardly felt discomfort.

Well…for a time. Soon Bonnie was coming at her with some other implement, running it roughly through her mane, and Estelle cried out with pain to have her head tugged. Had Ulysses not been there to hurry up and take her hands she would have fought the woman off, but the gentler spirit consoled her kindly. He clasped her hands together and kissed them, his lips soft beneath the bristles of his fur. Between those kisses he made hushing sounds, soothing orchestrations of noise that settled her down a little but hardly mitigated the yanks and tears at her scalp through which she repeatedly grimaced.

All the while Bonnie picked through her hair as if looking for the kinds of bugs Estelle herself used to pluck from the fur of her litter-mates and mother wolf. Once or twice the wild girl had dealt with such things on her own person, but she had quickly learned a few plants that these bugs truly hated to find ground into her scalp. It had been several years since the last instance of them, and Bonnie eventually commented with approval before resuming her rough tugging at Estelle's fur.

Gradually, however, bit by bit, the tugging became less painful; far smoother. It even started to feel good, and Estelle cooed to let them know they had finally figured out how to do what they were doing correctly…whatever it was, anyway. This made Ulysses smile all the wider—he had already been smiling since her mane had become de-tangled enough to hang straight and flat around her face, and the expression pleased her even more than did the gradually soothing application of what Ulysses coached her to call the 'nice brush.'

Another 'nice brush' and some foul powdery paste was applied to her teeth: both spirits worked together to keep her from swallowing the stuff, from slapping the brush out of their hands or from poking Bonnie in the eye to get her to stop scraping poor Estelle's mouth.

Then, with the exchange of a few words, Ulysses patted her hand and left the box in which they all stood. The girl cried out, especially to have the somewhat damp but still protective fur removed. It was only a moment that she stood in her bare skin, however: soon Bonnie approached her with something new, a long white fur that was soft to the touch but somehow also smooth.

The spirit extended her arms with this fur draped across them, apparently having learned from Ulysses that the best tone to take was a gentle one; she spoke more patiently to the wild girl now, saying pleasant things and once again using that word, 'nice.'

Biting her lip uncertainly, Estelle watched Bonnie pet the fur. The wild girl extended her own hand to slowly do the same. Bonnie smiled, then drew the fur away. She raised her arms in the air, producing some kind of sound a few times.

When the meaning was not immediately clear, she took Estelle's arms and lifted them for her. Estelle laughed to be manipulated into such a silly position, but soon produced another, more thoughtful noise of appreciation when Bonnie slid this thin fur over her head and arms.

Ah! These were the kinds of furs the spirits wore—spirits like Bonnie, anyway. Now the girl understood. She laughed down at herself, then had her attention directed to a strange plate of some kind gleaming upon the wall. There, Estelle balked to see herself. Though she had seen herself before, her own distorted reflection shimmering back at her in the trickling waters of a stream, she had never seen herself so clearly, nor so statically.

"Estelle," she whispered, stepping toward herself, reaching up to pet her own still-wet fur. With it so straight and neatly arranged, she could not help but marvel. Even accounting for the sudden stillness of her reflection, it went without saying that the wild girl had never seen herself this way. Not a bit of dirt clung to her anymore; the nails on her fingers and toes shone dully in light that came from sources she still didn't understand; the soft fur around her body clung to it while covering it at once.

How she smiled to look at herself! She suddenly wanted Ulysses to look at her, too. Would he think she resembled them, the spirits? Would it please him? She wanted to please him—her heart leapt in her chest at the thought of making him smile.

Of course, Bonnie was still doing things, or trying to. She approached with another pile of furs—but, seeing how burdened the spirit was by the many layers that had become evident to the girl over the course of the washing, Estelle attempted to politely refuse. When Bonnie went on trying to dress her in the rest of the stuff in her hands, Estelle slapped her away and growled, hoping she would get the message. With an annoyed expression and a terse sound of her own, Bonnie at last dropped the garments, waved her hands and mimed dusting them off.

Then, to the wild girl's delight, her temporary captor strolled to one side of the vast box and flung it open. As she marched out, Estelle hurried to follow, her fur gathered in her hands to keep it lifted above her feet. How low it hung! The man-spirits were lucky to wear furs that clung to their body more like wolves did; she at last noticed the difference when both males stood on the women's entry to a room rich with the warm scents of cooked food.

More than any food, Estelle found she wanted Ulysses. His eyes widened and his lips parted in pleasant shock to see her, expanding into a gentle laugh as she dashed across the floor to fling her arms around him.

"Ah," cried the girl, "nice Ulysses! Nice Estelle?"

"Yes, Estelle," said the good spirit with a fond smile and a hand that caressed her hair. "Yes—nice Estelle."

ULYSSES

ULYSSES WAS DOOMED.

Oh, dear. It hadn't fully occurred to him until he saw her dressed in her shift, hair combed and skin gleaming with the warmth of the water and Bonnie's careful attentions. He rose from his seat, somehow unprepared to look upon her even after the assistance he had provided.

After all—he had already seen her naked. The bath aside, the first time he set eyes upon Estelle was when she was in her natural state. One might have thought he had seen it all—that the electrical charge that seemed to rush between them whenever they made eye contact would dissipate, the mystery of her female form having been resolved even before he could be intrigued by it.

Yet somehow, seeing her in the white shift, arms bare and legs shining beneath the fabric with every fast step, his heart seized with a greater love than ever before.

How beautiful she was! What a mystery, women and their loveliness. What a mystery, Estelle. Though she now looked comparable to any other attractive young woman in America or England or the mainland of Europe, the anthropologist found some strange strain of exoticism in her more organized appearance.

The long hair streaming straight down her back leached some of its dampness into the wick of her gown and made its fabric cling to her all the more, tantalizing with all the questions beneath that his heart should have considered solved.

But there was no solving this feeling—this spark that immolated his soul whenever he set his eyes upon Estelle, sweet Estelle.

And 'sweet' was the word. She was so interested in everything, so patient in learning. Never having sat in a chair before, she had to be guided into it and fidgeted frequently as dinner was served.

Her night had been so overwhelming that Ulysses did not even bother trying to adapt her to the knife and fork with which Mark had optimistically set her place…yet, seeing the others at the table dined with the implements, the girl soon clumsily picked up her fork and attempted to make use of it. It was not too far off from a spear, he supposed; no doubt she saw the parallels very quickly and understood the concept even if she didn't understand the point. Yes—she watched everything very closely, Estelle.

Most of all, she watched Ulysses. What he did, she tried to do. When he set another dinner roll upon his plate, she gazed hopefully at him until he also provided one to her. When he wiped his hands and mouth with his napkin after his plate sat empty, she gingerly picked up her own scrap of cloth, laughed in surprise as it unfurled beneath the touch of her hand, then set about miming the same.

Her innocent and whole-hearted admiration was so dear to him. It would have been disingenuous if he did not admit it flattered his ego—but, more than that, it inspired him to watch over her. Her eagerness to please was such that he had to be surer than ever of that. No one could be permitted to take advantage of her...least of all, himself.

After dinner, while Mark tidied up, Ulysses showed Bonnie to her room adjacent the girl's. The suite was a comfortable apartment suitable for the long-term stay of an entire family; until the arrival of the girl and the presence of Bonnie, it had seemed a space far too big.

Now, it was far too small. While Ulysses sat at the writing desk in his room to draft two letters—one to Mrs. Halbrook, and the other to the Cambridge board that had awarded him the grant—each surprised noise or spate of laughter rang through the walls and rattled his skull.

Her joy, oh! He wanted to share in her joy. It was terrible to be cooped up, his pen scratching softly across the pages he filled with swirling handwriting. How pleased she would be to see her wolfskin arranged upon a comfortable bed! How pleasant he was sure she would find it to sleep through the night in an enclosed space, where no animals could sneak up on her and no cold wind could blow a fever into her bones.

Fever—ah, that reminded him. Quickly, he jotted off another note, this for the medical doctor he had seen on his arrival to the city when passage from Europe had left him with a bit of a flu. The girl would require a smallpox vaccination, her check-up aside; the last thing Ulysses wanted was to bring her into society only for her to die of some contagious disease. The mere thought twisted his esophagus into knots and he hurried out of his desk right away, finding Mark and urging him to deliver the note that night in hopes of bringing the physician around the next morning.

Then, Ulysses returned to his ho-hum room and his humdrum work. Had it always been this boring writing business letters?

Maybe he just hadn't noticed. It was so difficult to focus on all this nonsense when Estelle was nearby—even more difficult when, with the creak of a hinge, she appeared in the doorway with a noise of pleasure for her ability to work the knob.

Ulysses's heart leapt with joy at the excuse to take a break from his work. He lowered his pen and glanced over at the smiling girl whose drying hair revealed itself to be a rich brown once cleaned of dirt and grease.

"Hello, Estelle…my, you look happy."

Unaware of the meanings of his words, she beamed at him and hung back shyly behind the door. "Ulysses," she said, her free hand resting with a finger at the corner of her mouth. "Nice?"

"Not to everyone, but always to you." He chuckled at his own joke and glanced back over his shoulder to the Cambridge letter, half-complete at best.

Apparently, 'nice' had come to mean 'something that one could interact with' in the mysterious lexicon of Estelle. Leaving the door hanging open, she hurried into the room and, upon looking wildly around, darted right to his side to see what he looked at. Her eyes dashed so quickly over the letter that he had to wonder if she could even perceive the text upon the page—it seemed just as likely she saw only the page itself, the words upon it indistinct to her as the patterns of tree bark to him.

Rather than lingering upon any one thing in his domain, she instead took to studying him. Her small hand slipped into his and she tugged at him, saying, "Wolf, Ulysses! Wolf—"

"Want to show me your room, do you? Well…I could use a break." Chuckling at the persistence of her tugs upon his hand, Ulysses rose from his seat and followed her to the room down the hall. All the while she beamed, her expression eager with the anticipation of a young girl showing off her favorite treasures—or a young woman about to demonstrate her favorite dress. When Estelle flung wide her door and waved him in, she'd might as well have said 'Ta-da!'

He had seen the room already, of course, but she was so eager to show him he couldn't help but play along. "Ah, isn't this nice! Nice room," he added with little delay, his repetition already proving automatic. "Nice room, nice girl—nice Estelle."

"Nice Ulysses," she said with an approving pet of his hand. Then, hurrying over to the bed where her wolf fur had been arranged, she petted the pelt and said happily, "Nice wolf!"

"I wouldn't be so sure about *that*…wolves can be quite ferocious, after all. At least, they are in fairy tales…"

But—well, she did look at it with such love. She was very attached to that skull. And then, of course, there was the altar made of wolf bones.

His mind tried to make a connection that his human ego shook off. Life wasn't a Rudyard Kipling story. If a pack of wolves came upon a scrumptious human child, they would surely help themselves to an easy dinner rather than adopt it into their pack.

Still, as lovingly as she gazed upon the pelt, one would have thought her very fond of wolves.

"Ulysses wolf?"

She looked up at him questioningly and her eyes landed around his beard. He laughed at that, self-consciously stroking it.

"No, no…Ulysses human, I am human. Bonnie is human. Mark and Jason are humans. Human, see?"

"Oh…Ulysses human?"

"That's right. You are human—Estelle is human."

The girl pointed at herself in surprise. "Ulysses, Estelle human?"

"That's right. We're both human, Estelle…you and I."

"*Human*," she repeated with the soft, amazed realization of some obvious but un-grasped fact. The girl studied the flesh of her hand, then the fur of the wolf. "Wolf…nice wolf. Ulysses human wolf."

He laughed gently at that; she smiled with the weak patience of someone clearly having to deal with a less intelligent person. Ulysses eased down upon the edge of the bed and admired the fanged skull gazing upon him from the bedside table. There, also, sat the pocket watch he'd nearly forgotten about. While he smiled at it, the bed depressed beside him and he glanced over to find Estelle bouncing upon its surface experimentally. She giggled, then leaned against his body and slid under his arm.

"Ulysses," whispered the girl, gazing tenderly up at him. "Ulysses…Estelle nice?"

"Yes," he said softly, "very nice."

His hand stroked up and down her back, a gesture intended to be innocently affectionate. The sharp height of her pleasurable sigh, however, gave him a pang of inappropriate desire.

He had to be so careful here: had to walk all kinds of lines. The truth was that Bonnie was right. If he tried to reject affection with the wild woman, she might take it the wrong way and think he rejected *her*, but too much affection, and it would be all too easy for him to give into the molten heat that burned in the core of his heart every time he set eyes upon her. Lilac soap had left its powdery scent upon her body, and her neatened hair and features seemed to glow with purity. When she leaned her head against his shoulder, her soft breaths on his neck dimpled his flesh. He would have felt far guiltier about it if he didn't feel the identical goosebumps rising up her arm beneath his caresses.

"I can tell that you like me as much as I like you, Estelle," he told her softly, wishing she could understand. "I just wish I could reason with you—explain to you why it's not right for me to be too close to you. Even this close—"

He tried to lift his hand away but, whining, she caught it and drew it back to her side. Her hand fitting to his, Estelle encouraged him to pet her ribs, her waist, her lovely flank. Ulysses exhaled low and she mimicked the sound, permitting it to transmute to a soft moan of pleasure to experience this affection.

"Oh," he said, nearly holding his breath, "your body is so soft to the touch, even with all that sunshine…all these muscles underneath."

Emboldened by his obedience to her whims, the girl stared up into his face and stroked his beard, then his chest.

"Ulysses!"

She sighed, the sound of his name in itself a kind of moan upon her dreamily parted lips. Her legs drew upon the bed. In an attempt to get as close to him as possible, Estelle wriggled into his lap, then slid her arms tight around his waist. "Ulysses…nice Ulysses, oh…"

He wouldn't be so sure about that, either. Oh, it was insane what he was doing. And what frustrated him most of all was to think that, in another place or time or circumstance, it wouldn't have been insane at all. If he were a man as wild as she, there would have been no inequality in any love they shared. If she were civilized, a normal woman like Bonnie, well—there still would have been inequality, of course, but it would have been the acceptable brand of socially-enforced inequality.

Listen to him…'normal woman.'

The doctor barely repressed his scoff at his own thoughts. As though poor Bonnie, who had quite literally been brainwashed against her own cultural heritage, was normal! As if any woman was normal—any man, for that matter. All humans had been corrupted by the male ideal, whether they supported it or not. In just a few seconds of holding the affectionate wild girl in his arms, Ulysses saw more clearly than ever how mankind had betrayed and abused its feminine half.

His mind's eye whisked back in time across a sea of women who had been beaten, raped, neglected, forced to die in childbirth or outright murdered by their husbands. Women who struggled now to fit into corsets or whiten their faces with dangerous chemicals; who inhaled solvent fumes slaving over dry-cleaning, or had their organs torn out in the streets of Whitechapel, or who simply never got the chance to express an opinion that differed from that of their spouse.

And here was a woman who had never experienced any of that—a woman who did not yet even have the capacity to realize that such things went on. This, Estelle, was the only normal woman: it was Ulysses and all the rest of society that had made itself abnormal.

But did that change anything, really? Did it change their knowledge gap, their language gap? Even from the very basic standards of age, too much affection between them was improper. He was almost fifty and she surely couldn't have been far beyond twenty. Add atop it the fact that he was a researcher and she was his subject, and the power differential was so vast that simply petting her in a gesture of tender affection seemed the signpost indicating a dangerous road.

"I wish I could be natural with you," he told her, fondly patting her thigh through the fabric of her shift. The girl cooed, sweetly gazing into his face, hearing only his kind tone. "I wish I could respond to whatever you have to offer me without guilt or shame. But…of course, then we wouldn't be the same people we are now."

"Ulysses," answered Estelle, the word a sigh as soft as his heart.

She looked at him thoughtfully. He ached to know what she was thinking just then—yearned to hear her every idea, to answer all her questions.

A door opened in the distance and Mark called across the suite, "Is she still up, Ulysses? I have the physician for you here—"

Snapped in an instant from the enchantment the girl seemed to cast upon him, Ulysses smiled guiltily and slid her from his lap. She whined with displeasure, reaching out for him even as he stood. "Just a moment, just a moment…good girl, nice girl, wait for me please—"

Though she bit her lip in that adorably anxious habit of hers, she stilled at the lifting of his hand and let him walk away from her without following. By the time he made it to the hall, Dr. Dulcamara stood at the other end.

Opera fan that he was, Ulysses had settled on the services of Tom Dulcamara mostly owing to his name. Somehow, on first meeting the physician, Ulysses hadn't expected Dulcamara to be such a young man, nor so charming. With his clean-shaven look and sharp blue eyes, he resembled a barker more than he did a man of medicine. Nonetheless, his record was well-regarded, his spry young mind kept him up-to-date on all the latest medical advancements, and he had delivered a laudanum cough syrup that had really taken the edge off of Ulysses's spate of illness.

"Ulysses Cochran," observed the physician in his Appalachian twang, tipping a hat he had either already taken off or simply neglected to wear. "I was awful surprised to hear from you again! Thought you said you'd be on the boat back to Europe by the first of the month."

"Life is just full of surprises," answered the anthropologist while shaking the doctor's hand. With a glance down at the black bag that momentarily rested at their feet, he added, "I'm sorry to have disturbed you so late—I didn't mean for you to think it was any emergency, per se."

"Hey, now, it's no trouble! All part of the job description...though I have to admit, I was more surprised by the circumstances than I was by finding you here. I didn't realize you had a ward."

"Well—it's really somewhat complicated. Maybe you'd better come in and let me show you."

Ulysses guided the physician into the room where Estelle still sat upon the edge of the bed, now quietly contemplating the same wolf skull that drew a scoff from Dulcamara—of surprise or disgust, Ulysses did not know. "This is Estelle," explained Ulysses, "a feral woman."

"What? Feral!"

Perhaps fooled by her charming appearance now that she'd been bathed and put in modern clothes, the physician glanced back at the anthropologist with a somewhat dubious arch of his brow. As Ulysses went on to explain the situation, however, that brow was slowly joined by its partner. Soon both the young doctor's black eyebrows were creeping up to merge with his hairline, his eyes wide with astonishment and occasionally darting over to the staring girl.

"And so you see," Ulysses said, summing it all up, "it's really quite vital that she receive a smallpox inoculation post-haste. I'm not convinced she has ever been exposed to human germs—not since her birth."

"I see! I see..." Rubbing his bare chin, Dulcamara now stared steadily at the girl. "Doesn't know a lick of English, really?"

"Not a thing. I really am quite concerned that the in-oculation could be unpleasant for her, as unacquainted with the human world as she is—I don't want to betray her trust and let her think we're hurting her."

"Well..." Glancing thoughtfully down at his bag, then back at Ulysses, the doctor suggested, "You have any more of that laudanum tincture I gave you for your flu? I didn't bring any tonight, but—"

"You know, that's a capital idea—I actually do have some. Hold on, just a moment—"

With another hand raised to keep Estelle in place, Ulysses hurried back to his room for the bottle that sat in his bedside drawer. After fetching Bonnie, too, he in-terrupted a soft conversation with Mark and Dulcamara. Something rather unprofessional, going from the glance the physician gave his patient, but no matter, no mat-ter—that was why it was important Ulysses be there to care for her.

Soon Ulysses sat once more on the bed beside his wild wolf girl. "I have something for you that will help you, Estelle. Not as good as chocolate, but—"

"Chocolate?" The girl peered curiously at the bottle in his hand. Ulysses felt a pang of guilt.

"No—not chocolate. Medicine. Here."

With a spoon he had fetched along with the bottle, Ulysses poured out a small dose of the tincture and held it for the girl. After a cautious sniff and a curious glance, she opened her mouth and permitted him to slide the liquid in.

And, as she almost spit it right back out with a sputter of disgusted horror, poor Bonnie was charged with slapping a hand over her lips and forcing her to swallow.

Oh, dear! He still felt terribly guilty at the confused, helpless expression Estelle wore beneath that hand—at the rapid flicker of her eyes toward his face while he was forced to encouragingly coo and pet her lovely hand. But the guilt for this was not nearly so bad as would have been the guilt for letting the physician puncture her arm with her full awareness. As important as vaccines were, the last thing Ulysses wanted was for her to think it was some kind of cruelty, even a punishment.

"There, there," said Ulysses, which soothed her at last into swallowing. "There…see! Ah, all gone, what a good Estelle we have—what a good, nice human you are."

"'Nice human.'" The physician snickered.

"Well, now, she has to learn language somehow…I'm trying to leave her vocabulary simple at first, just to keep her from feeling overwhelmed or too confused."

"I know, I know…just sounds like you're talking to a cat. Hello, Estelle." Setting his bag upon the foot of the bed, the physician removed his stethoscope and smiled at the wild girl who quite literally growled at poor good

Bonnie. The maid had lifted her hand but was still looking set to be Estelle's least-favorite person at this rate. While Estelle then sought protection under Ulysses's arm, not realizing he had betrayed her with the tonic, she stared anxiously as Dulcamara knelt before them both. "My name is Tom Dulcamara. Why don't you call me 'Tom?' That's easy."

While Ulysses re-explained in his simple way that she could call the doctor 'Tom,' Dulcamara put his stethoscope in his ears and slowly lowered the cool disk upon her chest. She jolted a little, but, as Ulysses kept her hand held and she saw only encouragement in his face, she managed to keep still for the physician to listen.

"Well," he said, lowering the stethoscope away, "heart sounds good…skittish as a hare"—he laughed at this addition—"but healthy and strong. Let's check those reflexives now…"

On the appointment went while the laudanum did its work. Soon enough her head seemed awfully heavy; then, when the physician was satisfied that she was all around as fit as could be expected of a tough young woman who had spent her life living in the woods and eating mostly venison and berries, he backed off to wait for her to fall fully asleep. It was not long, and the droning conversation of the men seemed to ease her off very quickly.

"She doesn't seem very afraid," noted the physician while her eyes drooped shut.

"She's not, and I'd like to keep it that way if I can. God knows, most women spend their whole lives afraid… most men, too, if we're being honest. The world is fearful for too many reasons, and if I can shield her from that fear while also helping her to live a safe life, then I'll feel like I've done a service. If I bring her into the modern world and she can't adapt and can't be safe, then…well."

He didn't want to say 'then he wouldn't be able to live with himself,' but that was what sat on the tip of his tongue. It would be horrible to think of himself as having brought her into civilized society only to ruin her life. The idea was that civilization was supposed to improve one's reality, after all. If it didn't do that, the system was inherently botched.

Dulcamara didn't seem to think on it nearly half so deeply. "Now, I'm sure once she settles in and starts to appreciate the finer things in life, she'll be just fine…but it does seem almost a shame to take the forest out of her, as it were. Seems to me a man could benefit."

"Oh, the anthropological implications are incredible! It's not a pure example of the development of language from absolutely nothing, of course, but nonetheless—"

"Sure, sure, you can research all kinds of things. But, hell! If I'd been the one to find her, I'd be hard-pressed to keep my current job title. Think how easy it'd be to throw together a traveling show! Go from town to town and show her the world while making some good money. 'The Wild Woman of West Virginia,' say. You can keep that," he added with a joshing wink and a sweep of his finger.

Ulysses managed a sociable laugh for the success-starved American—this, in spite of the horror he felt at the notion of bringing Estelle around the states like a sideshow act. "Well, now, I don't know about all *that*…I just want to give her a good life and see what we can teach one another."

"Of course, of course. So—" The physician rose with a slap of his knee and strode to the bed where Estelle soundly slept, "You think she's out deep enough?"

She was, thankfully. Never having had so much as a drop of brandy, Estelle's liver was clearly unprepared for the task of processing the tincture. She snoozed on—having, Ulysses hoped, only the most wonderful and well-deserved dreams—while the vaccination occurred. Though by the third puncture she stirred with a beautiful scowl, she drifted back off a few seconds later and soon Dulcamara straightened up with a smile.

"There we go! She might feel a little feverish or tired tomorrow, have a little *mal*-aise…don't you worry about it, you know how it goes. Oh, but don't let her scratch it too much if it itches her, and remember she'll be sore there."

"I will, I will. Truly, Tom, I can't thank you enough."

"Ah, I'm just doing my job. Happy to help you." He smiled gallantly while Ulysses drew his billfold from his pocket. "Just send me another note if you need me again…I'll be ready to swing by any time."

It was reassuring to find such professionalism in the world!

ESTELLE

ESTELLE DID HAVE strange dreams that night—and some of them were even good. Others were not good, as when she dreamt that some great, fanged pincer bug had tunneled into the flesh of her left arm, or a bear had come and disrupted her camp despite her many heartfelt offerings to it and its kind.

But there were among them dreams that were only bad because they were dreams—because she awoke groggily the next morning to realize they were not real. She dreamt once that Ulysses brought her back to the camp and lived there with her, and hunted with her, and bathed in the stream with her, and touched her.

She had never dreamed of being touched before. After the wolves and before Ulysses, touch was a fearful thing: touch meant imminent danger was upon her; that her very life was at stake.

Now, knowing him, it meant something different. Something deeper. She wanted him to touch her—and every time he did, she wanted more and more. In the dream, he touched her everywhere. Then she awoke, strangely flushed and almost dizzy. She wondered if she could convince him to touch her in those ways while they were both awake. While it was something real.

The warmth of her face stayed on, however, and the dizziness did, too. With the bed warmer than even she was, she stayed bundled into the extraordinary softness of its furs and dozed back off to sleep until Ulysses came calling to check on her. Gently, softly, he lay a hand upon her forehead and over her cheek. She cooed and tugged at his other arm, hoping he would rest in the bed and hold her.

He did not, but he did look on her very tenderly and make that gesture that she had begun to believe meant she was to stay in whatever place she was when he made it. Very shortly thereafter he returned with a bowl of some kind of dark fluid.

After his last poor taste in 'treats' the night before, what with that acrid-tasting stuff Bonnie forced her to keep down for some reason, Estelle looked somewhat skeptically at him until he tried a few spoonfuls of his own. She deigned to try one, and—much to her surprise—found the salty stuff so rich and delicious that soon enough she had gulped down the whole bowl.

"Very nice human," he said, patting her hand. "Very nice Estelle."

"Nice human," repeated Estelle to him, smiling faintly before trying to get up.

"Ah-ah"—the human-spirit gently took her by the shoulders and she winced, glancing down at the sore spot he touched—"stay, Estelle."

Well, she was recognizing that word 'stay' well enough. She did, and once he had cleared away the bowl he returned with something else. A little square of some kind—another box of chocolate? She looked at him hopefully. Instead, when he opened this box, she frowned to see a strange sight indeed. Leaves of some kind, brittle and thin. She touched the top one, gingerly lifting it back and forth from where it was attached to a material not dissimilar from the one that made up her clothes back at home. When she tugged on it, he laughed softly and pushed away her hand.

Then, seated upon the edge of her bed, he began to make noise.

The leaves were stained somehow. It would be some time before she realized fully that the stains corresponded to the noises Ulysses made. It seemed an absolutely ingenious idea, yet even more overwhelming than the thought of simply learning to make all those deeply complex sounds.

At any rate, she was content enough to listen to Ulysses process and output them in the form of his melodious voice—smooth and low and comforting. She listened closely, looking for patterns in the words but finding it all too dense; her body, too exhausted. For a long time she dozed in and out while curled against Ulysses's side, her eyelids as heavy as the rest of her body.

Sometimes her arm would itch but when she tried to scratch it he would gently catch and kiss her hand, then hold it just to keep it still a moment. That was nice, too. Still, she was hot and tired. She had felt this way before sometimes, to greater or lesser degrees. Perhaps it was all just part of the process that the now visible man-spirit needed to put her through to—

What?

What did the spirits want from her, really?

What had they, it, anything wanted from mother wolf to take her in the night?

Between deep dozing sleeps with her arms around Ulysses's waist and his comforting hand resting in the small of her back, Estelle dreamt she stood on the bank of her old stream. From the other bank, mother wolf gazed upon her. She stretched, whined, wagged her tail, then turned and walked into the thick of the woods.

The wild girl had never needed language to understand her mother's thoughts; even now, Estelle found so many messages from her absent parent filling up that simple dream that she pondered it a long time on waking, always taken by the visions of her sleep but far moreso when it concerned her mother. After what seemed to the girl like a very long time, Ulysses used a small thing at the side of the bed to make a bright, happy noise. It pinged through the air and soon the door opened. Mark stuck his head in and Ulysses said some things until he disappeared.

More broth came. By then she felt better—at least less tired—and wanted to get up, but Ulysses fussed over her like mother wolf had once fretted over the pup that grew so slowly and had no fur to protect it. He insisted she remain there and continued producing his noise. She fidgeted, never having been still for so long in all her life except for a few times when she was very very hot, hotter than this and too aching with miserable exhaustion to move. Those times were far worse than this and, now that the worst of it had passed, she wanted to spring up—to hurry out and see this strange new world to which the spirits had taken her.

Alas, she had more than one more night to spend with Ulysses clucking over her. Bonnie sometimes appeared so as to roll her eyes, make noises in a funny sort of tone, and help the man-spirit by bathing Estelle while he waited outside. So far as Estelle was concerned, she didn't require anyone's help, let alone Bonnie's—but, well, the female spirit washed her hair in so soothing a way that Estelle didn't find she minded it too much.

Anyway, it was important that she get on the spirits' good sides. Just as the wolves could have torn her into pieces at any moment, these humans were unpredictable. They lived in strange ways in strange structures full of many strange, unnatural things, and the wild girl was never entirely sure what they were planning next. How bizarre to be counted among them! How queer to be called all these things—"human," "woman," "Estelle."

Only a few days before, she had been nothing but being. Not even 'a' being. She had just been the experience of existence, now somehow so distant from her; yet, far closer than ever.

Ulysses fussed over her a few days, at least until Estelle could no longer be contained. On the third day she refused to stay in bed and, when her benefactor came to check on her in the morning, she leapt up and met him at the door through which he'd barely stepped. Before he was ready, she flung her arms around his neck.

"Ulysses! Ulysses—" Not knowing the word she wanted, she pointed futilely at the portal that permitted her to look at the world through the same cool substance that had let her see fields of flowers and cows and lambs.

"Ah! Outside?" It took a few repetitions—and a special tactic—to make sure they were on the same page. When she looked at him uncertainly, he walked over to the cool pane and opened it. "Inside," he said, standing in the room, then leaning his head out. "Outside."

The girl hurried over while he straightened up. "Inside," he told her, gesturing to her before taking her hand

and guiding it to the other side of the portal. "Outside," he repeated while holding her hand out in the open air.

"Ah! Ah—Estelle outside. Ulysses, Estelle outside!"

"Ulysses *and* Estelle outside," he explained while she stuck her head out the window for a great, gasping breath of air that was not as fresh as her forest air but still infinitely fresher than the stuffy room. The girl sighed deeply, her body listing against the gentle warmth of her friend while she enjoyed the thought of going outside.

He made a short noise like an intake of breath, then, patting her back, said, "Wait," before disappearing toward the hall. "Bonnie!"

Blegh! Bonnie? Estelle didn't want Bonnie, Estelle wanted Ulysses. The wild girl scowled at the least generous of her helper-spirits as the woman appeared in the room, but luckily Ulysses returned, as well.

If Estelle had realized what was about to happen—that she was at last going to endure the ritual of being dressed in a poofy blouse, full skirt and (worst of all, in her opinion) the boots that contorted her feet as they'd never been before—she might have been somewhat less eager to go outside just then. How dreadful! It took both Ulysses and Bonnie to complete the task: Bonnie to do the hard work and Ulysses to convince the girl to accept the gown at all.

Estelle would not, however, abide whatever it was they wanted to do with her mane. Bonnie wore hers pilled up in curls that sat crookedly upon her head, and though Estelle thought she looked very nice, she also thought the woman always looked very uncomfortable. Whether that was due mostly to the furs she wore or the tension of her mane, Estelle couldn't tell—but from the first merciless tug Bonnie attempted on her locks to try to get them into place, the wild girl howled in protest.

Eventually the humans backed down. Estelle was permitted to leave her hair hanging down around her shoulders, the compromise for wearing the dress.

Then, at long last, Estelle was permitted to go outside.

Ah! Even in this strange new world, it was so nice to be beneath a blue sky. She sighed with relief to be taken out and see at last what had been kept from her during her period of confinement. There was so much to take in that she barely saw anything that first day, but that was all right.

It had never occurred to her that there was an 'inside' to the world, just as it had never occurred to her that where she lived could be defined as 'outside.' Things made the most sense to her when she was given opposition—counter-examples. Then, by comparison, she could see very clearly what it was Ulysses wanted her to know.

He seemed to want her to know as much as he could teach her, much as mother wolf once wanted her to know how to survive. As they walked on the strange, hard earth upon which humans evidently built, Ulysses brought Estelle around the dwelling where they had stayed and into a smaller, smellier one. But oh, how it thrilled her! She gasped with delight to see the horses—to see Mark there, leading out the spotted one from the other day.

"Horse," she whispered, pulling on Ulysses's hand. He chuckled warmly at that, patting her before gesturing to the horse and saying something else.

Estelle stared blankly at him until he lifted her hand. Saying it again, he gently caressed the backs of her knuckles. While the soft touch whizzed up her arm to electrify her brain, the smiling man repeated himself. "Pet—pet the horse."

Oh! So there were words for actions, just like for things? It was almost too much!

Her head swam, and not just with the increasingly overwhelming possibilities of her growing vocabulary. At the thought of petting the horse, she edged closer to Ulysses and stared anxiously up at him. In all her years of living in the forest, the only animals she had touched gently—and vice versa—had been the wolves. Deer were frightful, hateful things when you got up close and startled them; and then, of course, there were bears and rabbits and all number of other creatures that she had no business trying to touch until they were confirmed dead. Fretting at the thought of a confrontation with the large animal as she was, Estelle had to be guided over and once more gently taken by the hand.

"Pet," repeated Ulysses, guiding the wild girl's hand over the shivering neck of the beast. "Pet…nice horse."

"Nice horse," whispered Estelle, staring into the gigantic black eye of the animal that watched her. It shifted in place without warning, one great hoof lifting and clopping down, and Estelle winced away for a few seconds before realizing no harm was done. Emboldened, glancing at Ulysses only briefly for support, she reached out and once more petted the animal's mane. "Ah," she said with delight, astounded by the smooth fur of its well-kept coat and the gentleness that prevented the animal from responding to her touch with a buck and a gallop away. "Ah! Nice horse…"

"Yes, yes," said Ulysses, another word that she had noticed early on and that pleased her to hear. He sounded pleased, himself, and looked at Mark as though to emphasize some unspoken point. "Nice horse!"

"Nice Ulysses," she added, looking over at him while her hand trailed over the shimmering hide and tense muscles of the great animal.

Just slightly, Ulysses laughed.

He was always laughing, Ulysses. She liked to make him laugh—in fact, as pleased as she was by the horse's good behavior, she was infinitely more pleased every time she managed to make him so much as chuckle. Her heart burned with fierce joy for him, and whenever Ulysses wasn't around, he was all that she could think about.

Thankfully, he was not often gone. From the time she got up until the time she fell asleep he kept her company, teaching her words and phrases and showing her all the strange things that humans seemed to have created for themselves much as she had created her spears and her knives. He was always patient, always kind, and would repeat himself a thousand times were it required to make her understand.

Not everyone was as patient, nor as comfortable with her. Bonnie often got very exasperated when her meaning wasn't getting through, at which point she would turn to Ulysses for help; and Mark had never been in a room alone with Estelle, who liked him well enough but had the feeling that, like a few of her litter-mates now and again, he didn't really like her very much. Maybe it was just that, like those litter-mates, he took note of her strangeness and judged her somehow unsafe to be around. She certainly didn't want to bother anyone, so she left him alone in return and stayed focused on learning about the world to which she'd been brought.

And, anyway—Estelle just didn't like anyone as much as she like Ulysses. Not to listen to, not to be near, not to look at. Mark, Jason, the man who was always downstairs when they were on their way outside, all the people who were outside while they explored it: none of them filled her heart with such aching joy by nothing more than a glance. Sometimes, while Ulysses sat with the object he had called a 'book' and made his noises for awhile, Estelle would stare at him to absorb his features like a fish swallowing up the water through which it swam. Sometimes she thought she saw him looking at her, too, and that excited her very much—then he would look away, sometimes even leave the room, and she would worry she had done something wrong.

It never seemed to be her fault, though, whatever it was that occasionally sent him away from her. The next thing she knew he would be back and kinder than ever, taking her for walks or teaching her to ride the horse. What a development *that* was! Estelle was astonished the first time she sat astride the beast, and even more astonished when she got to see how fast it could run.

Her favorite part of it, however, was that Ulysses showed her how to ride. First he helped her up, then he climbed upon the animal's back along with her. At once, her body screamed with the same delight that washed over it when he held her in his arms. It made her think of that time when she had first arrived, when they sat together on the edge of the bed and he permitted her to sit on his knee the way they now sat together on the horse.

When she leaned back against his chest she swore she felt his heartbeat as clearly as she felt her own; and each time his hand landed upon her waist to steady her against a fast turn or a sudden gallop, those hearts both sped in equal measure.

How she loved it when he touched her! There was nothing on earth that made her feel this way, not in her world or in his. Every time he touched her, she wanted him to keep touching her. Every time he embraced her, she wished it could be forever.

That was something she noticed about this world, and the way humans interacted: they touched one another very frequently. When two humans met—two 'male' humans, anyway—they held each other's hands, then shook them up and down. Small humans, children, clung to their mothers or other female caregivers, often slung in their arms or at the very least holding hands.

But the interactions of male and female, adult humans were what interested Estelle most of all. Near the dwelling where Estelle lived with her friends was a place Ulysses called 'the park.' The park was a place where it seemed like humans had cut out a little part of nature and put it into the center of their constructions. If buildings had an outside and an inside, so did the place Ulysses called the 'town.'

Therefore, Estelle came to think of this park as a strange sliver of outside brought inside; a kind of three-dimensional window where she could catch her breath, because the city was a busy, noisy, often smelly place where people hurried along the street, and shouted to sell items Estelle didn't understand, and went in and out of buildings like ants hurrying about their hills.

Being in the park was soothing, then, and not just to Estelle. People in the park acted differently—as though they were the only humans there for miles. It was a nice, quiet place full of trees and grass, where the stream (she assumed—correctly—this was the same stream by which she had lived before, and was relieved to see it had joined her here) flowed more cleanly then it did elsewhere in the town. She enjoyed it, and so did everyone else; and, lulled by the soothing sounds of the water and the comfort of nature, people could slow down. They could behave differently.

Estelle noticed men and women went there frequently together, which was one of the few places—one of the only places, she thought—where these two types of humans mingled. There they walked hand-in-hand in the same way Ulysses and Estelle walked. They whispered quietly together upon benches or beneath the boughs of trees.

And sometimes—when they thought no one was looking because they had not seen Estelle—they leaned their heads together and kissed.

Seeing a kiss was not a regular occurrence, but it made Estelle feel so very nice whenever she got to see it. Watching two strangers kiss reminded her of being small; of being supported by mother wolf. When she tripped and cried for the pain in her knee or woke up from a nightmare or did something good during a hunt, mother wolf would hurry up and kiss her face with joy.

Estelle saw that kind of affection among human mothers and their cubs—not the same kind of kiss, of course, since wolves and humans had very different ways of kissing, but it was kissing all the same. But what drew Estelle's eye was seeing kisses exchanged between adults. Hand-holding adults, like her and Ulysses.

Wouldn't it be nice to be kissed by Ulysses! Oh, he was very reliable about praising her when she did something good. Yes, whenever she pleased him he would tell her she was good, then pat her hand or stroke her hair in a fond way. He would smile and compliment her. Sometimes he would even give her a chocolate, which was very nice.

But the longer they were together, the more all she wanted was for him to kiss her. When she watched him read to her, it was all she thought about. These thoughts swirled into her mind to fill up her heart and leave her body sizzling with that intense flame once felt while upon his knee. Sometimes her mouth ached the same way, as though it were an open wound that could only be healed by the application of his.

She leaned against his shoulder when she felt that way; he would slide an arm around her, and both of them would sigh as he went on.

One day, in that same park as usual, she saw another instance of affection between two people and quickly tugged her chaperon's hand. "Ulysses," she said, pointing toward them. "What?"

She had learned this word 'what' from Bonnie, who used it all the time when she didn't know what Estelle as trying to get across. The wild girl had taken it to mean a request for clarity, and it seemed to work when she used it in this way. Ulysses followed her gesture just in time to catch the end of the kiss and the lingering stare of the lovers who had shared it.

"Ah"—he chuckled a little while she stared at him curiously—"kiss? Is that what you mean? They're kissing."

Day by day she began to recognize more words, and though the meaning of each was not always precisely known to her, nor were the things Ulysses said always meaningless babble anymore. She could at least parse his statements into separate sounds and get a vague sense of his intention. In this case, satisfied he understood her, she nodded. "Kiss," she repeated, looking up at him. "Ulysses kiss Estelle?"

"What?" His eyebrows lifted and his lips parted in momentary surprise. "Oh," he began again, laughing a little, glancing away, "oh, well—well, yes, I suppose when we took you out of the forest I did kiss your cheek—"

She knew 'forest' and 'cheek' and now she knew 'kiss,' but so much had happened in the many day and night cycles since she was brought into the city that she hardly thought about the last day spent in the forest anymore.

"Now," she said, trying to explain to him that she wasn't referring to the last time it happened but instead hoping to make him kiss her again. "Now, Ulysses kiss Estelle."

"Oh—oh, my, well—" Clearing his throat, Ulysses glanced around. He shared a laugh with Bonnie, who almost always walked with them through the park. "Well!"

"Kisses are for marriage," Bonnie explained, talking extensively with her hands. This, she had found, helped her clarify herself with Estelle, making the process of communication far less frustrating between the women. She brought her index fingers together, saying, "Man and woman marry. They love. They kiss. Man and woman create baby, become mother and father."

"Oh," answered Estelle, understanding the family appellations she had been previously taught but not understanding something else. "Love?"

Again, the human man and woman shared a laugh in front of the wild girl. Ulysses tried first, starting "Love is…goodness." He laughed again and said something to Bonnie: Estelle caught none of it except for the words, "tall order."

"Love is a fire in your heart," Bonnie explained, eliciting a pleased sound from both Ulysses and Estelle at the description. "Mother and baby love, father and baby love. Mother and father love different."

"Different?"

"Different," agreed Bonnie.

"Estelle love Ulysses," the wild girl informed them both firmly. Now it was Bonnie's turn to laugh, but Ulysses simply looked somehow shocked—almost afraid. This made Estelle feel badly: it made her wonder if she had really understood what Bonnie was trying to tell her. "Love bad?"

"No," said Ulysses very quickly, taking up her hand again and holding it between both of his. "No, no, of course not. Love is good. Love is very good, Estelle, it's very nice. You are very nice."

Smiling, the girl admired Ulysses's pleasant face until he lifted her hand to his mouth. Her body stilled with joy as, upon the back of her knuckles, he placed a gentle kiss that made her heart flutter like a bird in a trap. When he lowered her hand again and looked up at her, she was warm from head to toe.

"There," he said, "a kiss for you."

Though she smiled—though she was grateful—that was not at all the kind of kiss she had meant. Did Ulysses really not want to kiss her the way she saw men and women kiss in the park? Did he really not want her to lay with him, curled with him, happy in his arms while he was happy in hers? Did Ulysses not look at her and feel the love-fire raging in his chest, like what she felt when looking upon him in her turn?

Somehow the thought made her very, very sad. Worse—well, it frustrated her. Why didn't he love Estelle? He had no one else to love. Maybe he loved Bonnie? That didn't seem right, though. Estelle had never seen them kiss or even hold hands—and Estelle, meanwhile, held Ulysses's hand every day. Estelle spent her days with him. Estelle ate with him and walked with him and rode with him and learned from him.

If Ulysses and Estelle were not made to love each other, then Estelle was clearly just not understanding what love was. It frustrated her; it saddened her deeper all the time. For as many things as Ulysses understood and could teach Estelle about the world, it seemed to Estelle that he knew very little about things that were truly important.

Maybe she just had to go out of her way to make him understand.

ULYSSES

ESTELLE'S PROGRESS ASTONISHED Ulysses more and more each day. She was smart as a whip, as Bonnie said. By the end of her first month she had developed enough of a vocabulary to respond to very simple sentences and come up with a few of her own. She had also begun to ask about specific things, terms like 'window' and 'bed' and 'building' joining her pre-existing mental dictionary as more and more items began to enter the field of her awareness.

Truly, it was fascinating. The girl was so accustomed to her wild life that she seemed to lack the frame of reference to fully perceive objects like buildings, trains, coaches until she had been around them for a few weeks and could consciously inquire. What she noticed before anything else in any environment was whatever was organic: women's furs, the feathers of hats.

Most of all, living animals. Each new such thing she saw was subject to a giddy point of her finger and the instant question, "What?" Lifelong mysteries, missing definitions were explained to her. Birds, divided into pigeons and ravens and chickadees and many other types, were named and defined for her eager eyes. Cats made her squeal with delight just to look upon and the antics of squirrels dashing through the park made her laugh every day.

Dogs, however, were by far her favorite. She would tear away from him at a second's notice to hurry over and pet a stray, often muddying her dress by hugging the animal and crying in grief when she had to be pulled off. The first time she saw such a creature, she had cried out with excitement.

"Wolf?"

"Close! No, not wolf. Dog, Estelle. That is a dog."

"Dog?" She had repeated the word with great curiosity, frowning. Later that night, when they were once more in the suite, she pointed at the skull on the nightstand. "Dog?"

"No, Estelle, that is a wolf. Wolf hunts lamb and cow," he added, trying to give her some idea of the chain of predator and prey. "Hunts for food, hunts for eating. Dog protects lamb and cow; Ulysses protects Estelle."

"Oh," she answered, looking thoughtfully at her trophy.

Ulysses did really wonder about that thing. As she was more articulate now, he tried asking her, "Did you hunt this wolf, Estelle?"

She looked at him, trying to fully understand his

question, and he repeated it more simply.

"Estelle hunt wolf?"

"Ah—no, human hunt wolf when dark." He did not understand her position on death, this notion she had developed of humans as death-spirits made visible. He took it to mean another human had literally hunted the wolf and Estelle had collected its skull and pelt until Estelle added with a sad expression, "Mother. Nice mother. Estelle love wolf."

His understanding struck him through like an arrow that was second only to the pain caused by the sorrow in such a delightful girl's expression. "Why—this wolf *raised* you? Your mother was this wolf?"

"Mother wolf," answered the girl longingly, extending a hand to pet the muzzle of the carefully tended-to skull to which she sometimes presented chocolates or little pieces of roast she had stashed in her napkin during dinner. "Mother wolf love Estelle. Nice wolf. Nice mother."

"Poor girl…oh, my, no wonder you had her bones this way."

How sad! How sad he was, especially, to think of some human hunter slaying Estelle's first protector. Someday he would uncover the truth of her perception and find it infinitely more fascinating—and somehow flattering to his ego—to think Estelle believed Ulysses some kind of death herald. After all, he had felt the same about her.

But love was a great killer. A great ender of old lives and beginner of new ones. And, Ulysses had to admit, this new life he was living was a far cry from the old one.

He had brought Estelle into civilization to study her and see how best to teach her, of course. In language she was quick, being as it was a tool like any other; but in most other things she was simply not interested, whether that included mores, manners, or fashions of dress. Every morning was a nightmare for poor Bonnie until the girl realized that in order to go out she had no choice but to be dressed, at which point she would grudgingly submit herself to be (wo)manhandled into this outfit or that bonnet.

How adorable she was! How beautiful. No man could have looked upon Estelle and resisted his urge to sigh with admiration.

It was almost hard to remember she was a wild girl—until she opened her mouth. Her unrefined speech gave her away and Ulysses suspected most in the town thought she was in some way mentally deficient. It annoyed him, really. She was maddeningly intelligent. The haste with which she learned language surprised him, and when they walked together through town he could see her mind working rapidly to absorb every detail of this new life around her. That the townsfolk held such a dim view of her intellect insulted him more than it ever would have her.

All this was just as well, however. Ulysses would have hated it had someone taken an interest in her. An unscientific interest, he meant—he himself was interested in her for research purposes, after all.

Though…one had to admit that sometimes he became very disconnected from the research aspects of teaching Estelle. It was hard to avoid. She lived so purely, as she moved moment to moment with no pretensions or plans for the future, that Ulysses—sometimes even Bonnie— was drawn into this way of effortless being right along with her.

Yes, of course, it was very interesting to see her intelligence adapt to the modern ways of life; but if he had been recording every little detail every second of the day as perhaps an anthropologist should have been doing, he wouldn't have been able to share in the simple joy of her successes, her comprehensions, her fun.

She had *fun*, Estelle. Ulysses had to wonder if he'd ever had fun in his adult life. Anthropological studies were fun to him, but when he was doing them for someone else—jumping through Cambridge's hoops for this or that grant—it became a duty instead of a matter of personal interest. He had lost his passion before Estelle, and he didn't even realize it until it came back to him.

Speaking of Cambridge: after a month, they returned his letter with great interest. Yes, they wanted very much to see his findings and meet the girl. They would send money to cover her travel expenses and be thrilled for an opportunity to interview both of them upon Ulysses's return home to Europe. This response seemed like an accomplishment when he received it, but soon he had to wonder if it really was something to be looked forward to.

After all…to the boys back on the board, Estelle was little more than a subject of research. Less than a subject: more of an object, an entity reduced to a walking artifact implying the history of mankind. And perhaps, at first, she had been partly that to Ulysses—but she had never been *only* that to Ulysses, and the truth was, as time went on, he found himself less an less interested in Estelle as a topic of research and more interested in Estelle as a human being. He loved her joy, he loved her small spates of melancholy, he loved to come upon her dozing peacefully in the window bench of her bedroom overlooking the cluttered city.

He loved Estelle.

And this notion made him feel terribly guilty.

What business did he have loving her, after all? He was a scientist. However he felt about her and however well he got to know her as a person, he was only in America based on the good will and scientific expectations of Cambridge. He was in a professional role with her, and just as it was his duty to see that she was never taken advantage of by someone else, it was also his duty to control himself and avoid his own foolish yielding to natural urges.

How he would have loved to hold her, to kiss her! To experience the raucous joy of her body as at last he gave her what he sensed she wanted, but what she did not even fully know she wanted.

That was the problem. If she had been aware of sex— of men, period—before all this began to happen between them, Ulysses would have felt a mite less boorish. But it seemed to him that, though she be a woman, her mind was more comparable to a girl's in terms of its understanding of the human world. She was used to the animal world; to primitive nature and its concerns of survival. Surely when it came to issues like romance she would have only gone along to please him. That idea kept him from acting on anything he felt.

What happened between them only happened because Estelle showed him that she had a much better idea love than he had given her credit for.

Their relationship began to change when he thought it would be a fun idea to take her out shooting. She had been sighing quite a lot, gazing dolefully out the window whenever she had a few minutes to herself. The girl needed something to do, a hobby or activity of some kind—and, suffice it to say, the traditional feminine pastimes of embroidery or letter-writing were not among reasonable options.

Ulysses wasn't sure what he could offer her in this way—not until he saw her perk while watching the city one day. "Hunt," she cried, pressing her face to the window. "Hunt! Bird hunt—"

He hurried to the window to see what she watched. Just as she'd said: a hawk was in a mid-air brawl with a few crows while more cawed on the nearby rooftops, egging their comrades on and no doubt throwing in their share of colorful language directed toward the raptor. Estelle watched eagerly, her breath held and her body poised forward as if at any second she might spring from the window to join the fray.

Soon enough the hawk flew off, the crows re-settled to groom one another in victory, and Estelle, her entertainment having vanished, settled back in her seat with another plaintive sigh.

This must have been the only form of entertainment she had in the forest, he told himself. Watching the shenanigans of animals—or busying herself with the maintenance of her camp. Engineering new tools, swimming in her stream, going on hunts of her own…

Ah! He gasped aloud at the realization, then laughed. How foolish he'd been not to think of this sooner! When she turned to find the source of his sudden mirth, Ulysses lightly nudged her shoulder. "Estelle loves hunting, yes? You love hunting."

The girl nodded at that. "Estelle good hunter."

"You want to hunt with me? Let's hunt together, Estelle."

Upon slowly taking his meaning, her face changed. She perked in her seat, expression bright and eyes wide with pleasure.

"Hunting? Ulysses, Estelle hunt?"

"Of course! Of course Ulysses *and* Estelle can go hunting together. Ah, what a fun idea that is. We'll teach you to shoot birds…capital idea. We'll try tomorrow.

Hm…but who will loan us a gun to go shooting with in this town…"

After some thought, Ulysses sent Mark with a note for Jason Blackthorn. Did Jason have a gun or two that the researcher could borrow? He did, it turned out—a pair of pistols—but evidently they needed cleaning before their next use. If Ulysses was willing to drop by the next day, Jason would have them cleaned by then.

Certainly! Ulysses thought it would be a nice chance for Estelle to meet Jason again, as well as for Jason to see that Estelle was no worse for the wear after spending over a month in Ulysses's care.

The researcher helped the girl into the coach the next morning and could see that she remembered it…even if she was no more comfortable than she had been the first time it rolled into motion. She gasped in shock and gripped Ulysses's arm, brow furrowing and eyes searching his for reassurance.

"It's all right, Estelle," he said gently. "Nice coach. The coach will take us hunting. Mark drives it up there, and the horse is there, too."

The notion that Mark drove the great moving box in which they traveled may not have occurred to her until that second. When illuminated by that notion, she made a noise of understanding and looked up at the front of the coach. Then, satisfied, she peered out the window. "Hunting…"

Oh, Estelle! He loved just looking at her—loved to see anticipation cross her face as she watched him fetch a bonbon for her, or the giddy delight that expanded her glittering features every time they set foot outside. He did try not to watch her too much, lest her maid make a comment or the girl herself take his looking the wrong way.

Now, in the privacy of the coach and Estelle distracted by the land through which they traveled, he could look at her with abandon.

And he did mean 'abandon.' When he observed Estelle, all his civilized pretensions fled him. His own qualms and quarrels with the world disappeared and there he was, simply a watcher. A lucky audience to a gentle-hearted, kind girl. A flower of the woods—a seed that he had been blessed to find and plant in the field of his heart.

Before leaving town, they stopped by Jason's cottage on the outskirts. Estelle, who followed Ulysses around like a baby duck even when they were back at the hotel suite, now insisted on clambering out of the coach and hurrying up to the door with him. He wasn't sure she would recognize Jason after the whirlwind month she'd had, but when the door open, her noise of pleasure said it all.

"Ah! Ah—Jason?"

"Well! Now that's a shock." With a dry laugh, the man rubbed his jaw and glanced briefly over Estelle's bright blue frock. "If you hadn't recognized me first, I might not have realized it was you, Estelle…amazing what a comb will do."

"And a bath," agreed Ulysses with a chuckle and a shake of his friend's hand. "How are you, Jason? Seems like it's been too long."

"Time whips by when you're busy…and I always keep myself very busy. Teaching her to shoot, are you?" While Jason stepped aside to permit their entry into his home, he caught Ulysses's eye and asked, "Sure about that?"

"Of course, I'm sure. She's been very eager to go hunting, and—"

Estelle's scream shattered both their peace. She

bolted back to the door, tugging on her benefactor's coat. "Ulysses!"

"Dear! What is it, Estelle?"

"What," she cried, vigorously pointing with one hand while trying to pull him back outside with the other. "What?"

Following her gesture, Ulysses soon realized she was pointing at the big stuffed grizzly that towered in the corner of the room. "The bear? Dear, poor Estelle! I didn't even think—"

While he consoled the girl, Jason looked at her with sympathy and only a touch of humor. "Poor thing. She's like a little kid."

"Now, now, she's a grown woman the same as any other…she's just a bit behind in her education. It's all right, Estelle, it's all right. The bear is dead. Dead bear, like mother wolf is dead."

At this analogy, her grip on Ulysses relaxed somewhat—though she still looked poised to bolt through the door any second. "Dead?"

"Yes, dead. Estelle and Ulysses and Jason, alive. Mother wolf and bear, dead."

"Dead," she whispered, the gears turning in her brain while looking the great beast up and down. Perhaps wisely, she remained unconvinced until Jason strolled over and patted the taxidermy display's great paw.

"Ulysses is right, the bear's dead. Shot him myself. Traded the rifle to Tom back in 1903…otherwise I'd have that to loan you, instead of the pistols."

Satisfied that the bear was not animate and not liable to attack, Estelle edged forward to examine it. Meanwhile, Jason crossed to his desk and lifted the rolltop. A pair of pistols sat, wrapped in handkerchiefs; he placed them in a box and passed them over along with a small container of ammunition. "I have to admit I feel a little nervous about this, Cochran."

"Now, there's no need to fret. We'll be back before nightfall no worse for the wear. The only real difference between a flintlock pistol and a flint-headed spear is a few thousand years of technological development." With the box tucked under his arm, he glanced over to see Estelle softly petting the fur of the lucky, lucky bear. Even if Jason hadn't interrupted his thoughts, he wouldn't have been able to disrupt the sight.

"Aren't you concerned with what these leaps in development are doing to her mind? You found her a wild girl, in scraps of hide and caked in mud. Now look at her."

The oblivious anthropologist answered, "She's much better adapted, isn't she?"

"Not from where I'm standing. Now she's a wild girl in a fancy dress and smelling of lilac. She might be able to produce a few more words than she could last time I saw her, but nothing's changed in her. She still looks like a girl waiting for a chance to go home—looks like Bonnie and I did when the boarding schools had us. Do you think she even realizes you intend to keep her 'civilized' permanently?"

"I don't think she knows what permanence is."

"Exactly." While the girl, upon seeing Ulysses's thoughtful stare, smiled and hurried over to his side to clutch his free hand, Jason examined them together before shaking his head. "I still think she would have been better-off staying in the woods. Unexposed to—" He waved vaguely toward the window that looked out over the town.

"Yes, well. And I think she's better-off with a smallpox vaccination. Only time will tell which one of us is right."

Ulysses hated to be curt, but he also hated it when

people second-guessed his decision to educate dear Estelle. With a tip of his hat, he said, "Thanks for the pistols, old boy. We'll be sure to bring them back to you before nightfall."

Then, they were off again: this time, beyond the boundaries of the town and somewhat closer to Estelle's forest. A large pond and smaller thicket of woods lay there, a perfect place for duck-hunting and frequented by a great many of the town's recreational hunters. Still early as it was, dawn having barely broken twenty minutes before, Ulysses, Mark and Estelle seemed the only humans for miles.

Carefully, the anthropologist showed the wild girl one of the pistols. "Gun, Estelle. This is a gun. Bear is dangerous, gun is dangerous. Gun makes animals and humans dead. Understand?"

The girl peered cautiously between Ulysses's serious face and the gun. "Gun?"

"That's right. Gun makes animals dead for hunting."

A curious gasp lit her lips and her eyes trailed up once more to his. "Gun hunt?"

"That's right…watch. Mark, you're a much better shot—would you show her?"

Having carried and arranged their picnic basket and its blanket beneath a nearby tree, Mark straightened up and came over to take the pistol from his boss's hand. He ensured it was loaded, then studied the pond.

A group of ducks quacked quietly among themselves, paddling through the water and occasionally dipping their bills in to collect a snack. Silent as night, Mark crept along the treeline and around the edge of the pond while Estelle watched in fascination. With the valet's back to them, Ulysses decided it was better if he preemptively supported the girl before the blast of the pistol; his arm slid around Estelle's waist and she gasped slightly, looking curiously (hopefully?) up at him while he pointed with his other hand.

"Now, watch," he told her, her body warm against his, its slight weight as she leaned into him inspiring once more that insatiable, dreadful hunger for her.

In what he evidently deemed an ideal location, Mark cocked the pistol.

Immediately, the ducks scattered; Estelle cried out in empathetic frustration for Mark's perceived failure, then jumped in place with a second, sharper crow of shock at the loud discharge of the gun. "Ulysses," she cried, her hands raising too late over her ears.

But then a duck fell—her eyes widened as it hit the water and she balked up at him.

"Hunting."

Her tone before while looking at the gun had been almost laughably dubious. For someone who knew relatively little language, Estelle was very good at conveying skepticism, sarcasm and derision, and all three of those had been blended into her initial impression of the idea that this small hunk of metal and pearl could serve any use in the art of killing animals. Now her eyes glowed with fascination; with promise and possibility. Ulysses swore he could see her mind racing through her memories, applying the potential of the gun against every animal that had ever evaded her more rudimentary tools: rabbits, foxes, yes, even bears all fell dead within the corridors of her mind until, gripping the lapels of Ulysses's coat, she begged, "Gun! Estelle learn gun?"

"Yes, but you must be careful. Very careful. Gun is for animals—never people. Never point a gun at humans. Do you understand? It's extremely important, Estelle. No humans."

Nodding eagerly, Estelle agreed, "No, Estelle nice girl—hunting, please?"

Oh, she certainly was a nice girl! His little darling. With her clutching the front of his coat, he slung his arms around her and was at once overwhelmed with the curious urge to kiss her. It was the purity of the hope in her lovely face; the sharp intensity of her desire to learn.

In the pond, Mark's victorious 'A-ha!' as he retrieved the fallen duck interrupted Ulysses's questionable thoughts. The researcher cleared his throat and, smiling, suggested to Estelle, "Well, come on, my dear…let's teach you to shoot, then we can have a bite to eat and wait to see if the ducks come back, or if we have to find them."

The truth was that Ulysses had always found hunting—well, a bit uncivilized. It was strange to him that men who claimed to be refined and thoughtful would then go out and take the lives of animals for sport. Ducks were one thing, or geese. Fox-hunting had always made him cringe, however, and he even had ethical questions about the decimation of wolves in the United States— especially now that his dear Estelle, his little wolf-girl, had come into his life. For his part, he had been hunting only once or twice.

Yet, teaching Estelle to shoot with the help of Mark and showing her the ease with which a human could now claim prey—yes, Ulysses almost saw the fun in hunting. Just learning to shoot the gun brought obvious joy to the girl, but having the opportunity to shoot it *at* the ducks made her laugh like a giddy child.

Not that she was very good at it. They waited quite some time before the ducks dared return to the pond from which their friend had disappeared, where all the cracks of practice gunfire and shattering tree-bark thundered through the air. By this point, far too excited to contain herself, Estelle dashed off after them, her skirt pulled past her ankles with one hand and the pistol haphazardly aimed in the other. "Careful," called Ulysses anxiously after her, ready to dash after her at a second's notice. Bullet on bullet whizzed harmlessly through the air between the fast-scattering birds. Estelle made a noise of frustration, her learning useless, a gun so small difficult to use for hunting without more skill than either she or Ulysses had.

But, of course, they were not the only hunters liable to take the opportunity of such a pleasant shooting location. Another shot rang through the air as Estelle lowered her hand with a noise of sad frustration; her head whipped up at the foreign discharge just in time to see a bird fall from the sky. She cried out in amazement, turning toward Ulysses and Mark to see if they had accomplished it, but neither had the second pistol in his hand.

Instead, Tom Dulcamara stepped from the woods, a smile on his face and a rifle against his shoulder.

The doctor looked between the threesome and laughed. "Well now! If I'd realized it was you three out here, I'd have let you have the space to yourselves instead of showing off. My, my."

His blue eyes glinted as they focused on Estelle, sweeping over her gown and across her face. "Estelle's sure learned how to wear the fashions of the time, hasn't she?"

At his first glimpse of the doctor, Ulysses had started forward to greet him; now there was an extra hint of speed to his step and, when he was within range, his hand landed upon Estelle's shoulder. While he smiled thinly and offered his other hand to the interloper, he said, "At the very least she hasn't bitten Bonnie Blackthorn in a few weeks…Estelle, do you remember Tom?"

"Tom," the girl said, peering into the doctor's face and attempting to place it. "Oh! *Tom.*"

She tapped her heart to indicate she remembered the visit from him; Dulcamara smiled at that. "That's right! Your friendly doctor. Always nice to be remembered by such a lovely patient."

With a very European flourish for such a West Virginian, Tom swept up the wild girl's free hand and bent to brush his lips across her knuckles. The audacity! Ulysses burned with envy despite the perfectly standard gesture; Estelle watched in faint confusion while the anthropologist caught himself trying to discern a hint of blush in her cheeks.

What did he care what she thought of whom? It wasn't his business; she wasn't his lover.

But oh, he had to admit he felt about as possessive as a man could be.

Still holding the girl's delicate hand, Dulcamara glanced down at the pistol and laughed slightly. "Now, you can't be teaching her to shoot with a little thing like *that.*"

"It was all Jason had to loan us, unfortunately…he said he traded that rifle to you, as it happened."

"That how he remembers it? Here I thought I won it in a poker match."

Chuckling slightly, the physician released Estelle's hand and made his way to the pond where the duck dropped. Wading a few feet in, the water barely rising halfway up his boots, the doctor stooped to claim his prize and shook the excess water from its feathers. "How about that! A very fine specimen, if I do say so myself. Tell you what—I've got mine, so why don't I teach your Estelle how to *really* shoot?"

Despite the odd strain of indignation burning inside

of him—totally irrational jealousy of which he could make absolutely no sense—the researcher forced a smile for the younger man. "Well, that would be incredibly generous of you."

"Ah, it's nothing. I'm a born teacher…come on, darlin', let me show you a thing or two."

Thus Ulysses found himself sidelined for the next hour or two, chest burning with bitter frustration to have been more or less ejected from his own outing. He stood near the picnic blanket, arms crossed over his chest while the physician taught Estelle how to shoot.

Somehow, the sly young man always found an excuse to have a hand on her. Adjusting this elbow, straightening that shoulder, even holding onto her waist and sliding a foot between hers—beneath her skirt—to encourage the widening of her stance.

"That's it," Dulcamara would tell her, his voice so low that only Estelle and a man with an ear tuned by the forces of obscene jealousy could possibly have caught it. "That's it…just like that. Now, don't tremble, breathe slowly out…like this, breathe out…"

His body against Estelle's body; his arms embracing hers to align the position of the rifle; his chin upon her shoulder; his unworthy lips brushing her hair.

Ulysses had to turn his eyes away from the scene and study the ample clouds that had crawled in throughout the late morning, transforming their lovely blue day into one of murky gray.

When satisfied with the wild girl's progress, the physician volunteered his duck for their midday meal as they waited for the rest of its companions to return. While Estelle continued practicing her aim, Mark started a fire and the doctor plucked a few feathers from the chest of the bird to make his work easier.

"I have to admit, Ulysses…I *am* impressed. Didn't think that girl had a prayer of learning anything about our way of life."

"Oh, now, she's very bright, very clever and eager to learn new tools and strategies for survival. If she wasn't, she wouldn't have made it this far."

"I suppose that's true. You just don't expect so much progress in a month. Seems like she understands an awful lot of words now." As the physician removed a hunting knife from a sheath hidden beneath his coat, he set to more thorough work on the fowl and said without looking at Ulysses, "She sure looks at you with stars in her eyes, too."

A bit of well-aimed praise soothed Ulysses's envious sting. "Yes, well—I have taught her quite a lot already, and plan to teach her more."

"If Cambridge lets you, I'd imagine."

"How's that?"

"Oh, well—it's just, I don't know. Seems to me they funded her discovery, your ticket here and back…don't you think that's going to give them the idea that they have some right to her? Some sort of claim over her?"

The knife slit along the bone in the center of the duck's breast and the physician pried a bit of purple meat from the depths of the feathers. Ulysses turned his eyes away, having little stomach for such things. "It's not as though she's an animal, Tom. The board wants to interview her, of course—they're as interested in learning from her as I am."

"Sure, they're interested. They're going to be so interested that they'll want access to her round-the-clock, and they'll want to see all kinds of things. How she problem-solves, how she learns…maybe even how she mothers."

Tom's eyes flickered significantly up to Ulysses, who had been forced by the level of his shock to look back at the man in the midst of dismembering his bird carcass.

"By no means do I intend to cast aspersions on the character of your fine European colleagues…yet I can't help but think of Jason's cousins stuck out in their territory, drinkin' themselves to death because it's easier than considering what they lost. If there's one thing a European hates, it's somebody who's truly free. That's why you all have such problems with Americans these days."

Though Ulysses scoffed lightly, a real fear grew in his breast.

The thought of Estelle being taken away from him by those very academics who permitted her discovery made his blood run like ice. "I do have to point out that it was, by and large, you Americans who did the most damage to tribes, and who shipped *them* to "Indian Territory" in the first place."

"Sure, but where'd we learn it? Not like we invented warfare, slavery, genocide…"

Tom tossed a few cuts of meat into a bowl of clean water that rested on the ground beside him. "We might have eagerly applied ourselves to the lessons, but folks in the old countries were just thrilled to teach us."

"Ah!"

Estelle's familiar cry of alert in the distance snapped them out of their conversation. All heads raised as she went hurrying toward the treeline. Ulysses rose from his place, calling out to her and starting after her—when the rifle discharged, the other men joined him.

Soon all three jogged to catch up to the wild girl, who they found standing with the rifle lowered and a supremely proud expression plastered across her face.

"Deer dead, Ulysses," she cried, pointing at the felled

buck who bled out amid the trees some yards away. "Estelle hunt!"

"Well, hell!" Laughing, scratching the back of his head, Tom glanced at Ulysses and said, "If Cambridge *does* want to keep her, looks like they'd better hope she doesn't have other plans."

That may have been so…but the idea that Tom had planted took root—and, in so doing, leeched the confidence straight out of Ulysses's soul.

Like most forms of untested confidence, it seemed what Cochran had been experiencing up until that point was really ignorance. Oh, it had crossed his mind that Cambridge might *objectify* her in some way, but he had been so caught up in the thrill of teaching Estelle and imagining their triumphant trip to Europe together that at no point had he realistically thought of what might happen when they got there.

Assuming they got there in one piece. There were more diseases than smallpox in the world, and Estelle had already caught at least one cold aside from the faint fever in the wake of the vaccine. Unexposed to humans for a lifetime, she was a sensitive girl with a relatively untested immune system. If something began to circle around whatever ship they boarded—a highly likely scenario—then she very well might have ended up dead before they reached Europe.

And that idea sickened him far more than had seeing her in the arms of Dulcamara…even for something as innocent as learning how to shoot.

Ulysses was very quiet for the rest of the day, though he tried to put on a pleasant face for Estelle while the other men broke down the deer carcass once through with lunch. She delighted in helping despite their chauvinistic protests, and soon they were both standing by to watch in awe as she expertly gutted and parceled out the animal; when she was done, she straightened up, hands bloody, beaming ear-to-ear until she saw Ulysses's distant, grim expression.

"Ulysses tired?" She asked this while hurrying over to him to have her hands wiped, which he often did after dinner or once she had been petting some stray mongrel. With a slight sigh, the anthropologist removed his handkerchief to oblige her.

"Yes, Estelle, just a bit tired…I'll be all right."

Frowning all the deeper despite his attempt to mollify her, Estelle sat down beside him and leaned her head against his shoulder. "Estelle love Ulysses," she told him softly, provoking from the man a low noise of something close to pain.

"You're a very good girl, Estelle," he said, sliding an arm around her and gently petting her arm.

Soon—not soon enough for Ulysses's liking—Dulcamara tipped his hat and excused himself with a stretch. "Well, this has been a lovely little diversion, but I must be heading home. Sure is a pleasant coincidence to have found you folks out here! Miss Estelle." After a nod and a somewhat theatrical bow to the girl, the hatless American nodded to the men. He made his way toward the road with his rifle over his shoulder.

"I don't like him," said Mark, idly smoothing the hairs of his mustache. "He's too familiar."

"Now, he's a perfectly nice fellow…you know how these Americans are, always coming on so strong. And, anyway—he did make a good point about Cambridge."

With a grim look over to Estelle—an expression he forced into a smile when she met his gaze—Ulysses clapped his knee and stood. "Well, let's head back home. Estelle could use a bath…and Lord knows I certainly could. Come along, dear."

"Deer," sang back his little bird of paradise, hurrying forward to take his hand. "Ulysses no hunt?"

"No," he agreed, "Ulysses doesn't hunt."

"Estelle hunt for Ulysses," she decided, squeezing his hand and looking into his face. "Estelle feed Ulysses."

Oh! What a sweet angel. His heart pulsed with love for her tender instinct to care for the man who cared for her in turn. Smiling fondly, Ulysses opened the door of the waiting coach and helped her inside while Mark led the horse, grazing in the nearby field through most of the day, up to the carriage's front.

Once shut into the coach with the girl, Ulysses found a sense of humor again. She had buzzed with energy since taking down the deer and now giddily flung her arms around his neck. One hand lifted to pet his beard, her eyes shining with the light of joy. "Ulysses! Nice Ulysses…Estelle love Ulysses."

"Sweet Estelle—"

He stilled; the girl, smiling all the while, had sat up straight enough to let her nose brush his in the lightest of nuzzles. "Ulysses," she whispered, her face flush with desire, hope, thrill. "Ulysses…kiss Estelle?"

The anthropologist's lips parted in a slight, fearful moan. At that short proximity he could taste the soft femininity of her breath—the humid warmth of her tongue. "Oh," he said, his diaphragm bundling into knots of longing, "oh, Estelle, but—"

Just be careful what you teach her.

Bonnie's wise words while washing the girl's back for the first time.

Ulysses stared into those hopeful eyes, that bright

doe-gaze as she waited for his answer. Waited for a buck to respond to the call of nature.

Body burning, Ulysses folded his arms around her, slid one hand up to cradle the back of her neck, and kissed Estelle's soft mouth.

Seraphim envied the incense of those eager lips, that avid tongue! At the first contact, she gasped and pushed herself up against him, her arms tightening around Ulysses's neck and her heart beating against his through her bodice. The anthropologist groaned beneath the annihilating weight of the pleasure—the simple ecstasy of holding her, kissing her, loving her. His tongue dared flutter against her parted lips, then quickly yielded as her unpracticed one emerged to slither into the raging fire of his mouth. Moaning, the wild girl wiggled in his arms, gave herself utterly to his kiss, and only drew her head back when the coach rocked to frightful life beneath Mark's climb to the driver's seat.

"Ulysses! Oh—Ulysses—"

"I love you, Estelle!" Words he could cry as passionately as his heart meant them over the crack of the reins and the thunder of the horse's hooves into action. While the coach lurched forward and Estelle swayed in his arms, pressing closer with a cry of fear at the motion, Ulysses inhaled and caressed her face to repeat himself at a softer tone. "Oh, Estelle, my wild girl, my dear, my wolf—I love you, how I love you."

"I love you," she repeated, her tone its own hushed whisper—an eager emulation of his, rather than an attempt to hide the words that she meant as purely as she said them. "Ulysses! Ulysses! Kiss, kiss Estelle—"

Groaning, as unable to refuse her in the semi-private quarters of the coach as he was unwilling to let the opportunity slip by after all the day's grim thoughts,

Ulysses sank his head over hers and obeyed. She writhed against him, sliding closer and closer until, for the first time in a month, she sat with her legs draped over his lap and her body all but fused to his.

How he ached to be rid of his clothes, her clothes, all the trappings of society! How he wished at once to be in the dark solitude of the forest, where he could lay her down on a bed of moss and make love to her—give in to what she was really begging for when she whispered between kisses, "Pet Estelle, Ulysses, oh, please, Ulysses, pet Estelle—fire, fire, Estelle fire everywhere—"

"My angel," he began, intending to rebuff her—but he found himself simply unable to continue along the train of thought when she caught one of the hands that had been caressing her back.

Taking this hand in hers, she looked him in the eye and guided his palm down her waist, over her flank, down as far as her knee. All the time she produced sweet, encouraging coos—soft, lovely gasps that echoed in his heart.

"Pet," she begged again, clutching the lapels of his coat. His heart swelled. She nuzzled her lips against his, kissing his jaw, tongue darting against the lobe of his ear to increase his ache to an unbearable extent. "Pet, Ulysses, oh, please?"

Nostrils flaring, the anthropologist kissed down the curve of her golden neck. His hand gathered the fabric of her dress and guided the hem above her boots, over her stockings, high enough that the same hand could trial under to stroke the flesh of her thigh. She cried out with the sharp pleasure of a woman who had just been wedded to her lifelong sweetheart, the simple touch of her limb enough to make her tremble in his arm.

"Ulysses! Oh—Ulysses, Ulysses—"

"No one will ever take you from me, Estelle—oh, Estelle, I won't let anyone harm you. Never! Not ever. I'll cut ties with Cambridge, become disgraced and stripped of every honor I have before I ever see that happen."

"Ulysses—Ulysses! Pet, please—oh, pet Estelle—"

Her legs splayed slightly. The researcher's head swam with bad decisions, but he then immediately corrected himself. This was not a "bad decision." This was love—plain, simple, thunderous love that quaked them both.

The caresses of his hand trailed higher, the fabric of her bloomers cool against him as her flesh was hot.

Gentle though he was, she nonetheless yelped in high surprise to discover the potentials of such pleasure. "*Oh*—oh, Ulysses—please, please, yes—"

Velvet, Jove! Oh, your tender Aphrodite was made of pure velvet. With a sharp sigh, Ulysses rested his forehead against her moaning jaw to occasionally let his lips brush the curve of her ultra-soft throat. "Ah—ah—yes, yes, love Ulysses, Estelle love Ulysses—I love you, please, please—"

Her whimpers filled him with a hunger so acute it brought with it a strain of remorse. Oh, what was he doing? What was he doing to himself? There was nothing impure in this moment—not to her. To her, to this innocent wild girl, such contact *was love*. One of love's many manifestations, as sweet as chocolate or walking in the park.

But Ulysses knew better. He knew if anyone discovered this, it would ruin him. No colleague would be able to look him in the eye again—and even the Blackthorns, even his household staff back in England, would have been right to take exception to his weakness.

Or perhaps that was just more ignorance. The girl panted against him, her body the trembling string of a harp from which his fingers elicited only the most sacred oratorio. The Blackthorns, the board, even wily Tom Dulcamara—they could all think as it pleased them and make themselves look more the fools for profaning a moment so holy. This long-awaited, long-resisted contact between them in the coach, it was pure and bright as the sun over Eden, and Ulysses would never believe it was anything else.

Her grip on him tightened. She cried out as though in fear until he lifted his head from her neck to watch the exquisite contortions of her face. A river flowed while the trunks of forest trees closed in around a lost man.

His kisses blotted out her scream of his name not more than sixty seconds before the coach came to a stop outside Jason's house, where Mark dismounted to bring the pistols, carried up front with him, inside.

Amid Estelle's whimpering, Ulysses eased his fingers away and kissed her perfect mouth. "Pet," she whispered, panting for air as they separated from their kiss. "Oh, love petting, love Ulysses…pet Estelle, Ulysses—"

"I want to, Estelle—ah—"

Throughout much of this, the girl had clutched and petted him in turn—gripping his coat, tugging at his shoulders, caressing his chest. Now those hands began to dip lower and, though it pained him, he caught her wrists. While she whined, he kissed her ear and murmured against her, "Soon, Estelle. Soon—I'll find a way. It must be while we are alone. We must be alone for love. Understand?"

Whining, shaking her head, nuzzling against him, Estelle curled more tightly in his lap and pleaded, "Now, now, again, please!"

"I want to, my God—oh, Estelle, I do want to. I love you—ah—"

The pain caught him in the heart, a bullet striking down a deer. He squeezed his eyes shut and pressed her all the more tightly to his chest, teeth clenched against the agony of his love for her. Feeling a teardrop escape against her neck, the girl cooed. She leaned back somewhat and took his face in her hands.

"Ulysses—not sad, Ulysses. Poor Ulysses! Nice, nice Ulysses."

Her gentle caress of his beard made him weep all the more. Hushing him tenderly, the girl drew his face down upon her bosom and rocked him slowly back and forth in her arms.

While Mark remounted to resume the trip to town, the coach rocked along with them.

11

ESTELLE

ESTELLE DIDN'T UNDERSTAND why petting her had so upset Ulysses. It had made *her* very happy—made her feel all kinds of funny things, like a bright sunburst dawned to shine upon her while she floated down a stream. Just hearing him say he loved her, oh!

She supposed that those words made her so happy she could have cried. She might have, if he had not been making her feel so good just then. Perhaps he was happy?

But, well—Ulysses didn't *seem* very happy. Not happy at all. From the moment they returned to their dwelling, in fact, he looked at her with a miserable expression and said something to Bonnie that Estelle didn't catch. Smiling pleasantly, Bonnie set her book aside, then got up and extended her hand to the girl.

"Come on, Estelle—time for your bath."

"Ulysses, please," the girl tried, wanting only to hold and be held by the man that she loved. Oblivious, Bonnie drew her toward the bathroom while Ulysses turned away to remove his coat and hat.

"Now, now, you know he'll read to you later…come on, let's get you scrubbed—ugh, how do you get so much dirt under your nails?"

Estelle only caught about one of every three words from Bonnie on the best of days, but at the moment she was so distracted that she couldn't focus on parsing any of the words. The wild girl frowned after Ulysses, smiling only when he turned to glance at her. Caught looking, his lips faintly upturned beneath his beard; seconds before she was more or less shoved toward the bath, he disappeared into his room and shut the door.

Estelle, sighing heftily, watched Bonnie fill the tub. All the while, the wild girl dreamed of Ulysses. How he'd touched her! How nice it had felt, how warm. How good it was to be so close to him, held by him. *Kissed* by him! Kissed!

Despite herself, the girl giddily laughed and rested a hand upon her astonished cheek. With a kindly smile, Bonnie tested the water, then came over to get Estelle out of her clothes. "Did you have a nice time hunting today?"

'Time.' That was one of those words that was used frequently, and one that Estelle just couldn't fully figure out. So far as she could tell, it referred to a chunk of experience, but even then she had the sense that she did not grasp its complete meaning. It might have helped if they had been able to provide her with a counter-example, much as she had figured out 'alive' and 'dead' with Ulysses's helpful comparison. 'Dead' was when another animal killed you, or when an invisible spirit came to take you from your body. 'Alive,' it seemed, was everything else. It was the animal state: the moving, breathing, being state in which humans lived. How funny! All this time she had thought she was dead, but seeing the bear made her understand the difference at last. What would finally teach her about the meaning of time, she wondered?

"Nice hunting," repeated Bonnie again, the question reduced to a few short words that the girl could focus on. At Estelle's lame nod, Bonnie hid a frown and stooped to help her out of her stockings. "Everything go okay?"

"Uh-huh. Mark hunt duck, Estelle hunt deer. Tom hunt duck, showed Estelle gun."

Looking surprised, Bonnie asked, "Tom—Tom Dulcamara was there? That's a weird coincidence." Then, seeing the girl's blank blinks at this big word, she cleared her throat and self-corrected, "I mean, it's strange. Lucky timing."

Still not wholly understanding, Estelle glanced worriedly toward the door and permitted Bonnie to help her out of the rest of her underthings. "Tom nice. Ulysses *very* nice. Ulysses—Estelle love Ulysses, Bonnie."

Her lips twisting into an almost sad sort of smile (how strange it was, the wild girl thought, to think of a smile as sad!), Bonnie took Estelle by the hand to help her into the tub. "I know you do, Estelle."

"Ulysses sad?" Estelle gazed up, searching Bonnie's face for some explanation of what had occurred in the back of the coach. Bonnie glanced sidelong, sighing faintly, wringing out the washrag and foaming up a bar of sweetly scented soap.

"Hm…how do I say this…Ulysses is smart. You and I are smart. Smart is hunting, building, listening. Understand?"

Strangely, she did. Estelle nodded, riveted to Bonnie's explanation as she said simply, "Sometimes, smart is sad."

"Why?"

"Because it sees," was her only elaboration before she set about scrubbing behind the wild girl's ears.

Maybe smart saw, but Estelle didn't. It was good to see, so far as she was concerned. Being in the dark was scarier—you didn't know what was there, and many things lived in it while looking for other animals to eat. But the light was sweet, and when it became especially warm in the spring and summer it made things grow, and during the day it frightened those things that most often liked to hunt wild girls.

Why seeing would make Ulysses sad, Estelle couldn't imagine. Not until after her bath. Bonnie brought her, wrapped in a towel, to get dressed again in her bedroom.

There, Estelle studied mother wolf's skull. The spark of mother wolf's life had disappeared in the darkness, and Estelle had only realized it upon the rising of the light.

Yes—Estelle supposed that seeing was a very sad thing, or could be. Not always, though. After all…some things were nice to see. Some things made seeing worth all the pain of seeing of other things.

So far as Estelle was concerned, the nicest thing to see in the whole world was Ulysses. When she looked at him, everything else faded away. When she was young and mother wolf had just died, Estelle often wondered why something so nice could exist but leave such a sorrowful feeling—such an awful burr lodged in the center of her heart.

Now it seemed almost like the pain from death's dagger was a low compared to a high: a great opposite by which Estelle could recognize the towering aperture of life to which this good man brought her simply by holding her in his arms. She wanted to rise upon those heights all the time: wanted always to feel like she had on the first morning she awoke beside him, sleeping in the forest together, the stars still faintly clinging over their heads and his warm body so close.

After dinner, when Ulysses had again excused himself to his quarters and Bonnie looked through a book quietly by the fire, Estelle went to see her finest friend in all the world. She cracked open the door and there he sat inside, his back to her while he looked over a piece of paper he'd filled with scratches of black ink. At the sudden intrusion, he glanced sharply up, then looked relieved.

"Estelle," he said softly, reaching out to her, "shut the door, sit with me—"

After the latch clicked beneath her hand, the girl drew her nightgown around her ankles and dashed on bare feet across the cold wood floor. With a low sigh of joy to do so, she threw her arms around his neck and slid into his lap. Ulysses produced a sigh of his own, his hands fitting at once to her body and sending another wildfire raging through it.

Nothing in the world made her feel like Ulysses had in the coach. Estelle had never known she could feel like that—that someone could make her feel that, or that she could make herself feel that. She wanted it again and gazed up at him in absolute adoration, but dared not beg too much for as sad as he had been after the last time. Instead, she petted his cheek.

"Ulysses smart," she said, eliciting a small laugh of surprise.

"I don't know about that…new word, eh? That's because you're smart, too…oh! My wild wolf girl—Estelle—"

A kind of pain struck his face, as if she had pinched or scratched him. Frowning, the girl asked, "Ulysses sad?"

"No—well—yes. But I'm happy. You make me very happy, Estelle. And that's why I'm sad. I have no business being made so happy by you."

Not understanding fully but hearing, amid all of that, that she made him happy, Estelle leaned her head against Ulysses's shoulder. "Estelle happy. Love you, Ulysses."

"I love you, oh, Estelle—sweet girl. But there's so much you don't know. Things you don't understand. You're very smart, but very—untaught. There are things you don't know."

"Can teach," she suggested to him, her lips pursing against the side of his throat. Goosebumps trailed down the flesh of his neck and she smiled softly to see them, nuzzling more closely against the beating heart of his pulse. "Ulysses can teach Estelle."

"I'd like to—I'd like to. I just don't know how. And if others, Bonnie or Mark—I just don't think it's right."

"Nice man," she told him, her skin burning to think of his kindness, her arms tightening around his neck. "Bonnie and Mark nice. Bonnie and Mark—see Ulysses nice."

"You're so articulate with the few words you know," he said, cheek pressing to the temple of her forehead, the precise meaning of each part of his sentence lost but the general emphasis more than clear to her. "But...it's my job to see *to* you, Estelle. Mother wolf protected Estelle before; Ulysses protects Estelle now."

"And Estelle protects Ulysses," she said firmly, thinking of what a pleasure it was to take down a deer and then watch him enjoy it for dinner. "Estelle and Ulysses, um—ah—" She leaned back to try to gesture, moving her hands in a circle around them. "Estelle and Ulysses, like mother wolf and baby, mother and father and baby—"

"Family?"

"Yes! Yes. Family." Estelle caught up his hand and, pressing his knuckles to her throbbing heart, gazed ardently into his face. "Estelle and Ulysses family. Like marriage."

"Yes. Yes, like marriage." Studying her very carefully, the tenderness in his face as clear as the trepidation, he asked after a moment, "Estelle—I'm sorry to have to ask this—do you understand where babies come from? Cubs, children?"

The girl bit her lip and shook her head. "Forest? Trees?"

"No"—he laughed slightly, his eye crinkling so beautifully with his mirth that she had to drop her gaze away for a second or else kiss him fiercely and silence him altogether—"no. A natural guess, though, I suppose. No, ah—well. Man and woman love each other, and kiss, and pet, and—the man, ah—oh, how do I put this?"

While Estelle stared blankly at him and waited for an answer, he at last suggested, "The wolves, for instance. Have you ever seen, ah, one wolf climb on top of another wolf? On top of mother wolf, maybe?"

"Oh! Yes, uh-huh, Estelle sees."

"Ahem, yes, well—that is where cubs come from, you see. And…it's much the same with humans who are in love. Some people call it making love, in fact. It is a mutual act. A gesture of partnership. It should be, anyway."

Just the thought of being held so tight by Ulysses, completely covered by him—it reminded her of the dream she had when she'd first come to this strange place, and she smiled. "Love you, Ulysses. I love you."

"Estelle! Oh—"

She feared she had made him sad again, or hurt him somehow owing to his tone; but he simply drew her down to his shoulder, his heart, then held her there with a hand gently resting upon her head. "I love you. *How* I love you. So bold and honest, brave and smart. And beautiful. You are so beautiful, Estelle. Beautiful to see. Beautiful to look at. I love to look at you, to listen to you. I want to listen to you forever. But—it's not fair for me to make love to you. You couldn't begin to know what to expect, could you? And—if you were left with child, and didn't understand…giving birth isn't easy, you know. Not even just carrying the child seems to be easy. If you were afraid, or hurt, I would feel terrible."

"Estelle understands," she said tersely, having garnered a mite more of his fretful words than he'd perhaps expected her to. "Estelle learns always. Lots and lots! Cubs from lovemaking—Ulysses and Estelle's cubs."

A giddy, almost shy explosion of giggles rose from her lips at the thought. How wonderful it would be! She had only liked being part of the pack so much. After all, being small as she was—and without natural claws or fangs, to boot—Estelle had been at the very bottom of the structure. But if she and Ulysses formed their own family, their own pack, why, wouldn't that be nice? Then she would be in charge, like mother wolf.

Better still: Wouldn't it be nice to love someone the way mother wolf loved her? To see him, Ulysses, loving those babies just as the tough male wolves became so gentle and kind when a pup came trundling along? It made Estelle's heart flutter and she petted his chest.

"Nice Ulysses," she whispered to him. "Estelle love nice Ulysses…want to make love. Want to have babies."

"Oh—oh, Estelle—"

Sighing painedly, Ulysses kept her pressed to his heart, then at last (at last!) slid a hand beneath her rump. With her carefully slung in his arms, he rose from his chair and brought her to the bed. Still in his clothes as much as she still wore her nightgown, he lay her down, smoothed the hair back from her face, and thrilled her with an unasked kiss upon her sensitive lips. So sensitive! It seemed almost that his kiss tickled her, stung her. She moaned, her hands running over his face and up into his hair while he nuzzled against her amid the working of their lips.

"Let me hold you, Estelle," he whispered, turning her over and folding his arms around her. "Let me hold you. Let me think."

A pleasant sigh drifted from her lips as Ulysses, one hand upon her hip, carefully eased her upon her side. Then, body fitting to hers, he folded his arms around her.

Oh! The richness of her love seemed to overflow from her very body. She felt as though the air buzzed with it, that love, and sighed to be held by him in what seemed a prelude to the act of lovemaking.

Alas, the civilized world was not as simple as the natural one. Estelle sensed that if she and Ulysses were in the woods together—alone in any true way, really—they might have made love that very night, and thereafter been a happy little pack of two. But for some reason, even after having explained these things to Estelle, he seemed nearly afraid to proceed. Instead they dozed off in one another's arms, the lights still on, her desire for him unsated.

What was a woman going to have to do to get a man to act naturally?

ULYSSES

ANOTHER CAMBRIDGE LETTER. Did he think the subject would be ready to travel before winter? If not, Dr. Cochran might have to wait for the following year. And if he could be so kind as to prepare a separate copy of his journals for review and admission into their library, it would be most appreciated. They did not want, of course, to take the original.

No—just Estelle.

Perhaps Tom had made the researcher paranoid…but Ulysses did now have to ask himself how he ever expected anything else when it came to the Cambridge. They were too formal, too professional, to see the human in Estelle, and by that stretch they would think nothing of taking her away from him.

Even once they met her, Ulysses couldn't believe they would see her as anything more than an abstract set of traits that piqued their interest. Ulysses knew her as a person and saw her as a person.

And he loved her as a person, too.

Oh, what a crushing sense of guilt washed over him every time he thought of it! And to imagine that she loved him back was unfathomable. Surely it was only because he was the first person she ever saw; the first and most prominent man in her life, the one who taught her and loved her. Clearly she was just confusing feelings of closeness and safety with those of love.

Yet, well—she seemed to feel safe enough around Mark, and even interested in a friendly way as time passed and they both got comfortable. The Irishman was very quiet and tended to keep to himself, but after Estelle had spent a few weeks as a part of the household, Ulysses observed a subtle change in the valet.

Once Ulysses had taught her the basics of riding, Mark helped to perfect her skills, and on clear days would often invite her to take the horse out under his supervision. After, he would teach her things about the horse's care, the brushing and the feeding of it. When Estelle would reappear up in the suite she would be bright-eyed and giggling with happy memories of the animal's lips collecting a sugar cube from the palm of her hand. Mark, in his typical quiet fashion, would say nothing but that the girl had listened well before he went about with the rest of his duties.

Ulysses felt none of the jealousy here that he had felt with Dr. Dulcamara teaching her to shoot, but he just couldn't put his finger on why that was until he observed a certain incident. One evening, Mark sat darning his socks by the fire; Bonnie was reading the evening paper and paying no more attention than was Ulysses, who was always aware of his darling Estelle in an unconscious way but at that moment occupied by returning a letter to Mrs. Halbrook.

The housekeeper had responded with much enthusiasm to the idea of a lady joining them in the household. Ulysses, at a small writing desk pushed against the break wall between the suite's living room and dining area, was just in the midst of a sentence inquiring if Halbrook knew offhand of any private passage back to England. A cry of surprise from the girl drew the researcher's attention, and he turned to see that Mark had caught her wrist with a frown.

Evidently, Estelle had wandered over to investigate the valet's sewing supplies and been pricked by a needle when she got too handsy. "Now, look at you," said Mark, his tone tersely paternal as he clucked to examine the little red dot on her fingertip. "You've hurt yourself. I've told you before to stay away from these needles."

"But Mark touch needles!"

"And Mark's been touching needles since before you were born. He knows how to touch 'em and doesn't mind if he pricks himself, but he minds if you do it. Ah, poor mite." At the girl's trembling lip and instantly watering eyes, Mark sighed and patted the back of her hand. "Sensitive as my little sister. No harm done, lass, but you keep clear of those needles, now. I won't see you hurting yourself."

"Sorry, Mark," she said, which was very interesting because it was the first time Ulysses had heard her apologize.

"Don't worry about me," said Mark, picking up the sock and resuming his work again. "Apologize to yourself. You're the one who's hurt. Let it be a lesson to you."

Frowning down at her hand, Estelle murmured, "Sorry, Estelle," at which point Bonnie took her off to have her finger washed.

No harm may have really been done, of course, but the incident stuck in the researcher's mind because Mark's behavior had rather reminded Ulysses of his own grandfather. The admixture of love and impatience, of protective instinct battling with the desire to foster independence—it was very familiar to him, and it had implications for the way Estelle felt about Mark in turn. That was to say, if there was a paternal figure in Estelle's life, it was more likely to be the distant and somewhat gruff valet who taught her how to care for horses than it was to be the man with whom she held hands while walking through the park.

Ulysses tried, then, to feel a little less guilty. It weren't as though he was corrupting Estelle, or instilling in her some perverse notion of what love truly was. She looked at him and felt what she felt, and there was nothing wrong with that. The true wrongness would come in if she was not equipped to understand what was arising between them…but, following the conversation in his bedroom and their innocent sleep together in his bed, Ulysses could not help but think that she did understand.

In fact…it seemed more and more that the only thing she didn't understand was why they couldn't behave in the ways that came naturally to lovers. He felt a pang of guilt every time they were in public and she looked at him with the obvious hope for a kiss, her head leaning against his shoulder and her eyes glued on his mouth. His heart twisted when she snuggled up against him while the suite was quiet and he then had to spring away from the intimacy because Bonnie had returned from her brother's, or Mark had come back from some errand.

If they could just be honest!

If Ulysses could just be honest with himself.

After all…there were other, more awful things than loving her and being loved in return.

It was not long after the duck hunting incident that they bumped into Dulcamara again—now, during one of their walks in the park. The physician had been mid-conversation with a pair of charming young ladies with whom he was evidently flirting, if their giggles were any indication. Only upon noting Estelle and Ulysses strolling together did he excuse himself with a half-bow, one hand upon his heart. Then, smiling with a greater pleasure, the doctor waved and called in a brash way typical of Americans, "Hey there! Ulysses, Miss Estelle, nice to run into you again!"

"Why, Tom." While the ladies wandered off, Ulysses and Estelle took their places. The doctors shook hands while the wild girl peered smilingly up at the man who had taught her to shoot a rifle. "Always good to see you, how are you? You do spend a lot of time outside for us to keep meeting like this."

"Fresh air, my friend. Makes all the difference to a man's health. And a lovely lady's! How are you, Estelle?"

"Well, and you?"

"Wow!" Amazed, eyebrows lifting, the physician didn't respond to the girl at all but instead looked at the anthropologist. "Get out of town. She sure is learning a lot under your guidance, isn't she?"

"Oh, well, we've just been practicing greetings this week, but she's a very quick study. She makes me very proud—"

"Ah! Doggie!"

At once distracted, Estelle dashed off in the direction of a lady who was walking a high-headed poodle around the promenade. Ulysses laughed a bit despite himself and glanced at Tom, admitting, "Though I fear she doesn't really care much for social niceties…only tolerates them to please me, it seems."

"I can tell! But you don't want to get her too educated, do you?"

With a light scoff, Ulysses asked that often fatal question, "What exactly do you mean?"

"Well, think of it from Cambridge's point of view. It's already pretty extraordinary that you'd find a girl like that in the woods and that she's such a fast learner when it comes to language. Who's to say you're not just faking it all—that you didn't just hire some urchin to act like a wild girl?"

"But why on earth would anyone do such a thing?"

"Ah, people'll do anything for acclaim…I still think the smarter thing is to forget Cambridge and just show her America. Put her in some leopard skin number like a cavewoman, get money for nothing but a looky-loo. Either way, whatever you do, it's important that you don't let her learn too much language. Otherwise, nobody'll believe it."

"That's a very interesting opinion, Tom." Ulysses tried and failed to keep the derision out of his voice, but he hoped his smile was at least a bit more convincing. Shaking the physician's hand once more, he began to turn toward Estelle and the dog over which she fussed. "I'll keep it under advisement—Estelle, dear, come along…"

"'Bye doggie," called the girl, dashing away without thanking the woman to whom Ulysses tipped his hat. Dulcamara caught his shoulder before he could complete the motion, drawing his attention back.

"Say, now, don't take it the wrong way! I'm only trying to be friendly. It's advice for your sake, too…I can tell you're working round-the-clock on this. Take it easy! There's plenty of time in the world—hey, here's an idea."

Nudging the researcher in the arm, the physician (about whom Ulysses increasingly suspected Mark's opinion to be quite valid) suggested, "Me and Jason Blackthorn are always after somebody new to play poker with. How about you and your valet"—a Southern pronunciation of the French 'valet' rather than the hard 't' British version, complete with improper emphasis on the first syllable—"swing by Jason's house on Friday for a little game? Get some time to yourself. A little recreation."

"Well…" Estelle slipped her delicate hand into his and he smiled faintly at her, then thought to himself that it had been quite some time since he had an evening where he was not hard at work teaching her basic linguistic conventions. "Yes, I suppose that would be nice. What time?"

"Great! How's seven? We'll have a few drinks, kick back. Just us men. 'Less you think Miss Estelle will want to learn how to play poker, that is."

Chuckling dryly, Ulysses assured Tom, "Maybe a few months from now…have to teach her the numbers a bit more thoroughly, first."

Although a queer feeling settled on Ulysses as he led Estelle away, he pushed it aside. For as long as he'd been alive, even going back as far as his schooling, Ulysses had felt a terrible sense of guilt for taking even a day off. He worked himself to the bone researching, writing and traveling for anthropological studies, yet he had never been able to justify leisure and only took a day off when he had pushed himself to the very brink of exhaustion and was left with no other choice. This constant labor was a large part of the reason why he had never taken a wife: he simply had no time to give attention to one.

In this way, it was really rather unavoidable that he should love Estelle. She was a woman who was also his job—the sole recipient of his undivided attention from dawn until dusk. That did make it all the more important that he take a bit of time to himself now and again.

Yet, when he invited Mark to come along with him to the game on Friday afternoon, the valet's dubious expression seemed to reinforce the queer feeling Ulysses had when agreeing to be social in the first place.

"You sure you want to go? Surely you can't trust that snakeoil salesman anymore than I do. Probably cheats."

"Now, Dr. Dulcamara is a bit of a fast-talker, it's true… but many Americans are. He's just trying to be friendly."

"I've seen friendly men, and I've seen shysters. I'll be the first to admit that telling the difference takes a bit of practice—but I'd think a man such as yourself, whose job is to study cultures, would be able to tell the difference a bit faster than the average…ah, hell."

Tossing down his newspaper with a sigh, Mark stood and said, "Guess I'd better come with you to make sure he doesn't rob you blind pulling cards out of his sleeve. You're too good-hearted, Ulysses."

"I'll take that as a compliment, because I'm in desperate need of one of late…I have to admit, I've been wondering about myself."

With a stroke of his mustache, the Irishman studied the researcher through a pair of dark eyes. After a few seconds of contemplation, he shook his head. "You need to worry less about what the world might think of you, and more about what the people you care about think of you."

Ulysses looked carefully at the valet—had he noticed Estelle's increasing affection for her protector?—but before he could ask anything, Mark fetched his hat and said, "I'll be back…better go get us an early dinner if we're to waste our time on this."

'Waste' was a strong word, but it certainly was an expenditure of energy. In true codependent, work-addicted fashion, from the moment Ulysses climbed into the driver's seat with Mark the researcher fretted about Estelle and how the time would have been better spent with her. It was a bad habit to be certain, all this second-guessing—but, well, Tom had made a good point when inviting him over. Ulysses had barely taken a day off for an entire month. He therefore wrote his intrusive thoughts off as his usual bad instinct.

And, anyway, the anthropologist was a study of cultures living as well as dead—he rather did want to see how Americans had fun, and couldn't help but be excited at the prospect of a bit of quality time spent with other men.

Much to his delight—and Mark's visible relief—Ulysses was not the only one who had been invited to the poker night. A few other men from around the town were there even before he arrived, and after greetings were exchanged, a mug of beer was shoved into the researcher's hands. Evidently the fellow who ran the local pub (or 'bar,' the Englishman reminded himself) was in the habit of bringing a cask of ale along with him to these occasions, a fact that somewhat softened Mark's stern disposition after about an hour. Tobacco smoke filled the air and money went around the table as steadily as did the cards. Laughter was on every man's lips even when he lost, and as the night grew on and everyone got a bit drunker, Ulysses relaxed more and more.

It really wasn't so bad taking a bit of time off now and again. Maybe Tom had been right about overworking himself. Why, the time was so grand that he was tempted to do it again the next week—tempted, until the other men began to trickle out.

One by one, people went home to their wives. The cask emptied. The barkeep took it when he left. The night grew darker and Ulysess's wallet was not quite so fat as it had been when he arrived. He began to think of going home and glanced at Jason's grandfather clock upon realizing that he and Mark were the last two guests remaining.

"Now"—Tom caught his gaze and leaned around the table to shove the researcher—"you can't be thinking about leaving us already! Come on, brother. Stick around for a few more hands, at least."

"Oh, I don't know—I'm really rather exhausted."

"Nonsense, come on! You never leave that damn hotel. Here, is it money you're worried about? Bet that tie clip. Looks like it's gold, is that right? Go on, throw it in the pot, let's play another hand."

A lucky hand: Ulysses won his tie clip back, along with an extremely solid fifteen dollars.

"Well, Mark and I really ought to be going now—"

"Ah, now, you can't just rob us blind and leave like this! Another round, come on, give us a chance to win it back."

Another round, another lucky break. Ulysses marveled to rake in more change and Jason watched his money go with a dry chuckle. "I never knew you were so good at cards, Dr. Cochran."

"Goodness, neither did I. I should probably quit while I'm ahead—"

"No, no." The drunk physician grabbed his arm and forced him back down into the table from which he'd tried to stand. "Come on, brother, stay, stick around. One more hand, one more, one more—"

One more turned into two more turned into three, and as the number of hands went on, Ulysses began to feel a new guilt. Good God, he didn't want to take advantage of the drunk man. "I really think I've taken enough of your money tonight," said Ulysses at last, trying to be firm.

"I'll tell you when you've taken enough, I—oh, hell." Laughing into his empty billfold, Tom raised his eyebrows and said, "Well, maybe you have taken enough. Looks like I'm out. Gotta bet something else. Look at this, got this fancy new French wristwatch here—they're makin''em for men now, can you believe it—beautiful silver, let me put it in—"

"No, no, really, I think I'd ought to—"

"You're right, it's not interesting enough. Oh! I know—here, I got this little, uh, this country place out in the woods there up in Southern Ohio. Pretty log cabin, cute as can be. Here."

Fetching his keyring from his pocket, the physician worked a brass key off. He tossed it into the center of the table. "I'm feeling so damn confident about my luck returning on this hand that I'll bet the whole damn house."

Ulysses scoffed and glanced at Mark, who glanced back from his own sizable pile of winnings. "Surely you can't mean that. You're drunk, Tom."

"Ah, I'm no drunker than you. Should I have cut you off from betting once you were a couple of beers in? Come on, now. One more hand. I'm fixin' to hit a hot streak! I can feel it."

Mark studied the physician's face as though in search of a trap. Detecting none, the valet glanced over at Ulysses and lifted his eyebrows. "Don't know if I'd mind a shot at winning a house, myself, Ulysses."

Tsking somewhat playfully, the researcher relaxed and

said to his employee, "Want an excuse to quit your job, do you…very well. But if I win and you come back to your sense tomorrow, Tom—"

"Hell! Didn't I tell you I ain't got no more cents? It's why I bet the cabin!" Laughing uproariously, nudging Jason Blackthorn beside him, Tom slapped the table before he looked more seriously at Ulysses.

"Man's only as good as his word, Ulysses, or at least that's the way we see it here in America. If I'm betting the cabin, I'm betting the cabin, and drunk or sober I'll give it up if I lose. But I won't, of course. On the wild off-chance somebody bests me, I swear on my life you can take the key tonight and I'll send you the deed tomorrow."

"You better learn not to lose your ass like this, Tom," said Blackthorn with a wry shake of his head amid his casual vulgarity. "Your gambling is going to be the end of you."

"End, nothing! This, coming from the Injun who lost his rifle to me."

While Ulysses and Mark shared a discreet glance for a term that they both agreed was lazy, somewhat pejorative and outright geographically incorrect, Jason ignored the physician's terminology and set about shuffling the cards. "One of these nights, you'll be desperate enough to put it in the pot again…I can wait to win it back."

As Jason dealt the hand, it occurred to Ulysses that, however absurd the deal was, surely Estelle would have greatly enjoyed an opportunity to stay in a cabin in the woods. In fact—well. That might have resolved quite a few problems for them.

It was a perfect intersection of civilization and wilderness; a chance for them to at last be truly alone. He could have Mark drive them up and drop them off with the stated intent of Ulysses having a chance to observe Estelle in as close to her natural environment as possible. Then, when she realized they had some time alone, wouldn't Estelle be thrilled! Ulysses was a little excited, himself.

He was interested.

He played.

He actually won.

The anthropologist couldn't imagine what strange contrivance of fate permitted him this boon. When at last the physician threw down his cards with a hefty sigh of displeasure, he shook his head and said, "Hell, Ulysses, I just don't know how you do it!"

Mark, who had folded a moment before, watched Ulysses's eyes brighten to take the key. "Must be very lucky tonight, eh, Ulysses."

"I must be—but really, Tom, are you sure? I'd be glad to just rent it from you a few weeks, I don't—"

"Hey, what'd I say? A deal's a deal. I never bet anything I'm not willing to lose…that place is a chore to take care of, anyway. Basement full of preserves from my aunt, maybe, but it gets cold in the winter and it's a million miles from anyplace I'd like to visit. If you want the burden, be my guest. Should have let you quit, shouldn't I have!"

Tom burst into an uproarious spell of laughter at that, slapping the table as he stood. "All right…I'd ought to go sleep off my loss. God willing, we'll have a smallpox outbreak or somesuch soon—I need a few patients!"

Laughing, clapping Jason on the shoulder and then nodding to Mark, Tom took his coat from the rack by the door and enthused, "You're a good player, Ulysses…I'll send somebody by with the deed tomorrow, but don't look for me to be the one to do it…the way I feel, I think

I'm going to be lucky if I wake up early enough to get to the bank when it opens and get some cash in my wallet again."

The door shut behind him. Ulysses glanced between Mark and Jason. The host of the night gathered up his cards with a shake of his head.

"Some men would stake their whole lives just for the thrill of a moment," said Blackthorn in the patient disapproval of one old friend for another. "You should have been there the night he bet his mother's jewelry…have to hand it to him, though. For all his mistakes, he somehow manages to waltz through life with nothing even resembling regret. We should all be so lucky!"

ESTELLE

ULYSSES WENT OUT with Mark one night and didn't come back for a long time, which made Estelle very worried because it had never happened before. When she'd first come to this place, Ulysses had sat up with her every night until she fell asleep; after that very nice day in the coach and the subsequent evening, he often slept with her for most of the night, sometimes all the night.

Her favorite thing in the world was when he fell asleep so soundly that she woke up to find him still there, still holding her, his face more peaceful in sleep than it ever was during the day. She would pet him gently to wake him up, caressing his beard until he stirred—and the first thing he would always do on such a morning would be to smile.

But he had never been gone in the evening before; certainly not so long, so late. Estelle tossed and turned and fidgeted in bed before, in the dark, she sat up and drew mother wolf's skull into her arms. Her hand stroked up and down the bony crown while she stared into the darkness, wondering, waiting.

Worrying.

More than once she had to remind herself that, so far as she had seen, no animals lived in the city but stray dogs, and owned ones, and sometimes also cats. Surely none of those were big enough to have hunted Ulysses—

The front door of the suite opened. She sprang upright in bed, only delaying her clamber out of it to set mother wolf down upon the nightstand. The sort of noises Bonnie called "a ruckus" filled the living room, and although Estelle was amazed to realize until that moment that she had never heard Mark laugh, she was far more captivated by the laughter of Ulysses.

It was the first time she heard him so unrestrained, so open, and her heart throbbed in her chest as she opened the bedroom door to peek into the hall.

While, at the far end, Mark entered his bedroom with of a wave of his hand around the corner, Ulysses appeared with a wave of his own. He stopped only when he saw Estelle.

Like the first time all over again, his hand drifted to his heart; now he was far faster in smiling, especially as the girl burst from her room and rushed over to him.

"Ulysses! Home, Ulysses."

"My angel, oh, Estelle—of course I'm home"—he kissed her briefly on the mouth before she was ready to fully appreciate it, and his breath smelled like sour bread—"were you worried? I'm sorry you're still up! You should be asleep."

Not knowing the word 'worried,' Estelle could only catch parts of the last two sentences and clutched the fabric of his shirt. "Sleep with Ulysses," she told him, begged him.

With a tut and a fond stroke of her hair back from her face, her dearest friend told her, "Of course, of course. Let me settle you down. Come now, Estelle..."

Soon the wild woman had snuggled back into her bed, cozy in the dark while Ulysses moved about the room. Her eyes, which had already adjusted to the light of the hall, now struggled to re-adjust to the darkness.

For all the times they had rested together, she had never seen him relax enough to so much as take off his shirt. Now he unbuttoned it with a sigh of relief, asking as he did, "Have a good night, Estelle? Fun with Bonnie?"

"Uh-huh."

"Did she read to you for me?"

"Yes," answered Estelle, who had wished all the while it was Ulysses reading to her but didn't know how to express the thought to him. "Love you, Ulysses."

"Oh! Dear. I love you, too, Estelle—and guess what?"

Now he sat upon the bed with her, and from the pocket of his trousers he withdrew something that clinked. She peered through the darkness until he leaned over to light the small gas lamp beside mother wolf's skull. Its tiny flame illuminated a small brass key in his palm.

Estelle studied it, then looked into his face. "What?"

"How would you like to go stay in the woods together, Estelle?"

Woods! Oh, the woods! She knew that word. 'Woods' and 'forest' were the words humans used to describe the place from which she'd come: the old world where she lived alone with trees and animals and teacher mushrooms.

The small cluster of mushrooms she had picked on her way out of the forest had dried in the now almost two months since her coming to live with Ulysses, and she hadn't been sure she would ever be able to learn from them again because she just couldn't imagine doing it in a strange place like the city. Somehow she had the sense that their lessons wouldn't be able to reach her, or would be corrupted by the noise, the concrete, the strange buildings.

But maybe now she could receive a lesson from them—something that might help her adjust more to her new world, and to her new role (or forthcoming role, at any rate) as leader of a pack alongside Ulysses. Better, she could show Ulysses all the things she loved about the forest: she could commune with him in nature, in a real and meaningful way that just wasn't possible in civilization.

And maybe she could even convince him to see the benefits of her old way of life. After all—now that she understood she wasn't dead and that she had not literally transitioned into a new world, she thought it more possible than ever that maybe she could go back. Maybe Ulysses would go back with her.

"Woods, Ulysses? Forest?"

"Yes, dear, the forest. Just you and me and the birds. I won a cabin tonight! These Americans really are a bit too bold for their own good…fine by me, though. It's an opportunity to see you in the forest. To be alone together… if you want to be."

Suddenly looking concerned, he put the key away again and asked her, "You do *want* to be alone together, don't you, Estelle? I would hate it if—"

He didn't finish his thought and instead settled on saying, "I want you to want to be with me."

"Yes! Oh, Ulysses, please—Ulysses and Estelle in forest. No Bonnie, no Mark. Ulysses and Estelle."

His eyes seemed as though to twinkle with joy while he told her, "Okay. No Bonnie, no Mark. Just Ulysses and Estelle."

Smiling, nodding, Estelle leaned against her friend and marveled to see him without his shirt. She had suspected on their first encounter that he was not just an invisible spirit, but some kind of wolf—the effect was now even more noticeable, for she discovered a great patch of graying but still mostly dark hair over his chest and trailing down his stomach. Biting her lip, Estelle slid out from beneath her blankets and into his lap to press herself against his body. She pet the fur of his chest, his beard.

"Estelle sad, Ulysses."

"Sad! Whyever are you sad? Oh, poor dear—"

While his arms enfolded her body, she told him earnestly, "Ulysses not home, away with Mark."

"Now, now…I'll always come home. Really, I will. There's no need to be afraid—oh, but I suppose it *is hard* for you to wait when you don't know what time even is, let alone what time to expect me home! Here…where's that pocket watch I gave you—ah—"

He noticed its silver glint through the eye holes of mother wolf's skull. Reaching toward the bone, he thoughtfully glanced at Estelle and asked, "May I?"

Understanding the meaning less than the individual words, she nodded. There was something nice about how reverent he was when lifting mother wolf's head to reach beneath her fangs. He lowered her back just as gently once he had the small device. As he had upon giving it to her, Ulysses pushed the latch to flip it open, then once more demonstrated the marked face to Estelle.

"Time is how we measure change," he said carefully. "And time is measured by clocks, watches, sundials. Time is a measure of how the sun travels—how long it takes the sun to go from one point to another and then disappear and come back. Time is a measure of experience. When I left, it was about six-thirty."

He fidgeted with one of the little knobs on the watch until the hands had glided into a new position, the short hand pointing down with the long one. Estelle looked at it quizzically, puzzled somewhat by the purpose of all this until, as usual, the opposing factor was explained to her.

"Now that I'm home, it's 12:04—or was when I turned the time back just now. See…as the big hand counts the minutes, the minutes become hours. The hours become days. Depending on what time of the year it is, the sun might be up for about 9 hours, or 12, or more in other parts of other countries. The sun goes around and around the earth, the planet where we live, and the clock goes around and around to count out time. Understand?"

The girl frowned somewhat at the stopwatch. She understood what he meant about measuring the journey of the sun and in fact found the concept to be an extremely novel one, because she had wondered how it was that people were able to keep track of the daylight when they didn't go outside or open a window. She was only accustomed to tracking the rises and falls for benefit of predicting her blood's flow, rather than the actual journey of the sun itself. But as to the process of measurement, she was still not quite clear. Smiling faintly at her confusion, patient Ulysses shut the pocket watch and set it down again.

"Well, we'll have to teach you your numbers more thoroughly before we can deal with time. One, two, three, four, five…I know you know it a little, but you'll understand it better soon. Ah! I do go on, listen to me."

Chuckling faintly, Ulysses shut off the lamp again. Then, sighing, he settled down upon Estelle's pillows. "Ah," he said softly, "smells like you—come here, Estelle, my greatest joy in life is just to hold you—"

Understanding that far better than any notion of time, Estelle threw herself down into his waiting arms and beamed to kiss his slightly sour mouth. She loved the taste—somehow it made him all the more exotic, all the more male.

Her tongue slid past his lips to explore the sacred cavern that poured out words and kisses of love. Ulysses sighed, his great jaw relaxing a bit more to permit the conjoining of hers, his hands sliding over her back and down her rump as their kisses intermingled.

Slowly, steadily, his tongue became bolder than she had ever felt it. Its assertive caresses probed into her mouth in a way that was usually her purview, and soon his breath grew heated as it filled her lungs with his essence. He rolled her upon her side, his hand sliding over her leg and drawing it around his waist. Estelle moaned softly, her body suffused with that white hot burn that overcame it when he kissed her like this—when he kissed her in the coach and his hands trailed up and up beneath the fabric of her skirt.

Her heart throbbed like her body. She reached down and drew her nightgown up her legs, pulling and pulling until the limbs were free of their lacy enclosure. As his hand happened to slide down over the flesh, his breath hitched. Ulysses's head leaned back and he studied her face in the dark, looking, reading. She pleaded with her eyes to be touched again, touched as he had touched her in the coach. Bare skin to bare skin.

His head lowered over hers once again, the avid explorations of his tongue taking on a new and far more urgent heat that only stoked the one in her body. That heat seemed focused almost entirely between her legs and, meanwhile, his fingers trailed up the flesh along the back of her thigh. Then higher, higher. She wore nothing beneath her nightgown but still felt the gown was far too much: soon she had wiggled it up over her head and Ulysses gasped to see it go, groaning slightly, his hand fitting to her rear.

"We should stop," he murmured between their kisses. "We should wait, wait until the forest—"

Estelle couldn't wait—didn't want to wait. Especially not as, at last, for the very first time, she pressed against him flesh to flesh. He still wore his trousers, but the heat of his body, his naked skin clothed only in the light layer of fur across his chest…it was beyond compare to anything Estelle had ever felt. She moaned to feel him, moving against him, her hands catching his face to hold him there for her kisses. Ulysses groaned and submitted to her utterly, his palm patting and petting her backside to stoke the ache between the front of her legs.

"Estelle love Ulysses," she whispered, clinging to him, twisting her head aside to kiss his powerful neck and his broad shoulder as he had kissed her in the coach. She had loved the feeling of those kisses, had been driven to a point of unbearable ecstasy by them; they had brought about the queer flow of some strange new fluid between her legs, some substance whose slickness had only increased the pleasure of Ulysses's touch.

That same stuff flowed from her though he did not just then touch its source—it was merely enough to kiss him and to be petted by him elsewhere. It was enough to trail her lips along his throat and to know by the depth of his rumbling groan that he experienced an ecstasy similar to the one he inspired in her.

Yes—similar. Because she could not believe anything, not even what she caused when she kissed him, could feel as good as Ulysses made her feel.

Her legs tightened around him. His hips arched against hers and she gasped to feel something in his lap she had never felt before except for once, briefly, in the coach. While her hands trailed over his chest and his explored her rump, he ground gently against her. The pressure made her moan, made her whimper and beg, "Ulysses, Ulysses—pet Estelle, oh—"

"Estelle, Estelle—oh, darling, I don't want to wait for the forest—oh, my love—"

The pressure of his hips relented and she cried out in frustration—until the hand that had most avidly squeezed and petted and patted her rear now trailed around her thighs. She released a gasp, flowers blooming all across her body at the light tease of his petting fingertips gliding between her legs. Moaning, her fingers tightening through his short hair and nails scratching against his scalp, Estelle spread her legs, opening her body to the man she loved. He exhaled, saying something under his breath in a tone that seemed to indicate astonishment at the fluid against which two of his fingers swirled, and stroked, and caressed.

Soon enough, between his kisses and his hand and his admiring, absorbing gaze, he had worked Estelle into a state of frenzy from which there was no return. It had almost frightened her in the coach, this sensaticn—it made her feel like her body was going to burst, disappear. Like she might simply die because the pleasure was just so much. Now knowing that no harm had come to her that first time, she submitted to the euphoria with absolute adoration for the sensations themselves—and for the man who produced them in her fragile nerves. Soon his caresses hastened; soon, his tongue grew more possessive with its hunger.

Soon she burst into flames, the flowers of her body searing beneath a sudden golden sun.

"Ulysses," she cried, a near scream that made him laugh and hush her nervously. He pressed kisses to her mouth while she whined, her thighs closing around his hand to keep it there as the climax fluttered through her. "Ulysses, Ulysses, love you, love you, oh—"

"God, Estelle—I love you, too." His voice was so different from its normal timbre—low and dreamy, like he had just woken or was in the middle of falling asleep. While he lifted his head from their kiss to say that, his low-lidded eyes searched her face through a darkness penetrated by love. "I adore you. I worship you. We'll be together soon, Estelle. Oh, Estelle! Were I as wild as you, I would have already taken you for my mate. I've never seen a woman that's your like. Never in the world. I love you, love you—oh, how I love you!"

ULYSSES

THE NEXT MORNING, Ulysses awoke with a splitting headache, a raw stomach, and the key to paradise in the left pocket of his trousers. His heart leapt to remember it and, carefully so as not to disturb the girl who slept soundly with her cheek upon his chest, he eased a hand into his pocket to ensure the whole business with the foolhardy American had not all been a dream.

No—there it was, cool and real. Real as the naked body of the girl who fidgeted slightly amid her dreams, her face rubbing against his chest at even this slightest motion of the arm opposite. Ulysses sighed and stowed the key away again, his lips grazing over her hair while he prayed the American did not wake up and immediately decide to go back on his ill-made deal.

Much to the anthropologist's relief, Tom really did follow through. It was something of a shock when they were called on by the front desk clerk, who appeared at the door of the suite with an enveloped containing a letter and a deed.

The letter, in nearly illegible physician scrawl, read *Fair's fair*, and thereafter contained a set of very specific directions about the way from their current town to the cabin in Southern Ohio.

And the deed, ah! It was beautiful, real, almost unbelievable to look upon. Ulysses showed it off to Bonnie and Mark that evening, prompting the former to frown and take it from his hands while the latter lifted bushy eyebrows with a slight grunt of surprise.

"Have to give it to him…I thought for sure he'd change his mind."

Estelle hurried over from where she watched the city to see the paper Bonnie held. While the girl frowned at her lack of comprehension for the written contents, Bonnie looked it over and said, "What is this supposed to be?"

"I won it from Tom Dulcamara at the poker game last night, along with his money, his watch, and probably his immortal soul. That poor man has a serious gambling addiction."

"What? You won a *house* at a poker game?" Scowling, Bonnie handed the deed back to him and said, "It's no wonder you men never allow women at games like these…we'd learn them just to win the property that should be ours and you'd never let us play again."

"Look, Estelle." Smilingly extending the deed for her to see, Ulysses said, "This is for our home in the forest. A nice place for us to stay a little while. Time for Bonnie to get a vacation of her own!"

Now fully understanding the implications of this, Bonnie looked between them—the eagerly smiling girl and blissfully expectant man. Ulysses swore he heard the beads of an abacus clicking together in her brain.

"You really won't need my help?" Bonnie glanced one more time at scrutinizing Estelle before focusing entirely on Ulysses. As he regarded her as innocently as was possible, the maid arched her brow. "You don't want my help bathing her? Dressing her?"

Clearing his throat, the anthropologist responded, "Well, of course, there comes a point when independence must be learned...one step at a time, and you know what they say. There's no time like the present. So on, so forth. Careful with that, dear." Ulysses slipped the paper from the hands of the girl who had been experimenting treacherously with the fold lines of the somewhat aged document. "Rather brittle, we wouldn't want to break it and then have to go down to city hall to explain the circumstances and get their help with a new one."

Oh...but if such an incident had occurred, Ulysses would have hardly minded. He was simply so overjoyed with the opportunity to at last be alone with Estelle that he just couldn't think of anything that might have taken the wind out of his sails.

After packing a bag at the end of the week, he jotted off a quick thank-you note to Tom and had the valet bring it by. Then, as he stood in his room trying to decide if he needed to pack anything else, Bonnie knocked on his door. Upon entering at his invitation, she assessed him with a somewhat stern expression and her arms crossed over her breast.

"Bonnie," said Ulysses, "is something the matter?"

"Nothing specifically, but, well—I was just wondering..."

Her firm jaw grinding back and forth with the teeth she nervously worked, at last Bonnie forced herself to ask, "Just what are your intentions toward Estelle, Dr. Cochran?"

The phrasing of the question was so much like what one would have expected from a concerned parent that the researcher laughed fondly, truly appreciative of the love Bonnie seemed to have developed for the wild woman. "Well—I want to educate her, of course. I want to see her blossom in the world and see how language develops in the human mind when one goes from the worst-case to the best-case scenario."

"Uh-huh. And then? After she's learned enough language to get by—then what are your intentions for her? No matter how much language she learns and how much she comes to understand about the modern world, you don't think you're going to be able to—what, set her up in an apartment and teach her to sew for a living, do you?"

"You don't think that she could?"

"Well—I guess to a certain extent, maybe. But there are so many little problems a woman runs into in the world—little problems, and big ones. It takes a lifetime of preparation to ready a girl for the things she's going to face in the real world. Do you really think she can rely on herself in a city like this? Any city?"

"She was extremely independent in the forest. Exceptionally tenacious."

Bonnie frowned at that. "That may be so, but—"

"Bonnie." Speaking gently, Ulysses stepped toward her to take her hand. "I know what you're asking. The trouble is that the answer just isn't professional, and it's important to me that you and I maintain a professional relationship. I don't want you to think you've been involved in something sordid or manipulative."

"That's not what I'm worried about!"

Surprised by her tone, Ulysses released her. She wrung her pinafore with tense hands while explaining, "Estelle is so sensitive, Dr. Cochran. I'm worried—I think she really loves you, you know. And I'm worried that you just see her as a research subject, or—or a pet of some kind. A human pet."

Now he was just appalled—not at Bonnie, of course, but at himself. Did he really seem so crude, so abhorrent and thoughtless, when viewed from the outside? "Dear! Bonnie, I would never think such a thing. Oh—Estelle is my greatest joy in life."

"Well, you're hers. That other night during the poker game, with you gone, she seemed so lonesome. I don't think she'll ever be the same if you let Cambridge interview her and then just—I don't know, remand her to their care or try to set her up in some apartment by herself."

"I know. I know. Trust me...I would never be the same, either."

"Will you at least set my mind at ease and tell me that, whatever you do, you're not going to abandon her?"

"Never! Oh, Bonnie, of course—I will never, ever abandon Estelle, no matter what happens. I mean it when I call her my joy. You know...I think I was really very unhappy before Estelle.

"It's so hard to tell because I feel like I'm still learning exactly just what happiness is—but I can tell you, at least vaguely, that it's the light I feel when I hear her laugh, or see her dance, or turn to find she's run off to ruffle the ears of some mongrel. She is a source of emotions I never truly thought I'd feel, and losing her—oh, it would devastate me.

"I love Estelle deeply. Very, very deeply. She is a good person, a funny and kind person, and without her I would have no joy at all. If I can, and if she'll have me, I want to keep her with me for the rest of my days."

Nodding carefully, Bonnie glanced down at her own feet, then again at Ulysses. "I don't meant to second-guess you, Dr. Cochran, it's just—"

"Please, no, oh, don't worry about it at all, Bonnie—I'm so glad that you care about Estelle."

Drawing the lady's maid into his arms to embrace her as he would a sister, Ulysses patted her back and said, "And I'm so glad you're there for us. So glad that Estelle—ah! Estelle."

Outside the cracked door of the bedroom, a floorboard creaked. His heart skipped with joy to see Estelle peering in, her arm frozen in motion upon the door.

Their eyes met, and for the first time he had ever seen, she scowled—not at some difficult lesson, or at some silly rule, or some long word. No.

She scowled at *him*.

The girl disappeared from view and Ulysses called out after her, baffled, releasing Bonnie to follow his dear wild wolf. Soon enough he found her in her room, her skirts spread out upon the bed where she lay gazing at the window.

"Estelle!" When she didn't respond to the pleasure in his tone, Ulysses frowned in concern, shut the door after him, and went to sit upon the edge of the bed with her. "Why, whatever's the matter?"

"Ulysses and Bonnie," muttered Estelle, not looking back at him. "Ulysses love Bonnie?"

This gave him such pause that he laughed, though the girl only grew incensed with that and sat up just to strike him with a pillow. "No laughing," she snapped, flopping back down and hugging that same pillow to her breast. "Ulysses and Bonnie love?"

"No, dear, of course not—I mean, of course I love Bonnie as a friend. But there are different kinds of love. Ulysses loves Bonnie the way Ulysses loves Mark. Do you see?"

Still slightly scowling, her shoulders nonetheless began to relax. "Friend?"

"Yes, exactly. Bonnie and I are friends; Mark and I are friends; Mark and Bonnie are friends. You, Estelle, and I—we are lovers. Lovers, Estelle. Like mates, like two mated wolves."

Her breath produced a sharp intake at that. Lip bitten uncertainly, she turned over and set the pillow aside to look at him.

"Wolves from outside?"

Somehow, he understood that question. "No, my beloved," he told her with a caress of her free-hanging dark hair. "No, there are no other wolves for me. I love you too much to be satisfied with anyone else. I haven't been with a woman in years. No one I would want to call my mate, anyway. There are things you and I will do that no one else will ever do with either one of us. We'll travel together, we'll try all kinds of foods together, we'll play games together—make love and have children together, God willing."

Her nostrils flared, those lovely dark eyes of hers all the darker for the expansion of her pupils at the thought. "Mother wolf and father wolf."

"That's right. Mother wolf and father wolf of our own litter. Not now, but someday—whenever it happens, it will be the right time. Until then, we can always practice…and I will never make love to anyone else, Estelle." He caught up her hand and bent his head, kissing her knuckles while she sighed. "I swear it: you are the only beauty I see in this life, this world. You are a treasure beyond all compare. No one will ever stand between us... and God help those who try."

Thankfully, Estelle seemed satisfied by that. Nodding, then reaching over to pat mother wolf's snout, she asked, "Mother wolf in forest?"

"Of course, my dear, of course she can come with us... here, let me help you pack her so we can make sure she gets to enjoy the trip."

Then, it was one more sleep. One more long, agonizing, constantly interrupted sleep that was filled with dreams of excitement, anticipation, things going terribly wrong. In one the cabin was situated on a mountainside and subject to an avalanche; in another, it was missing a wall entirely. Yet, when he awoke as early as he could, not even a missing wall would have kept him from enjoying privacy with his beloved.

And anyway, she was so lovely in the dark pink silk of her newest frock. He would have thrown himself out of a window if that was what was required to look at her in the dress into which Bonnie had put her first thing that morning. Now the nursemaid stood giving the girl valuable advice in a soft hush, each positioned before the hearth in the living room. Both looked up like startled groundhogs when Ulysses emerged in the room, travel bag in-hand, and each at once softened to see him. Estelle left Bonnie's side and darted into his free arm, eliciting a laugh from him and earning a cluster of kisses from his lips. He let Bonnie see the act to reassure her, and let Estelle be kissed before Bonnie so she would know for certain where his heart lay.

The poor dove! Now more than ever he saw it was important to truly love her—to let himself love her completely in defiance of all professional standard. He couldn't stand the thought of her doubting his love; of misunderstanding his intentions in even the slightest way. Estelle was a jewel. She deserved to know beyond a shadow of a doubt that his entire heart lay with her. That all his love was hers to have, no matter the environment around them. No matter what Cambridge did or didn't have to say.

And if Cambridge didn't like that, well…then Ulysses was just going to have to alter his own priorities.

The trip from the town where they stayed in West Virginia seemed extraordinarily long—longer, even, than its eight hours ought to have felt. All the roads were dirt, long and winding and wobbling. He and Estelle bounced around the coach and the poor girl complained of nausea, holding her stomach and leaning against him with a decidedly green tinge to her face. He savored the opportunity to fold her in his arms, console her, pet and pat her back.

That did not keep her from eating her fill when they stopped for lunch, however. While the girl ate, Mark looked over them, then asked Ulysses in a tone that was only half-joking, "When I come back for you in two weeks, will I find you? Or will she have convinced you to come live in the woods as a pair of wild animals, Adam and Eve?"

"Oh…we'll be there when you come back to pick us up again, but you're right. I think this trip will be as beneficial for me as it will be for Estelle."

Yes, he could feel it. It was the crystallization of the change that Estelle had begun to set into motion deep within his heart. She was so different—so extraordinarily different from any other human he had known, man or woman. It was impossible to know someone so radically apart from one's fellows and not be transformed utterly by the knowing.

Especially when it was intimate knowing.

His heart thundered in his breast with all the anticipation of a bridegroom long-denied. At last, the coach drew down the final road that had been indicated in Dr. Dulcamara's notes. Estelle pressed her face to the window with a noise of pure, angelic joy for the trees that gradually sprang up around them, by the second growing thicker in number and higher in trunk. Soon the coach rolled through the woods; and Estelle, with giddy pleasure to find the other side of the carriage also enclosed by trees, gripped Ulysses's hand and cried into his face, "Happy, Ulysses—oh, Estelle happy! Love woods, love Ulysses. Love you!"

Before he could respond, she threw herself against his chest and kissed his lips with pure delight. Ulysses sighed, the soft taste of her feminine sweetness overwhelming to his senses. The taste of absolute love. When she drew her flushed face away to smile into his, their noses brushing, she seemed as though to glow.

"Ulysses nice," said Estelle, petting his cheek, his beard, his ear. "Ulysses very nice."

"You deserve nothing but the kindest treatment, Estelle," he told her in return, clasping her to his heart as the coach began to slow. "I want to give you all of this and more—everything I can, for the rest of our lives. How I love you…oh! How I love you!"

15

ESTELLE

HOWEVER LONG THE coach ride felt to Ulysses, it was an eternity to timeless Estelle. She still had not mastered the measure of time's passage and therefore could only observe the movement of space around her—the sudden development of the woods through which they drove like a signal of all the bliss that was to come.

How happy she was! How good it was to be home, though she understood just owing to the trees that these were not the forests of her youth. It didn't matter. All of nature had been her home then, and still was. Wherever civilization was not, that was where she belonged.

Her conversation with Bonnie rolled mysteriously through her head all morning, doing nothing to lessen her excitement and only adding to the litany of questions that had to go unspoken.

"You love Ulysses, right, Estelle?" The woman looked at her carefully while they stood before the fire, perhaps making sure Estelle meant her adamant response. How nice it was to tell Bonnie that time! For the first moment Estelle could think of, Bonnie seemed to understand how deeply that love was meant.

"Well," said Bonnie upon this answer, her glance darting toward the skirts of Estelle's dress, "just be ready, okay? I won't patronize you by worrying whether or not you know about sex—what men and women do together, when they're alone together. Just make sure, whatever you do with Ulysses, it's something you really want to do. Oh—and make sure he takes care of you after, and still treats you the same. Nicely, you know. Whatever happens, never let him treat you anything but nicely."

But Estelle was never worried about that. It didn't seem physically possible for Ulysses to treat her anything but nicely. As he helped her down from the high coach while Mark fetched out their bags, his very smile was an expression that filled her with warmth unending. She hurried up to the building the men called 'a cottage' with joy in her heart, ecstasy throbbing through her to look at it.

The trellis of unkempt wild roses rising up the side of the building, the great stones and logs that made up the structure, that happy little windows that looked to her somehow like smiling eyes…she pressed her face to the glass and peered inside, her hands around her temples to afford her a glimpse while Mark set down their bags and the men shook hands.

"Mark," Ulysses was saying, "I can't thank you enough for the trip. What will you do with your time off?"

"Stay in and give the horse a break, for starters..."

At that, Estelle whipped around and hurried up to the horse, her smile now for it. She and the kind beast of burden had developed a closeness during her time in the world of men, and as her hand raised, its nose lowered. She petted it, kissed it, softly told it, "Nice horsey...nice horse. Have good time! Love you."

"Oh, Estelle." The fondness dripped from Ulysses's words to see her with the horse, though she wasn't quite sure why. She turned to smile at him and see if he had something to explain to her, but instead he simply extended his hand and said warmly, "Come on—let's see the inside."

The truth was that, to Estelle, city and forest were two such distinct states that it gobsmacked her to think of a human structure amid the wild things of the wood. These great square buildings didn't fit amid all the natural curves of trees and roots and earth. Yet, by the same token, this structure—clearly made of the contents of the forest in which it dwelled in a way that was much more obvious than the materials of other buildings in which humans resided—was so much a part of the forest that, despite its rigid form, it did seem fully natural to her.

Especially once the door opened beneath Ulysses's hand and he gestured for her to step inside.

The sight of the place was so pleasing to her that she barely heard Mark's snapping reins, or the beats of the horse's hooves into the distance. From the stone floor to the furniture that was mostly made of wood, it was such an inspiring sight that she had to ask herself why she had never thought of doing such things while she lived alone. Oh, she'd had her little den...but she had been so busy trying to survive in other ways that it never occurred to her to make a proper building, one big enough to walk around in. Maybe it was just because she had never seen a building before the gentle man who carried her wolf-skin to the loft above the living room took her from the solitude in which she lived.

There were things she missed about the forest, and things she didn't miss. She didn't miss the bugs, the heat, the cold, the anxiety. The constant anxiety still tightened her body on a daily basis and now that they were back in the forest it was almost unavoidable that she felt it again. But there was relief in a homecoming here, too—relief and beauty, and excitement. At last, she could share the wonderful, enriching things that the forest had to offer with the man she loved!

Upon returning to the ground floor, Ulysses found her pondering the timepiece: a heavy metal thing upon the mantle. Pointing at the still face, she asked him, "Dead?"

"Hm—oh, no, it's just wound down. And items aren't 'dead,' they are 'broken,' my dear…here—"

Estelle watched in amazement as Ulysses very casual-ly shifted the device around and, with a key resting near-by, wound it a few times until its hands ticked to life. Was there nothing the man couldn't do?

She marveled. Even if this was something everyone else in the world knew how to do, somehow Estelle thought she would still find Ulysses's ability accomplish it as proof of his superiority.

He checked the watch on his wrist, then used a fin-ger to move the little arms of the clock. After shutting the glass door over its face with a pleased expression, he turned his smile upon Estelle—

And it was like they both realized the same thing at the very same second.

They were alone together.

With a shy grin, hopeful and excited as her heart, Estelle raised her hand to her mouth as though to hide her mirth. Her thumb pressed to her lips and she asked, "Ulysses sleepy?"

"I was…but I find myself very awake suddenly."

Her eyes turned toward the clock. "Time?"

"It's seven fifty-two. See—"

He pointed out the big hand and the little hand, and this and that, and at some point while he explained it all to her his hand came to rest upon her shoulder. She leaned into him and he inhaled sharply, but still continued, "Why don't we practice your counting a bit? Here, Estelle…we've been sitting in that coach all day I know, but let's lay down on the sofa here."

Her heart throbbed while he drew her gently into the soft cushions that had been arranged upon the wooden support of the sofa. Holding her breath, Estelle settled in his embrace and permitted him to take her hands in his. Once he had folded them into fists, he did the same thing with his own and raised one finger.

"One," he said before lifting a second, "two—"

She followed along with him, her fingers raising, her lips silently miming the words. She wanted to burn these things into her brain, and not just for him anymore. The human world had become an insane curiosity to Estelle, and she wanted to comprehend its greatest secrets as soon as she could.

She wanted to learn how to tell time; she wanted to learn how to read. There was so much that she wanted to learn, and it made her happy every time she managed to grasp something knew. Ulysses and his teaching, that was what made her happy.

Estelle looked up at him, interrupting the lesson.

"Ulysses?"

"Yes?"

That low, almost tired tone of his voice. But he was not tired, he said. This was the tone that his voice had found on that recent night when he had come home so late; when he had touched her so sweetly.

"Thank you," whispered Estelle, looking into his face.

But for the delay of a few seconds wherein he absorbed what she had just told him, he didn't hesitate.

He kissed her.

ULYSSES

SOMETIMES, LIFE WAS grand. Ulysses was embarrassed to admit that he hadn't really seen it that way before he and Estelle were free to love one another… but, oh! Now he saw it with bright, shining clarity. Yes! Sometimes life was revealed, in all its purity, as the gift it truly was—and in those sweetest, most wrenching moments, it was a gift so great that it caused him a kind of physical pain to contemplate.

In his youth, he had seduced a handful of women before he realized how silly it was to chase people that he didn't have time for. Modern ladies were coy and embarrassed. The air was always rusty with shame.

No woman was like Estelle, however.

Estelle did not have any expectation, and so he was able to doubly thrill her. The sensual pleasures they shared were entirely unknown to her, in theory as well as in practice, and he felt at times as he had when he guided her from the woods and she first saw that bountiful sea of lavender. Then, as now, he had the sense that she had never conceived of such a thing—the potential for so much wonder all in one sprawling location.

And they sprawled together, Ulysses and Estelle. Their bodies intertwined and their hearts raced in time and their limbs and hips and minds seemed to match pace together. Best of all, he felt as if he had suddenly come into her domain—though she, of the two of them, was the one less-versed in all these matters.

Yet, she was a natural. Of course she was a natural. And, better still, she made him natural in turn. They did not speak except for names. Instead their bodies grew so close that they seemed all the time to be two parts of a single invisible entity. One soul, united in the current between these two splendid bodies.

Oh, to hold her! To hold her. He loved to hold her, before and during and after. With her warm body pressed naked against his own, he stroked her cheek and pushed her hair back from her face. He sang to her, which she had liked since the first time they met; and oh, how she smiled through her sleepy drifting-off.

The best part of all, though, was not that blurred consummation. Yes, of course their union was an achievement worth celebrating—but the real glory, the real moment that mattered most to Ulysses, was waking up to nude Estelle still in his arms the next morning.

Ah, he had waited for this since the first night he spent with her! When he had wooed her with chocolates and furs on behalf the modern world as though he were making a pitch in the stead of Duke Orsino; and as it had happened to Shakespeare's displaced messenger, Estelle had instead fallen for Ulysses.

But oh, there was no trepidation on his side as there was on Viola's. Once they were away from the city, his every last doubt dissolved as if by some form of primitive magic. He watched her doze in the early morning half-light and, as she slowly stirred, he kissed the eyelids that seemed to shine in the dark.

With a soft sigh and a long, almost feline stretch, Estelle opened those lovely eyes and batted them slowly up at him.

"Good morning," he told her very gently.

"Good morning," she said. Then, smiling—remembering the night before, it would seem—that dear wild woman trailed her fingertips over his chest. "Again?"

Again, and again, and again! She was as eager to celebrate their love as he was, and it was a terribly refreshing opportunity for them both. While her screams of joy echoed through the empty little cabin, his rapid panting filled his mouth with the humidity of her flesh. Those little claws of hers sank into his back but somehow the sting only served to make the pleasure that much better.

Soon they were dozing again, and then again they made love; and only when they became insatiably hungry for something more than one another did Ulysses at last force himself to get up and prepare them some food. He set the fire to blaze in the hearth, then made a stew with the ingredients they had brought along plus water from the well out back. That and a jar of peaches later and suddenly it was nightfall again.

Suddenly one day had passed by to find them that much closer to the one when they would be forced to return. This was where a fragile sense of time did a person a favor. If only Ulysses were not so keenly aware of the ticking of those hateful clocks!

Ah, but it was an invaluable lesson in its own right. Noticing as he did his own preoccupation with the future, he had the opportunity—the choice—to turn his mind to present matters.

It became an exercise to keep himself bound there with the pleasure, the joy, of Estelle.

And Estelle took such joy in life—especially now that they were where she, like all the other plants and animals around, blossomed.

It was not that Estelle had been depressed while in the city, per se. But being with her in the forest made him realize how cautiously reserved she had become when around the creations of Man. No doubt she had somewhat withdrawn into herself out of caution, putting emphasis on observing and absorbing rather than interacting. She daydreamed frequently, and sighed often, and gazed out of the nearest window to watch the world at every opportunity.

But now, in the forest, it was as though she had become an entirely different girl. Every step she took was a kind of dance—a celebration of wonder. With wide eyes and the drumbeat of excitement to her movements, she drew Ulysses into the forest the second morning while refusing shoes and anything more than her shift.

This white lace ghost moved silently through trees, and caressed the moss, and got down on hands and knees to see closely the bramble-tangled tuft of gray fur that made her declare with bold excitement, "Wolf, wolf!" How filled with effervescent ecstasy she was to examine the flowers, the insects, the mushrooms!

The mushrooms.

He noticed right away, as he had not had the opportunity to before, that she seemed to especially revere mushrooms. He did not know how it was with her before she was brought out of the forest the first time, but now when she saw a clutch of the little things she would bend her head and whisper, "Hello!" as though greeting an old friend.

After hearing this a few times, and having taught her the word for mushroom after the first instance, he asked, "Did you eat mushrooms often while living in the forest?"

The girl parsed his sentence in only a handful of seconds this time, then shook her head. "Mushrooms smart. Smart, like Ulysses."

He laughed at that just slightly, not understanding what she meant. She was magical to him—a mystical being, a wood sprite. While he watched, she climbed trees and found streams and picked berries that she pressed into his mouth. And when she found a spot she liked (for the plush bed of moss or the view of the stars through the supple fingers of trees) she would draw him down to the earth and beg him for his love.

Yes, oh, Estelle! She was so pure. So natural and simple and *happy* out there in the forest.

And the thought of bringing this happy wild girl back to England with him—where nothing at all seemed natural anymore and where Cambridge would want to wring from her every last shining organic quality—made him feel sick.

It was difficult to say how he felt about what he had done to Estelle by bringing her from the wild. That it had been altogether a mistake? No, of course not—without bringing her from the woods and teaching her at least the amount of English he had already taught her, they never would have had the chance to fall in love.

Yet it did make him realize that the beauty of Estelle's nature—her true character—lay in her innocent heart and sinless perception the world. It was in her freshness, her levity, her movement from moment to moment without that burden of the long-term future felt by Ulysses every day.

And the more time she spent in the city, educated in the means and mores of men, the more he squelched and tamed and restrained that gleaming inner nature until it was doomed to be a shadow of itself. What he was really doing, he realized, was not educating her, but domesticating her.

Worse…domesticating her for Cambridge.

Yes: during the first few days of their consummated romance, these initial periods of time as a couple, the researcher realized that all he had done was ultimately fruitless. He could never, would never take her to Cambridge. He would never chase the acclaim or the credit of her discovery.

But he would never let her go, either.

This resolve fomented in him on the day that she convinced him to try the mushrooms—not the ones out in the woods where they stayed but ones that, going by their brittle, dried-out appearance, she had evidently brought from her original home.

They had been out through the woods on their fifth day of solitude when she nearly screamed with delight and hurried to see another bunch of mushrooms gathered on a log. "Aha," she cried, trying to pick them. He gasped and caught her hand.

"Oh, no, no, Estelle—we can look, but we'd ought not to touch. Many mushrooms are poisonous, you know."

The girl gave him a cross look at that, a young lady looking at an out-of-touch old man.

"No," she corrected, repeating with an avid point, "mushrooms *smart*. Teach Estelle. Teach like Ulysses, and more."

Not understanding at all, he insisted again, somewhat lamely, "But they're toxic, dear. Everything but the buttons and the morels are in question to the layman, even mushroom experts occasionally pick the wrong kind and die."

Her eyes rolled and she looked at him somewhat sourly—but, with a huff, she did leave the fresh patch in the log. The girl gripped his hand. "Come, come," she said, having picked up on one of his many manners of speech.

Soon they stood again in the cabin, where Estelle dug through her bag before producing something that quite shocked him. The dry and twisted mushrooms she extended looked like little phalluses, or maybe some kind of desiccated flatworm; he looked at them in astonishment, plucking one up and examining it in the light.

"Now these are interesting, but I would still have to talk to a friend in the field before I—Estelle!"

Making eye contact with him, the girl crammed about half of the dried mushrooms into her mouth with a high, wicked laugh. He dropped the one in his hand to grab her, insisting, "You must spit them out, Estelle—no! Don't swallow—"

Too late. She gulped the chewed mushrooms down and then extended the rest, insisting, "Ulysses eat. Mushrooms smart. Make ideas, tools, dreams."

Frowning, he accepted the mushrooms she insisted on holding for him, including the one she had picked from the floor and blown off in a habit learned from Bonnie whenever a pin was dropped in the wild girl's dressing. Estelle waited, expectant, and he studied the things in his hand again.

"I don't understand," he told her after a moment. She rolled her eyes.

"Estelle eat mushroom lots. Estelle not hurt, Estelle happy—happy with Ulysses."

In other words: *I eat these things all the time! Aren't I still here?*

He supposed that was true, but it still didn't make a lot of sense to him. Why would one eat a toxic mushroom and take the risk? What could the pay-off possibly be? Ulysses turned the twisted fungus over between his fingers. While Estelle clambered down the ladder from their loft to leave him to his decision, he recalled records of a strange case from a little over a hundred years prior.

In 1799, a family had picked mushrooms in London's Green Park and, upon preparing a meal with the things, experienced all manner of bizarre but euphoric mental effects. Their pupils had expanded; they had burst into long bouts of spontaneous laughter; they had experienced what had been noted as delirium; but, ultimately, they had recovered just fine after the incident with no ill effects to speak of.

The whole thing had brought to mind recorded instances of mass ergot poisoning, where whole towns were simultaneously stupefied—but not necessarily harmed—by the effects of fungus-infused grain.

The researcher frowned once more at the mushrooms that Estelle had given him: mushrooms that, unlike the fresh ones in the woods, he had not been able to stop Estelle from taking because they were already on her person.

All at once, thinking of those historic incidents and of the girl wandering about downstairs with some kind of toxic fungus working its way through her system, Ulysses suddenly had to ask himself—

Why did he think he knew more about nature than someone who spent her whole life a part of it, rather than apart from it?

This was the first of many revelations that the night would hold for him. With a reluctant sidelong glance at the girl who had taken a position near the front wall of the cabin to see him from where she waited, Ulysses picked up one of the mushrooms and sniffed. It didn't smell like anything, but oh, the taste of the first was so acrid that his mouth began to water and the nausea was evident at once. Somehow, Estelle had overcome that effect and managed to eat her entire palmful in a few enthusiastic chews. Ulysses had a hard time, especially as his saliva softened the dried things and left them repulsively slimy.

But then, from her watching vantage, she called, "Hooray, Ulysses!"

And, well…Ulysses was far from the first man in history who ate something stupid because a beautiful woman seemed to approve.

At least he'd be able to write a paper about this someday, assuming he survived. With the bitter taste still clinging to his mouth, Ulysses lowered down the ladder and laughed as Estelle more or less threw herself upon him.

"You're quite sure this won't hurt us?"

It was a useless question to ask, owing to the fact that he had just eaten the things one way or another…but Estelle's rapid nod did soothe his fearful mind. "Nice mushroom," she assured him in approval. Then, stroking his face and smiling, she added, "Nice Ulysses."

Ugh. Ulysses may have been nice…but as to the niceness of the mushroom, the jury was still out. Estelle had insisted on going outside right away, and hand-in-hand they resumed their natural explorations. Paying careful attention to both his condition and Estelle's, Ulysses noticed after something on the order of half an hour that the girl's pupils had grown to the size of dish plates. Worried, he examined her flushed cheeks and throat, then asked, "Are you sure you don't want to go back?"

She laughed at that and shook her head. Soon, sighing with pleasure, the girl found a lovely clearing where a few small patches of wildflowers had grown up around a tiny crystal pond. Just large enough to wade into or maybe even swim without much risk of drowning, the secluded body of water housed a cluster of little frogs who hopped happily about until seen—at which point, they promptly disappeared into some reeds and fell completely silent. Giddy with the thrill of it, Estelle slipped her shift over her head and waded into the water: naked, lovely, her golden skin dappled with sweat and sweet pink blush.

"Be careful, Estelle," he said, unable to help fussing after her, still wondering what those mushrooms were supposed to have done. Where was the ecstasy? Where was the delirium?

All things in their time. He noticed it first when he turned his head a bit too quickly and reality seemed somehow to lag—a bit like being drunk, he thought, although the novel qualities of this substance soon revealed themselves. Namely, as he sat amid the wildflowers to watch his true love splash around, his mind began to somehow float. It seemed to raise above him, away from him, into a new momentum of thought that was totally uncontrolled by the force of his will. He barely noticed how sweaty he was for quite some time: he was focused almost entirely upon his own mind, the chain of consciousness that sped off into the distance.

Look! The mushroom was perfectly harmless, wasn't it? Didn't seem to do anything, as it happened—maybe made Estelle a bit giddy, made the world sway around him. Other than that, what was the problem? Why had he really been so ignorant, so unwilling to listen to Estelle? His ego really was getting in the way. That Freud fellow in Vienna, he was really onto something with all that chatter about the ego and the superego and the id. Maybe not completely right, but onto something all the same.

A person's conception of themselves was often completely removed from the way others perceived them—the true, shining light of being was buried underneath all the stuffy pretensions of social expectation and political goals and career ambitions.

Why, Ulysses was so obsessed with proving himself 'right'—proving his way of life was superior to Estelle's—that for all his yammering about wanting to teach her and be taught by her, he really hadn't learned a thing. No, no: he just saw a girl in need of education. Really she was a *woman*, more competent and wiser than he in the ways of basic human instinct and natural survival.

Hadn't he been struck with terror at the mere idea of starting a fire on his own when he was lost in the woods and came upon her that first time? Hadn't he become completely detached from his roots? Darwin, now there was another fellow who had a thing or two to say—why, he and Estelle and the monkeys and apes of the jungle all shared some shining common ancestor, some true Eve whose pedigree lay in all of them.

Was his way of life not a disruption of all of that? An improvement, yes, but still a cloistering disruption to natural order? Was there not some balance that could be struck between a completely wild life of simian intelligence and the existence of the conscious human being with his buildings, his electricity, his clothes?

His clothes—Ulysses became aware of his clothes and the sweat plastering them to his body. He rose to take them off. Estelle, her smile as bright as the noonday sun, hurried over with a happy cry to assist him—then, just as soon as he was free of all these foolish human contraptions, she made fierce love to him. Under the effects of the mushroom it took much longer than normal, felt much more powerful than even that first time, and seemed to take him to a transcendent dimension of consciousness about which he thought he might like to write a paper someday.

By the time it was over, the psilocybin had gripped hold of both their consciousnesses and the sun began to set.

He was almost worried about getting back to the cabin because he of course had no idea of the way—then he realized that was how Estelle probably still felt every time they went to the park. To her, the buildings of the city were as wholly indistinct as he found the trees of this forest. Estelle, however, had no worries. It seemed to him that the only time he had ever seen her worry was when he was out playing poker with Tom and Jason. Oh, they'd never believe this story! He wasn't sure how he would describe it to anyone.

After all—it was such a personal, intimate experience, not just between one another but with themselves. Sometimes each one of them would lapse into intense silence, whether they were embracing or on different sides of that lovely clearing. Mostly, though, they communicated in whatever way felt right, through speech or silent caress. Eventually they ended up on their backs together, watching the stars.

"Look, Estelle—you see, the stars, I named you after them."

"Stars?"

"Yes, that's what 'Estelle' means. It means 'star' in another language."

"Stars," she repeated pleasantly, looking over at him. "What?"

"They're suns, you see—suns like our sun, but very far away. Miles and miles, whole lifetimes away. Imagine! Totally different planets swirling around them…maybe even with beings, totally different beings. Think of all the possibilities! Sometimes I try to imagine such things, but I don't even know where to begin. How different their cultures could be…how differently they could *look* from us.

"How strange! I wonder if we'll ever go? I saw a moving picture a few years ago…it told the story of a bunch of astronomers—researchers who are interested in the stars, I mean—who go to the moon and see a funny race of people there. I just thought it was a silly story then… suddenly, though, I wonder if it's possible. Maybe we jolly well could go there…oh! But why? Why do we want to escape ourselves so much, Estelle? Why can't we be satisfied?"

He looked over to find Estelle watched him very closely, listening and absorbing what she could of his romantic diatribe. "London, where I'm from, feels far away as the moon…Cambridge, even farther. Estelle! Oh, Estelle—I love you so much, I—"

His eyes filled with tears. The mushrooms made some thoughts flow easily and others difficult to complete. Cooing, the girl sat up and wiped his cheeks, gradually bending her head to kiss away the tears that flowed ceaselessly.

"Love you, Ulysses…it's okay, it's okay…"

"No—no, it's not okay. There's no difference between what I intended to do to you and Tom's idea to put you into entertainment." She looked at him blankly, never having been made aware of the physician's proposal to exploit her as some sideshow attraction; pushing it all out of his mind, Ulysses cradled her cheek in his hand.

"I don't want to take you back to England. There's nothing for either of us there. I want to stay here. I want to live a simple life with you. I want to—to start a pack. A family with you, Estelle."

Her eyes brightened and she lifted her head to see him better, peering through the moonlit dark as he said, "I want to spend all my days with you. I want to be myself, be a *human*. Not a gentleman, an anthropologist, no, none of it. By God! Maybe I'll just start studying these mushrooms, these amazing things—"

"Mushroom smart," said Estelle, nodding in encouragement. Her smile widened and she asked, "Ulysses and Estelle live in forest?"

"Well, why not? If Tom changes his mind and wants this cabin back, I'll just buy it from him…write to Mrs. Halbrook, sell the estate, pay her off to let her retire. Oh, but you don't care about all that—let's look at the stars, Estelle, at the—sh!"

Both leapt at the snap of a twig; both looked up with animal fright. Their eyes focused in the direction of the sound and, after some study, Ulysses's tear-blurred gaze discerned another pair of stars gazing from the line of the trees. He sat up a bit to better see: by then, Estelle had already recognized the thing that looked at them, and gasped.

"Oh," she cried with joy, "oh, wolf! Hello! Oh, cousin, hello!"

The great timber wolf looked steadily into them. Ulysses's heart rested firmly in its mouth.

Without another sound, the animal disappeared once more into the trees.

Its movements were so utterly silent as it left—so like a phantom despite its massive size—that Ulysses had the strange sense that the wolf had wanted them to hear it. He would never be sure why he got that impression; but, even once the mushroom wore off, it was destined to remain.

The psilocybin seemed to remain in their systems for almost twelve hours; by the time the vibration of his body had calmed enough to sleep, Estelle was already drooping against his chest with heavily-lidded Pre-Raphaelite eyes. He disturbed her only to ask, "Do you know the way back, my love?"

"Uh-huh," said the sleepy girl, forcing herself upright with a great yawn. She began to make for the trees, but he laughed and gently caught her hand. After quickly dressing himself, he drew her shift over her head; then, together, they returned the way they had come, with Estelle's wandering gaze seeking signs in trees and stones as to the best route to the cabin.

It somehow still astonished him how easily she found it. After the invaluable lessons the mushroom had imparted, he should have been ready to give her more credit; but now more than ever he marveled at her—or anyone else's—ability to survive. The will of the human was a triumph! Yes, truly a triumph. But what he and so many other humans had forgotten was that it was possible for the will to triumph *with* nature, rather than over it.

Soon, despite Estelle's sleepy grumbles, he convinced her to join him for a proper washing-up in the washtub. By the time dawn had rolled around, they were both exhausted, and each slept soundly most of the day through. By the time Ulysses awoke it was already after noon, and though he might not have described himself as 'hungover,' he was certainly wired and thirsty.

With a kiss upon the temple of Estelle's forehead, he made his way down to the main floor of the cabin, put on a pair of trousers, and went around back to draw water from the well.

The cold muzzle of Tom Dulcamara's rifle against the back of his head was the first indication that they were no longer alone.

"Don't turn around," said the physician while Ulysses slowly put his hands in the air, "and don't get smart. If I were you, I wouldn't start a fight about this."

"What—Tom? What's going on?"

"Consider this a trade. I give you my cabin, and you give me a better life. Sound fair?"

Uncomprehending, Ulysses tried after a few bleary seconds, "I'm—I'm afraid I still don't understand."

The physician's laugh was dark as the gun he pushed against Ulysses's head. "You really think I'm that bad at poker? How the hell you think I won this rifle, Cochran? I'm great at poker. I hardly ever lose—not unless I want to lose."

Though the researcher's stomach had already sunken into a hideous swamp of remorseful understanding, Tom went on. "I've tried to talk sense into you for two months now, and all the time I just see you letting your opportunity fade away. So…I decided, since I'm the only one who's seeing it, I might as well make it *my* opportunity.

"Couldn't make it my opportunity with all those folks around all the time, though—Bonnie, that valet of yours…hell, even the front desk clerk at the hotel. So, I let you have my cabin for a few days. Figured when you'd had time to settle in we'd swing up here, grab the girl and that'd be that."

"'We?'"

"Jason Blackthorn, of course…thinks we're saving the girl to let her roam free in the wild again, but"—the alleged physician produced an ugly, hateful sound that couldn't really be called a laugh—"that's because I thought I better get some back-up along in case you proved *really* disagreeable. I'll shake him loose one way or another when the time is right."

"Going to kill him, you mean."

"Like I said…one way or another. Now, unless you want me to kill *you*, too, you just come along quietly with me. Let's go talk a little walk in the woods, friend…it is one hell of a beautiful day."

ESTELLE

WHAT A NIGHT! What a perfect night. Estelle had feared the night as a girl but, with Ulysses by her side, the night was its own sort of beauty to her now. Especially after it was blessed by her cousin wolf.

They were far away from her pack's old territory—she knew that only because it seemed they had spent the whole day in the carriage—but somehow, Estelle found herself wondering if the beast was a relation. Wolves lived a long time so far as she was concerned, and in that time they could wander far and wide. Who was to say one of her siblings had not made it up here, up in this forest that was so different and yet so much the same as her own?

It was such a happy sight, that wolf. It made her feel like she was being told something: reassured by both the mushroom and the animal. All things aligned as though to demonstrate that she and Ulysses were perfectly fit for one another: that this good and patient man who loved her was something, someone, for whom she had been waiting all this time without realizing she even waited.

She was glad he took the mushroom alongside her, and gladder still to go to bed together to sleep it off—but oh, how she hated when he left! Estelle sighed as he kissed her forehead and then got up, maybe to get food or water or relieve himself. Hopefully he would be back soon.

Still among the pillows, she reached for the silver watch on the bedside table with mother wolf. This, she drew into her palm as though in lieu of her lover, pressing the switch that opened the face to her uncomprehending eyes.

Not entirely uncomprehending, though. When Ulysses had practiced counting with her while the mushroom teacher rushed through her blood, the numbers he taught her suddenly became more than meaningless sounds associated with the fingers she held up.

They were tools just like language—yes, the language of amounts and of logic! The language of things that did not move or speak, but were observed from the outside. Now, peering at the face of the clock, she tried to understand the numbers there.

She still could not read. That was the biggest problem with her time-telling—even more than the numbers themselves, linking the sounds of the numbers to written symbols still seemed somewhat beyond her. But she did now sort of understand the motion of the steady 'minute' hand, as Ulysses called it.

She stared at the watch, its second hand ticking around at a pace that was the fastest of the three. When it reached the top symbol, the minute hand ticked forward once.

A-ha!

Yes, ah, *now* she saw. Now she understood. She sat up a little and waited for the hand to twitch forward another time, once again when the second hand reached that top numeral. Excitement grew in her. Yes! Now it made sense. She beamed as the minute hand aligned with the number at the bottom of the watch; then, satisfied, she shut the silver door and rested her hand upon her heart. Wouldn't Ulysses be so excited, so proud, to see what she had learned?

Estelle dozed and dreamed of his pride—dreamed, too, of how they would make this pretty cabin their new home. All his talk of 'Cambridge' and 'London' was talk of things she had never really understood, especially when he tried to show her a map and demonstrate where they were. It all made no sense—not that there should be so much world out there, and not that Ulysses should consider his home anywhere but where he was staying at a given moment.

But that seemed to have changed. Her heart raced with the joyous thought that she had finally gotten through to him—yes! Finally, he understood what she wanted. All that she wanted.

Yet…something was wrong.

Estelle drew out of her doze; the pocket watch ticked away on the pillow where she had expected to find Ulysses's dreaming head. The girl sat up in bed and looked around, leaning over the edge of the loft that served as the bedroom.

Nothing. No Ulysses downstairs.

Frowning, Estelle returned to bed and peered out the window overlooking the yard. Once more, nothing: no sign of him bent over the well or doing anything at all.

Something strange was afoot, though she wasn't sure what. Her lower lip disappearing between her teeth, Estelle eased back into bed and ran her hand nervously over her leg. She took up the watch and opened its face.

The minute hand had moved forward a quarter of the face, now pointing left. That was an awful lot of ticks of the second hand between the time when he left and this time: an awful lot of seconds to be drawing water from the well.

Her frown deeper by the second, Estelle climbed up out of bed and threw her shift over her head, because it was the polite thing to do and it pleased Ulysses when she was polite. She didn't want to go outside only for him to tut to her about her nudity—but she was almost glad she had dressed when she stepped out to the porch.

Estelle had never thought twice of her nakedness before being taught that the proper thing was to wear clothes in the presence of others. But when she crossed the threshold of the front door and found Jason Black-thorn waiting there for her, she almost felt that the shift was not enough.

"Estelle," said the man, touching the brim of his hat. "May I come in?"

"Ulysses?"

She searched Jason's face in vain but found no answer there. Jason stepped toward her and, when she stepped back, he raised his hands to show they were empty. His jacket shifted and the pearl handle of the gun beneath it shone from its holster.

"You don't need to be afraid of me, Estelle. I just came here to talk—talk to you, talk to Ulysses."

"Where Ulysses?"

"I imagine he's off having a conversation with Tom… so let's you and I do the same."

With slow, broad steps, the man approached, hands still raised. Estelle backed anxiously into the cabin and gritted her teeth as Jason removed his hat, pressing it to his heart and shutting the door behind him. He lowered slowly into a rocking chair by the window and looked at her very carefully.

"You can't be happy here."

The words sounded less like a supposition and more like a command—as though by being happy in the cabin, in the world to which Ulysses brought her, she was proving something unacceptable.

"Love Ulysses," she answered simply. "Love Ulysses, and Mark, and Bonnie. But—*love* Ulysses."

The man before her heaved a hefty sigh. He leaned forward in the seat, hands folded between his knees. "I understand what you're saying…and I know why you would think those things. But there's a difference between loving someone because you want to, and loving someone because you *have to*."

"No!" His eyebrows lifted at her shout but she ignored his expression completely, one bare foot stamping upon the floorboard. "Ulysses nice, Ulysses good—smart and fun and teacher. Estelle love Ulysses first time!"

If Ulysses had been around to hear her use 'first,' he would have been so proud: that thought made her all the sadder and she bit her lip while Jason shook his head.

"You didn't even know what love is then. You probably still don't, not really. You were better off in the woods, Estelle. Don't you think it's unreasonable for these people to come and take you away?"

"*You*," she said sharply, pointing at the man before her.

"You and Ulysses, not just Ulysses."

Jason's eyes drifted askance. "That's right…me, too. I had a chance to talk Ulysses out of it, or at least refuse to cooperate. I didn't—you know why?" He looked at her pointedly now and sat up a little straighter. "Because of the money he offered me, Estelle. The money. Do you know what money is, yet?"

The girl faltered at that, then tensed as Jason reached into his pocket. He lifted his free hand and drew out a leather square like the one Ulysses sometimes took out for various reasons. "This is money," he said, pulling out a green rectangle of paper embossed with a silver stamp. "A silver certificate. It's the kind of money that's easiest to carry around—it's as good as silver, real silver that men use to trade. Do you know what silver is?" At the shake of the girl's head, he said, "It's a kind of metal that men decided was valuable. Not as valuable as gold, but still valuable enough to kill for…still valuable enough to sacrifice every other value for."

Jason put the bill away and said, "I've always been bad with money. It runs through my fingers like water. That's what they want, you know—white men, the government, they want you to be bad with money so you have to work for them. Tom, he's a little like that. Pretends to be your friend while robbing you blind during a poker game until all you have left to offer is a rifle."

Able to see that he had begun to discuss topics somewhat beyond Estelle's understanding, Jason sighed heftily and looked at her with obvious sorrow.

"My ancestors were robbed of everything—everything they had. Land, culture, life. They didn't even realize what it was to be robbed until it had already happened to them. As soon as Ulysses and I took you from those woods, I realized we had done the same thing. We had robbed you. We robbed you of peace, of simplicity. When I was a boy at boarding school, we learned about the white men and their Christian faith. My teachers loved to tell us a story about the first man and the first woman, who it is said lived in a beautiful garden together until the day a snake came and gave them too much knowledge. Then they knew what shame was, and fear, and toil. It's said that, because of what they did, all human beings are now sinful…and my teachers *loved to remind my people of that.*"

Jason's hand rested over his smooth jaw. He studied Estelle long and hard, his eyes trailing over her shift as he suggested, "Maybe it's too late. Maybe you already know too much to go back to the forest and be happy. We were snakes. We opened eyes you never asked to be opened; taught you things you never asked to know. 'Course— nobody asks to be born, either, but in this world?" Jason shook his head. "If there were an alternative—if we could know then what we know now—I'm not convinced we would want to suffer through it all. The worry, the stress, the pestilence and heartache. No, Estelle. I'm not convinced. And I'm sick at the thought that I let Ulysses convince *me* to put you through all this, when the fact is that you were better-off than any of the rest of us."

Standing, the chair rocking behind him in his absence, Jason made his slow way toward Estelle. "Don't worry," he said, "I'm not going to hurt you. I'm just going to take you—"

The girl leapt on him, her hand snatching the pearl handle of his gun from beneath his coat before he could even realize what happened.

Shock widened Jason's features: he lifted his hands in the air once again, this time in self-defense and helplessness before his own pointed pistol.

"Love Ulysses," insisted Estelle. "Love the town,

and—and words, and thinking, and being Estelle! Love *being*. I love it." Her brow furrowed and she gestured with the pistol, calling on the lessons given to her on the day of the duck hunt. Carefully, slowly, Jason stepped back in the direction that she indicated. "Ulysses loves me."

"Ulysses wants to cart you off across the sea and—"

"No! Not smart—you're not smart. *You* don't know! Ulysses wants to stay. Ulysses wants to stay with me, here. Me and Ulysses in the forest—loving, being, a pack. A family. No money. No bad. Just love."

Nostrils flaring, Jason said, "Well, I'm glad Ulysses changed his mind, but—"

His step forward was interrupted when Estelle shot at his feet. He leapt back; she did, too, almost having forgotten the volume of a gun's discharge in the time since the duck hunt.

But that leap gave her momentum, much as it widened the gap between the two of them. Without the least delay, the girl dashed through the front door of the cabin and into the tree-filtered sunlight.

Her heart pounded in her breast. Estelle looked around, searching for any sign of Ulysses. Two horses pawed anxiously at the earth where they had been tied to a tree some ways down the leaf-littered path to the cabin; she looked around, all across the ground, in search of Ulysses's tracks. Her hunter eyes soon found them—drawing not just his from relief with the grass and moss, but someone else's. Estelle followed, her sweaty palms forcing her to tighten her grip on the gun or lose it entirely.

What had happened here? Where had Ulysses been taken? She feared for his life but somehow thought that, if he were really dead, she would feel it in the center of her heart. Yes—she would have heard a cry, a gunshot, anything.

Someone else had heard a gunshot, though. At motion in the distance, Estelle skidded to a stop, the pistol raised in time to train on Tom Dulcamara.

He worked his way in pursuit of the sound of the discharge, but stopped short when he found himself all of twelve yards from the girl whose eyes blazed behind the merciless gun.

"Well, now, Estelle! Wild girl...what're you doing running through these woods alone?"

"Ulysses! Where?"

"I see you already met up with Jason."

Tom considered the pearl-handled pistol in her hands, then slowly lowered the rifle he held to the earth. "Don't you go pointing that thing all around, now...liable to hurt somebody."

"Just you," she told him, pulling back the hammer. "Ulysses! Where, where?"

"Back that ways a little, sugar, out for a nap in the trees. No harm done, I promise you."

Relief washing over her, Estelle gestured with the gun again. "Show me."

"Right this way," answered Dulcamara, turning his back to her with his hands both lifted in the air. Breath held, Estelle followed him at a distance, the gun trained always on his back.

All the while the cruel and evil man continued talking, yammering on as if he really expected his words to make a difference.

"You know, Estelle, you're an awful special girl. I'm not rightly sure Ulysses knows how special! He was just telling me all about how he wants to live here in the woods with you, but now—you don't want that really, do you? Haven't you seen enough of the woods? Wouldn't you rather see America? *All* of America?

"It's a wild country, little sister, I'll tell you that for sure…different everywhere you look. Bet you've never seen a desert, for instance, or a swamp. I can name a few things that I think you'd find to be quite—"

She got so sick of his voice that she fired the gun past him, eliciting a yelp and high spate of nervous laughter.

"All right! Hell's bells, all right, point taken…guess Dr. Cochran hasn't finished the process of your education, else you'd know nice young ladies don't go around shooting guns at gentlemen."

"Ulysses is gentle man," she corrected tersely. "You, Tom…animal. No—toxic mushroom. Make Estelle sick."

"Phoo-ee! You don't need a gun to shoot a man through the heart, Estelle, that's for damn sure…"

It wasn't long, thankfully, before they broached the boundary of the very same clearing where Estelle and Ulysses had shared the powerful lessons of the good-natured mushroom the night before. There, Ulysses lay face-down among the wildflowers.

A gasp escaped her lips and Estelle dashed forward, shoving Tom aside to reach her lover. Beside his prone form, she threw the gun down and hurried to draw him into her arms.

"Ulysses," she whispered, relieved at least to hear his breath but not able to relax until she saw him conscious. "Ulysses!"

"Ah…Estelle…"

As he stirred, grimacing against her, she cooed in sympathy at the welt upon the back of his head.

This was the mark to which his hand began to lift, but she stopped its trajectory to hold his fingers gently in hers.

"Careful, Ulysses—oh, Ulysses hurt!"

"Oh, dear…ah, I'll be all right. Just a knock on the—Tom!"

The physician's shadow fell across her before she could so much as react to the sound of her true love's cry. In one second, Dulcamara had the pistol and stepped back from the couple to aim it properly at them.

"You silly little fool! See, now, you're just an ape-girl after all…hey, maybe that's what I'll call you! 'Ape-Girl of Appalachia,' much better than 'Wild Woman of West Virginia.' What was I thinking!"

Laughing cruelly, Tom relaxed his posture in overconfidence and gestured casually with the gun. "That's the thing about inspiration, I reckon…you never know when it's going to strike. A little like when first I heard about you, Estelle! I would have gone in on a partnership with you, Ulysses, but you're just too damn stubborn…can't trust a man like that not to change his mind even once he's finally been convinced. Yes, I think it's better this way. Don't go thinkin' it's all bad for you, though…you still have the cabin. Come on, Ape-Girl…get on up, you leave him there and let's hit the road."

"No," said Estelle sternly, her arms tightening around Ulysses. "Estelle hates Tom. I hate you, Tom."

"We're going to need you to dial back the English in public, honey…can't have the crowds thinking you're educated, or even educatable. Now, come on." The hammer clicked back and his face grew darker while he said, "Get up or I shoot your hero. I won't say it again."

But he didn't have to. He would never get a chance. The click of the hammer was followed by another noise—one that came from the trees and filled Estelle's heart with a throb of wild joy.

Only when the girl laughed did Tom turn around to search for the source of the sound: and only when Tom turned around did the great gray wolf spring from the trees, its growl pealing into a snarl of absolute rage.

The next few seconds were such a blur of blood and fur that Estelle could hardly keep up. The physician cried out, firing wildly into the trees, his gun soon clicking empty while the wolf, with its grip on his arm, shook its head to break the bone. When at last the emptied pistol tumbled from his hand, Tom was driven to his knees by the pain. He cried out, "Please," as though the wild animal could speak—as though it cared about his suffering, his miserable human life.

It didn't.

While Estelle watched in amazement, her arms still around Ulysses, the wolf dragged the duplicitous doctor into the trees.

No one would ever see Tom Dulcamara again.

While his screaming receded into the distance, Estelle forgot him immediately. Her entire world became absorbed by Ulysses and her concerns for him. While she helped him over upon his back and drew him up until he was seated properly, she begged to know, "All right? All right? Oh, Ulysses! There, there…"

While she gently petted his back, Ulysses, a hint of tear in his eyes, nodded and said, "Yes, Estelle—yes, I'm all right. Oh, God! I'm so glad you're okay—kiss me, Estelle, please, I was so frightened for both of us—"

The girl dipped his head over his, their hearts meeting as intimately as their lips in that sacred second. He reached up and gripped her face while her fingers sank into his shoulders, their breaths like the warm summer wind that whistled through the trees around them.

When Estelle lifted her head, the breath of that kiss froze in a stifled gasp. Jason Blackthorn stood at the edge of the clearing, the rifle in his hand.

Estelle's arms tightened defensively around Ulysses.

Unmoving, Blackthorn studied first the man, then the woman.

"Got my rifle back," he said, gesturing with the weapon that pointed off to the side, rather than at either of the lovers. "Sounds from that scream like Tom won't have any argument about the matter."

The couple said nothing. Jason looked hard into Estelle's face; at the arms that cradled Ulysses to her breast.

"I guess if this is really how you want to live, well… then that's your choice. Like Bonnie. I'll never understand Bonnie. I'll never understand her…but I wouldn't make her live any way she didn't want."

He glanced at the pearl-handled revolver lying in the bloody grass.

"You can keep that," he said, "in case Tom comes back. But…I don't think he will."

Voice hoarse, Ulysses said, "Thank you, Jason. Thank you."

"Please don't thank me, Dr. Cochran. I'm ashamed. I'm disappointed in myself. I think maybe I'll see if Bonnie wants to buy my house with the money you've been paying her…or maybe you will, if you'd like to spend your winters closer to town."

"I'd like that."

Just once, Jason nodded. He turned on his heel and made his way into the trees again. "Come and see me when you're back in town, Ulysses. I'll probably still be there. Estelle—I'm glad you're happy."

The crunching of the leaves beneath his boots faded into the far distance of the forest. Estelle held her breath until her lungs burned: until she couldn't hear anything anymore except for the slow and anxious breathing of Ulysses.

Alone, the pair looked at one another. Ulysses, whose eyes were already filled with tears, began to weep with relief.

While kissing his cheeks and his beard and his eyelids, Estelle followed suit.

EPILOGUE

ROAST GOOSE FILLED the city house with a scent so divine that not even Bonnie, who claimed whole roasted animals upset her to look upon, could argue with the effect it had on her appetite. Ulysses beamed with pride and set the golden fowl in the center of the table, laying it reverently amid poinsettia and holly that had been arranged with a few small red candles.

"There," he said with sincere pleasure. "If that isn't the finest Christmas feast I've had in years...what do you think, Estelle?"

"I'm *hungry*," Estelle lamented, her complaint tinged with a miserable, girlish moan that brought a smile to her husband's lips. "Can we please eat? Please?"

"Almost," said Bonnie, patting her hand and laughing at her impatient scowl.

Mark shifted forward in his seat, hands folded. "Have to say our prayers first, haven't we?"

Mark, in his Irish Catholic way, was trying to teach Estelle about God, but Ulysses had a feeling that this was one of those areas where his dear wife would never fully adapt. To her, God was the forest, the sun—the wolf that had dragged Dulcamara into the trees. God was the mother wolf that had raised her and the bear that had chased Ulysses into her camp. The divine was an experiential, impartial force of nature to the girl, who simply could not seem to relate at all with images of the crucifixion or icons of a bearded man raising a pair of crossed fingers.

It was just as well, really. That was where the true anxieties of modern life came in, so far as Ulysses was concerned. Every culture in the world had its own form of religion, and, with maybe one or two small exceptions, nearly all religions were deeply invested in prescribing human behavior.

The last thing Ulysses wanted, ever, was to control Estelle's behavior. He loved that even after six months together she was still so wild and free—still broke out of his arm to pet a dog or chase a cat. Still wanted to walk in the forest barefoot whenever they were at their cabin. Ah...soon it would be springtime, and they could be there again.

Mrs. Halbrook had just managed the movement of his London estate to a very happy French couple looking to explore the possibilities of other countries. Seeing Estelle admire the goose with a glow in her eyes made him wonder what the staff members of his old home were doing for their own Christmas dinners.

Maybe Halbrook could share when she came to visit him, if she wasn't so enthusiastic about getting to know Estelle that she forgot Christmas had ever happened.

Ah, but Ulysses would never forget Christmas. This, Estelle's first Christmas with them all, it was the most important one of his life thusfar. The only more important one would come in the future, when they had children who could appreciate the season with them.

Ulysses had just begun to saw into the bird when a knock echoed upon the door of their home. The postman with another letter from Cambridge, begging him to reconsider and return to England with the girl during the spring? Surely not…no postal service ran on Christmas, not even the best-paid private ones.

After getting Mark to take his place carving the goose, Ulysses excused himself from the table to answer the door.

On the other side of that door stood the home's former owner, Jason Blackthorn. Ulysses fell back upon his heel at the unexpected surprise, his eyebrows lifting as he said, "Jason! Why, I didn't know you were coming."

"Hope I'm not imposing," said the fellow, gesturing with the fat tin in his hands. "I brought a fruitcake to make up for it."

"Oh, goodness, isn't that kind—come in, come in, Merry Christmas."

"You, too…hey, Bonnie."

"Jason!" Laughing with delight, Bonnie leapt from the table to throw her arms around her brother's neck to kiss his unready face. Eyes aglow with joy, she leaned back. "I thought you were up looking for work in Cleveland!"

"Yeah, well, I thought better of it now that it's the wintertime…believe me, that's the wrong place to spend December."

"Well, this is the right one, even if it seems just about as cold." Smiling with a yuletide pleasure of his own, Ulysses guided Jason toward the table and fetched him an extra seat. As Bonnie went about getting together another place setting, Ulysses, "Hope you approve of what we've done with the place…I think it's quite cozy, myself."

"Oh, it looks much nicer than I ever had it…bigger, too. Say, where's the bear?"

"He's in my apartment," answered Bonnie, laughing.

"It was giving poor Estelle nightmares." Glancing over at the girl who peered shyly at Jason, Ulysses smiled. "You don't mind that Jason's come to spend Christmas dinner with us, do you, dear?"

Even now, it was sometimes hard to read what whirled through Estelle's seemingly boundless mind. Was she happy? Unhappy? Anxious? Maybe a little of all three—nonetheless, whatever she thought, she eventually reached across the table and touched Jason's hand. "Merry Christmas, Jason," said Estelle, the greeting as unpracticed upon her lips as it was whole-heartedly meant.

"Merry Christmas, Estelle," Jason responded, perhaps almost as unaccustomed to using the phrase if only out of spite for his terrible childhood. With a faint smile for the sister who set the place before him, Jason patted Estelle's hand, then leaned back in his seat to smile at the center of the table. "That's some goose!"

"Estelle bagged that monster of a thing," Mark explained, still audibly impressed. He stroked his mustache while Jason lifted his eyebrows in surprise. "I was amazed, too…but I knew it had to be her, soon as I saw it. No way is Ulysses a good enough shot to hit any kind of bird. An ostrich, maybe."

"So you want to be fired and sent back to Europe, do you…" Ulysses shared a teasing grin with his valet, who sipped from his mug of spiced rum to hide his cheeky smirk. "Well, that would be quite a way to start a new year…"

Soon enough the impromptu little family sat around the table, sawing the goose to pieces and devouring suet pudding. Bonnie and her brother caught each other up and Mark chatted with Estelle about her latest adventures in bird-watching and herb-growing, this latter hobby being somewhat stalled by the cold depths of wintertime. At last, Jason glanced up at Ulysses.

"And how are you doing, Dr. Cochran? I heard you and Estelle got married."

"Very well, thank you! Happier than I've been in years."

"Still in the anthropology field?"

"Mm, in small ways. I think I chose Estelle above all that, but—well, do you want to tell him what we're up to, dear?"

Estelle beamed, her smile as pretty as the curls in which she'd permitted Bonnie to set her hair. "We're writing a book!"

Jason lifted his eyebrows in astonishment, not just to hear Estelle's advanced grasp of language but also at her bold declaration. He glanced back at Ulysses. "Is that so?"

"It is, it is indeed…Estelle knows much more about plants than I do. Mushrooms, too. I've taken something of an interest in entheogens—sacred plants, vision-inducing or otherwise. Estelle lends her knowledge and experience, and I do the hard work of the writing down."

"I'm learning to write, too," she advised quickly, smiling all the wider when her husband took her hand to kiss it.

"Yes, you are, my dear—ah, she learns more and more every day. Faster than I ever dreamed. I'm a lucky man to have such a smart wife."

With a surprised but ultimately pleased little smile of his own, Jason took a sip of his drink and said, "Well, Dr. Cochran…I have to hand it to you. This is quite a home you've made for yourself here in the states."

"Without Estelle, I would still be wandering the world. Never, not even as a boy, did I dream I could be so happy in one place."

Sweet dimples appearing in her cheeks with the breadth of her smile, Estelle reached over and stroked Ulysses's arm. "You make me so happy, Ulysses."

Heart swelling with pride, with love, with the blessings of his good fortune to have found this woman at all, Ulysses leaned over and kissed her waiting mouth. "Merry Christmas, Estelle," he told her, looking deeply into her eyes. "Thank you for being a part of my life."

"Thank you for teaching me, and being my husband."

The two exchanged a heartfelt gaze until, at the foot of the table, Bonnie said, "All right, that's enough—I'll either lose my appetite or start to cry. Besides, we haven't even made it to dessert! Save it for the mistletoe, you two."

While exchanging a laugh, the Cochrans settled back in their seats and finished Christmas dinner.

ABOUT THE AUTHOR

Regina Watts is the penname of a woman who certainly is not also M. F. Sullivan, founder and flagship author of Painted Blind Publishing. From her cozy home a few universes away from this one, Watts transmits stories to Sullivan that are then transcribed and published online and in paperback. Her available titles range from transgressive erotica to psychedelic fiction to erotica to romance. Be sure to check out her website and sign up for her mailing list at hrhdegenetrix.com!

ABOUT THE PUBLISHER

Painted Blind Publishing and its erotic imprint, Painted Blue Publishing, are the brainchild of author and devoted editor to Regina Watts, M. F. Sullivan. Founded in 2015 while Sullivan resided in Tucson, PBP is a house dedicated to bringing readers the finest in consciousness-expanding fiction. Be sure to check out the wide variety of essays available for free at paintedblindpublishing.com to learn more about the company, Watts, and Sullivan.

OTHER PAPERBACK WORKS
FROM PAINTED BLIND PUBLISHING

REGINA WATTS

INDUSTRIAL DIVINITY (2020)

DOTTIE FOR YOU SEASON 1 (2021)

SEDUCED BY SABINE (TBD)

M. F. SULLIVAN

DELILAH, MY WOMAN (2015)

THE LIGHTNING STENOGRAPHY DEVICE (2017)

THE DISGRACED MARTYR TRILOGY (2019-2020)